Asymmetry

Asymmetry

Lisa Halliday

GRANTA

Granta Publications, 12 Addison Avenue, London W11 4QR

First published in Great Britain by Granta Books, 2018
First published in the United States by Simon & Schuster, New York, in 2018

This book is a work of fiction. Any references to historical events, real people, or
real places are used fictitiously. Other names, characters, places, and events are
products of the author's imagination, and any resemblance to actual events or
places or persons, living or dead, is entirely coincidental.

A CIP catalogue record for this book is available from the British Library.

1 3 5 7 9 10 8 6 4 2

ISBN 978 1 78378 360 1 (hardback)
ISBN 978 1 78378 396 0 (trade paperback)
ISBN 978 1 78378 361 8 (ebook)

Offset by Avon DataSet Ltd, Bidford on Avon, B50 4JH

Printed and bound by CPI Group (UK) Ltd, Croydon, CR0 4YY

www.granta.com

MIX
Paper from
responsible sources
FSC® C020471
FSC
www.fsc.org

For Theo

CONTENTS

I

Folly

1

II

Madness

125

III

**Ezra Blazer's
Desert Island Discs**

245

I

FOLLY

We all live slapstick lives, under an inexplicable sentence
of death . . .

—MARTIN GARDNER, *The Annotated Alice*

ALICE WAS BEGINNING TO get very tired of all this sitting by herself with nothing to do: every so often she tried again to read the book in her lap, but it was made up almost exclusively of long paragraphs, and no quotation marks whatsoever, and what is the point of a book, thought Alice, that does not have any quotation marks?

She was considering (somewhat foolishly, for she was not very good at finishing things) whether one day she might even write a book herself, when a man with pewter-colored curls and an ice-cream cone from the Mister Softee on the corner sat down beside her.

"What are you reading?"

Alice showed it to him.

"Is that the one with the watermelons?"

Alice had not yet read anything about watermelons, but she nodded anyway.

"What else do you read?"

"Oh, old stuff, mostly."

They sat without speaking for a while, the man eating his ice cream and Alice pretending to read her book. Two joggers in a row gave them a second glance as they passed. Alice knew who he was—she'd known the moment he sat down, turning her cheeks watermelon pink—but in her astonishment she could only continue staring, like a studious little garden gnome, at the impassable pages that lay open in her lap. They might as well have been made of concrete.

"So," said the man, rising. "What's your name?"

"Alice."

"Who likes old stuff. See you around."

The next Sunday, she was sitting in the same spot, trying to read another book, this one about an angry volcano and a flatulent king.

"You," he said.

"Alice."

"Alice. What are you reading that for? I thought you wanted to be a writer."

"Who said that?"

"Didn't you?"

His hand shook a little as he broke off a square of chocolate and held it out.

"Thank you," said Alice.

"You're velcome," he replied.

Biting into her chocolate, Alice gave him a quizzical look.

"Don't you know that joke? A man flying into Honolulu says to the guy in the seat next to him, 'Excuse me, how do you pronounce it? Hawaii or Havaii?' 'Havaii,' says the other guy. 'Thank you,' says the first guy. And the other guy says, 'You're velcome.'"

Still chewing, Alice laughed. "Is that a Jewish joke?"

The writer crossed his legs and folded his hands in his lap. "What do you think?"

The third Sunday, he bought two cones from Mister Softee and offered her one. Alice accepted it, as she had done with the chocolate, because it was beginning to drip and in any case multiple–Pulitzer Prize winners don't go around poisoning people.

They ate their ice cream and watched a pair of pigeons peck at a straw. Alice, whose blue sandals matched the zigzags on her dress, flexed a foot idly in the sun.

"So. Miss Alice. Are you game?"

She looked at him.

He looked at her.

Alice laughed.

"Are you game?" he repeated.

Turning back to her cone: "Well, no reason not to be, I guess."

The writer got up to throw his napkin away and came back to her. "There are plenty of reasons not to be."

Alice squinted up at him and smiled.

"How old are you?"

"Twenty-five."

"Boyfriend?"

She shook her head.

"Job?"

"I'm an editorial assistant. At Gryphon."

Hands in his pockets, he lifted his chin slightly and seemed to conclude this made sense.

"All right. Shall we take a walk together next Saturday?"

Alice nodded.

"Here at four?"

She nodded again.

"I should take your number. In case something comes up."

While another jogger slowed to look at him, Alice wrote it down on the bookmark that had come with her book.

"You've lost your place," said the writer.

"That's okay," said Alice.

On Saturday, it rained. Alice was sitting on the checkered floor of her bathroom, trying to screw tight her broken toilet seat with a butter knife, when her cell phone beeped: CALLER ID BLOCKED.

"Hello Alice? It's Mister Softee. Where are you?"

"At home."

"Where is that?"

"Eighty-Fifth and Broadway."

"Oh, right around the corner. We could string up a couple of tin cans."

Alice pictured a string, bowing like a giant jump rope over Amsterdam, trembling between them whenever they spoke.

"So, Miss Alice. What should we do? Would you like to come here, and talk a while? Or should we take a walk together another day?"

"I'll come there."

"You'll come here. Very good. Four thirty?"

Alice wrote the address down on a piece of junk mail. Then she put a hand over her mouth and waited.

"Actually, let's say five. See you here at five?"

The rain flooded the crosswalks and soaked her feet. The cabs churning a spray up Amsterdam seemed to be traveling much faster than they did when it was dry. While his doorman made room for her by pressing himself into a cruciform position, Alice entered purposefully: long strides, blowing out her cheeks, shaking out her umbrella. The elevator was plated top to bottom with warped brass. Either the floors it climbed were very tall or the elevator was moving very slowly, because she had plenty of time to frown at her infinite funhouse reflections and to worry more than a little about what was going to happen next.

When the elevator doors opened, there was a hallway containing six more gray doors. She was about to knock on the first door she came to when another door, on the other side of the elevator, opened a crack and a hand came through, holding a glass.

Alice accepted the glass, which was full of water.

The door closed.

Alice took a sip.

The next time the door opened, it seemed to swing wide on its own. Alice hesitated before carrying her water down a short hallway that ended in a bright white room containing, among other things, a draughtsman's desk and an unusually wide bed.

"Show me your purse," he said from behind her.

She did.

"Now open it please. For security reasons."

Alice set her purse down on the little glass table between them and unlatched it. She took out her wallet: a brown leather men's wallet that was badly worn and torn. A scratch card, purchased for a dollar and worth the same. A ChapStick. A comb. A key ring. A barrette. A mechanical pencil. A few loose coins and, finally, three portable tampons, which she held in her palm like bullets. Fuzz. Grit.

"No phone?"

"I left it at home."

He picked up the wallet, fingering a bit of stitching that had come undone. "This is a disgrace, Alice."

"I know."

He opened the wallet and removed her debit card, her credit card, an expired Dunkin' Donuts gift card, her driver's license, her college ID, and twenty-three dollars in bills. Holding up one of the cards: "*Mary*-Alice." Alice wrinkled her nose.

"You don't like the Mary part."

"Do *you*?"

For a moment, he alternated between looking at her and at the card, as though trying to decide which version of her he preferred. Then he nodded, tapped the cards into alignment, snapped a rubber band from his desk around them and the bills, and dropped the stack back into her purse. The wallet he lobbed into a mesh-wire wastepaper basket already lined with a white cone of discarded typescript. The sight of this seemed to irritate him briefly.

"So, Mary-Alice . . ." He sat down, gesturing for her to do the same. The seat of his reading chair was black leather and low to the ground, like a Porsche. "What else can I do for you?"

Alice looked around. On the draughtsman's desk a fresh manuscript awaited his attention. Beyond it a pair of sliding glass doors gave onto a small balcony sheltered by the one above it from the rain. Behind her the enormous bed was made up so neatly as to look aloof.

"Do you want to go outside?"

"Okay."

"No one throws the other one over. Deal?"

Alice smiled and, still sitting five feet from him, extended a hand. The writer lowered his eyes to look at it for a long, doubtful moment, as though listed there on her palm were the pros and cons of every handshake he'd ever made.

"On second thought," he said then. "Come here."

His skin was lined and cool.

His lips were soft—but then his teeth were behind them.

At her office, there were no fewer than three National Book Award certificates in his name framed on the lobby wall.

The second time, when she knocked, several seconds went by with no answer.

"It's me," Alice said to the door.

The door opened a crack and a hand came through, holding a box.

Alice took the box.

The door closed.

Lincoln Stationers, it said on the box, tooled smartly in gold. Inside, under a single sheet of white tissue paper, lay a burgundy wallet with a coin purse and a clutch clasp.

"Oh my goodness!" said Alice. "It's so pretty. Thank you."

"You're velcome," said the door.

Again, she was given a glass of water.

Again, they did what they did without disturbing the bed.

Over her sweater, he put a hand on each breast, as if to silence her.

"This one's bigger."

"Oh," said Alice, looking down unhappily.

"No no; it's not an imperfection. There's no such thing as a matching pair."

"Like snowflakes?" suggested Alice.

"Like snowflakes," he agreed.

From his stomach all the way up to his sternum ran a pink, zipper-like scar. Another scar bisected his leg from groin to ankle. Two more made a faint circumflex above his hip. And that was just the front.

"Who did this to you?"

"Norman Mailer."

While she was tugging up her tights, he got up to turn the Yankees game on. "Ooh, I love baseball," said Alice.

"Do you? Which team?"

"The Red Sox. When I was little, my grandmother used to take me to Fenway every year."

"Is she still alive, your grandmother?"

"Yep. Would you like her number? You're about the same age."

"It's a little early in our relationship for you to be satirizing me, Mary-Alice."

"I know," laughed Alice. "I'm sorry."

They watched as Jason Giambi slugged a three-two pitch into left center.

"Oh!" said the writer, getting up. "I almost forgot. I bought you a cookie."

When they sat looking at each other, across his little glass dining table or she on the bed and he in his chair, she noticed that his head pulsed sideways ever so slightly, as though with the beating of his heart.

And, he'd had three operations on his spine, which meant there were certain things they could and couldn't do. Shouldn't do.

"I don't want you to get hurt," said Alice, frowning.

"It's a little late for that."

They used the bed now. His mattress was made of a special orthopedic material that made her feel as though she were slowly sinking into a giant slab of fudge. Turning her head to the side, she could see, through his double-height windows, the midtown skyline, looking huddled and solemn in the rain.

"Oh, God. Oh, Jesus. Oh, Christ. Oh Jesus Christ. What are you doing? Do you know . . . what . . . you're *doing*?"

Afterward, while she was eating another cookie:

"Who taught you that, Mary-Alice? Who have you been with?"

"No one," she said, picking a crumb off her lap and eating it. "I just imagine what would feel good and I do it."

"Well, you have quite an imagination."

He called her a mermaid. She didn't know why.

Propped beside his keyboard was a tent of white paper on which he had typed:

You are an empty vessel for a long time, then something grows that you don't want, something creeps into it that you actually cannot do. The God of Chance creates in us. . . . Endeavours in art require a lot of patience.

And below that:

An artist, I think, is nothing but a powerful memory that can move itself at will through certain experiences sideways . . .

When she opened the refrigerator, his gold medal from the White House, tied to its handle, clanked loudly against the door. Alice went back to the bed.

"Sweetheart," he said. "I can't wear a condom. Nobody can."

"Okay."

"So what are we going to do about diseases?"

"Well, I trust you, if you—"

"You shouldn't trust anyone. What if you become pregnant?"

"Oh, don't worry about that. I'd have an abortion."

Later, while she was washing up in the bathroom, he handed through to her a glass of white wine.

Blackout cookies, they were called, and they came from the Columbus Bakery, which he passed every day on his walk. He tried not to eat them himself. Nor did he drink; alcohol didn't mix with one of the medications he was taking. But for Alice he bought bottles of Sancerre or Pouilly-Fuissé and, after pouring her what she wanted, put the cork back in the bottle and the bottle on the floor next to the door for her to take home.

One evening, a few bites into her cookie, Alice took a sip and made a daintily revolted face.

"What?"

"I'm sorry," she said. "I don't mean to seem ungrateful. It's just that, you know, they don't really go."

He thought for a moment and then got up and went into the kitchen for a tumbler and a bottle of Knob Creek.

"Try this."

He watched hungrily as she took a bite, then a sip. The bourbon went down like a flame.

Alice coughed. "It's heaven," she said.

Other gifts:

An extremely sensible, analog, waterproof watch.

Allure Chanel eau de parfum.

A sheet of thirty-two-cent stamps from the Legends of American Music series, commemorating Harold Arlen, Johnny Mercer, Dorothy Fields, and Hoagy Carmichael.

A *New York Post* cover from March 1992 with the headline "Weird Sex Act in Bullpen (Late City Final)."

The eighth time, while they were doing one of the things he wasn't supposed to do, he said:

"I love you. I love you for this."

Afterward, while she sat at the table eating her cookie, he watched her in silence.

The following morning:

CALLER ID BLOCKED.

"I just wanted to say that it must have been strange, hearing that from me; you must have been reeling—that's R-E-E-L-I-N-G, not R-E-A-L-I-N-G, which isn't a bad word, either. What I'm saying is that it was meant in the moment, but it doesn't mean anything should change between us. I don't want anything to change. You do what you want and I do what I want."

"Of course."

"Good girl."

When Alice hung up, she was smiling.

Then she thought about it a little longer, and she frowned.

She was reading the instructions that had come with her watch when her father called to inform her, for the second time that week, that not a single Jew had reported to work in the towers on the day they came down. But the writer did not call her again for many days. Alice slept with her phone next to her pillow and when she wasn't in bed carried it around with her everywhere—to the kitchen when she got herself a drink, to the bathroom when she went to the bathroom. Also making her crazy was her toilet seat, the way it slid to the side every time she sat on it.

She thought of going back to their bench in the park, but decided on a walk instead. It was Memorial Day weekend and Broadway was closed for a street fair. Already at eleven the neighborhood was smoky and the air sizzling with falafel, fajitas, French fries, Sloppy Joes, corn on the cob, fennel sausages, funnel cake, and fried dough the diameter of a Frisbee. Ice-cold lemonade. Free spinal health exams. "We the People" legal document administration—Divorce $399, Bankruptcy $199. At one of the stalls peddling brandless bohemian fashion, there was a pretty poppy-colored sundress lolling on the breeze. It was only ten dollars. The Indian stallholder got it down so that Alice could try it on in the back of his van, where a watery-eyed German shepherd watched her with his chin on his paws.

That night, when she was already in her pajamas:

CALLER ID BLOCKED.

"Hello?"

"Hello, Mary-Alice. Did you see the game?"

"What game?"

"The Red Sox–Yankees game. The Yankees won fourteen to five."

"I don't have a television. Who pitched?"

"Who pitched. Everyone pitched. Your grandmother pitched a few innings. What are you doing?"

"Nothing."

"Do you want to come over?"

Alice took off her pajamas and put on her new dress. Already a thread needed biting off.

When she got to his apartment, only the lamp on his nightstand was lit and he was propped up in bed with a book and a glass of chocolate soymilk.

"It's spring!" cried Alice, pulling the dress over her head.

"It's spring," he said, sighing wearily.

Alice crawled lynxlike toward him across the snow-white duvet. "Mary-Alice, sometimes you really do look sixteen."

"Cradlerobber."

"Graverobber. Careful of my back."

Sometimes, it could feel like playing Operation—as if his nose would flash and his circuitry buzz if she failed to extract his Funny Bone cleanly.

"Oh, Mary-Alice. You're crazy, do you know? You're crazy and you get it and I love you for it."

Alice smiled.

When she got home, it had been only an hour and forty minutes since he'd called, and everything was exactly as she'd left it, but her bedroom looked too bright and unfamiliar somehow, as though it now belonged to someone else.

CALLER ID BLOCKED.

  CALLER ID BLOCKED.

  CALLER ID BLOCKED.

  He left a message.

  "Who takes the greatest pleasure in leading the other one astray?"

Another message:

  "Does anyone smell mermaid in here?"

CALLER ID BLOCKED.

  "Mary-Alice?"

  "Yes?"

  "Is that you?"

  "Yes."

  "How are you?"

  "Fine."

  "What are you doing?"

  "Reading."

  "What are you reading?"

  "Oh, nothing interesting."

  "Do you have air-conditioning?"

  "No."

  "You must be hot."

"I am."

"It's going to get even hotter this weekend."

"I know."

"What'll you do?"

"I don't know. Melt."

"I'm coming back into the city on Saturday. Would you like to see me then?"

"Yes."

"Six o'clock?"

"Yep."

"I'm sorry. Six thirty?"

"Okay."

"I might even have some dinner for you."

"That would be nice."

He forgot about dinner, or decided against it. Instead, when she arrived he sat her down on the edge of his bed and presented her with two large Barnes & Noble bags filled to the handles with books. *Huckleberry Finn. Tender Is the Night. Journey to the End of the Night. The Thief's Journal. July's People. Tropic of Cancer. Axel's Castle. The Garden of Eden. The Joke. The Lover. Death in Venice and Other Stories. First Love and Other Stories. Enemies, A Love Story* . . . Alice picked up one by a writer whose name she had seen but never heard. "Ooh, Camus!" she said, rhyming it with "Seamus." A long moment followed in which the writer said nothing and Alice read the copy on the back of *The First Man.* When she looked up he was still wearing a gently startled expression.

"It's Ca-MOO, sweetheart. He's French. Ca-MOO."

Her own apartment was on the top floor of an old brownstone, where it caught the sun and stoppered the heat. The only other tenant on her floor was an old lady called Anna, for whom ascending the four steep flights was a twenty-minute ordeal. Step, rest.

Step, rest. Once, Alice passed her on her way out to H&H and when she came back the poor thing was still at it. From the shopping bags she carried you would have thought she ate bowling balls for breakfast.

"Anna, may I help?"

"Oh no dear. Been doing it fifty years. Keeps me alive."

Step, rest.

"Are you sure?"

"Oh yes. Such a pretty girl. Tell me. Do you have a boyfriend?"

"Not at the moment."

"Well, don't wait too long, dear."

"I won't," laughed Alice, running up the stairs.

"Capitana!"

His doorman greeted her chummily now. He called the writer down and saluted them off as they set out for a walk. Swinging a bag of plums from Zingone's, the writer asked whether Alice had heard about the city's plan to rename some of its luxury residences after major-league baseball players: The Posada, The Rivera, The Soriano. "The Garciaparra," said Alice. "No no," he said, stopping her importantly. "Only Yankees." They entered the little park behind the natural history museum, where, biting into one of his plums, Alice pretended to chisel his name under Joseph Stiglitz's on the monument to American Nobel Laureates. But mostly, they stayed in. He read her what he'd written. She queried the spelling of "keister." They watched baseball and, on weekend afternoons, listened to Jonathan Schwartz swoon over Tierney Sutton and Nancy La-Mott. "Come Rain or Come Shine." "Just You, Just Me." Doris Day wistfully warbling "The Party's Over." One afternoon, Alice burst out laughing and said, "This guy is such a cornball."

"'Cornball,'" repeated the writer, eating a nectarine. "That's a good old-fashioned word."

"I guess you could say," said Alice, searching the floor for her underpants, "that I'm a good old-fashioned girl."

"*The party's over . . . ,*" he sang, whenever he wanted her to go home. "*It's time to call it a d-a-a-a-a-y . . .*"

Then, going cheerfully around the room, he would switch off the phone, the fax, the lights, pour himself a glass of chocolate soy-milk, and count out a small pile of pills. "The older you get," he explained, "the more you have to do before you can go to bed. I'm up to a hundred things."

The party's over. The air-conditioning's over. Alice would stagger a little, taking herself home in the heat, her belly full of bourbon and chocolate and her underwear in her pocket. When she had climbed the four increasingly steamy flights up to her apartment, she would do exactly one thing, which was to move her pillows down the hall to her front room, where, on the floor next to the fire escape, there was at least the possibility of a breeze.

"So listen darling. I'm going away for a while."

Alice put down her cookie and wiped her mouth.

"I'm going back out to the country for a bit. I've got to finish this draft."

"Okay."

"But that doesn't mean we can't speak. We'll speak regularly, and then when I finish, we can see each other again. Should you want to. All right?"

Alice nodded. "All right."

"Meanwhile . . ." He slid an envelope across the table. "That's for you."

Alice picked it up—*Bridgehampton National Bank*, it said on the front, next to a logo of a sailboat regatta—and took out six one-hundred-dollar bills.

"For an air conditioner."

Alice shook her head. "I can't—"

"Yes you can. It would make me happy."

It was still light out when she left for home. The sky had a stagnant quality to it—as though a thunderstorm were due, but had gotten lost. The young people drinking on the sidewalk were just beginning their evenings. Alice approached her stoop slowly, reluctantly, one hand on the envelope inside her purse, trying to decide what to do. Her stomach felt as if she were still back in his elevator and someone had cut the suspension.

There was a restaurant one block north with a long wooden bar and a mostly civilized-looking clientele. Alice found a stool at the far end, next to the napkin caddy, and arranged herself as though she were there primarily for the television mounted high in one corner. New York led Kansas City by four runs in the bottom of the third.

Come on Royals, she thought.

The bartender dropped a napkin down in front of her and asked her what she wanted to drink. Alice considered the wine specials listed on the wall.

"I'll have a glass of . . ."

"Milk?"

"Actually, do you have any Knob Creek?"

Her tab came to twenty-four dollars. She put her credit card down before picking it up again and taking out one of the writer's hundreds instead. The bartender returned with three twenties, a ten, and six ones.

"Those are for you," said Alice, sliding the ones toward him.

The Yankees won.

IN THE RELUCTANT, MUSTY current of a secondhand Frigidaire:

> *. . . I didn't believe we could lick such a crowd of Spaniards and A-rabs, but I wanted to see the camels and elephants, so I was on hand next day, Saturday, in the ambuscade; and when we got the word, we rushed out of the woods and down the hill. But there warn't no Spaniards and A-rabs, and there warn't no camels nor no elephants. It warn't anything but a Sunday-school picnic, and only a primer-class at that. We busted it up, and chased the children up the hollow; but we never got anything but some doughnuts and jam, though Ben Rogers got a rag doll, and Jo Harper got a hymn-book and a tract; and then the teacher charged in and made us drop everything and cut. . . .*

In the night, rain fell on the part of her air conditioner that extended into the air shaft with the sound of metal arrowheads shot earthward. Thunderstorms came and went, their patter crescendoing into sharp cracks and lightning that penetrated the eyelids. Water siphoned off gutters like spring water off mountain boulders. When the storm retreated, what was left of it counted out the early-morning minutes in slow, metronomic drips. . . .

> *I had the middle watch, you know, but I was pretty sleepy by that time, so Jim he said he would stand the first half of it for me; he was always mighty good that way, Jim was. I crawled into the wigwam, but the king and the duke had their legs sprawled around so there warn't no show for me; so I laid outside—I didn't mind the rain, because it was*

warm, and the waves warn't running so high now. About two they come
up again, though, and Jim was going to call me; but he changed his mind,
because he reckoned they warn't high enough yet to do any harm; but he
was mistaken about that, for pretty soon all of a sudden along comes a
regular ripper and washed me overboard. It most killed Jim a-laughing.
He was the easiest nigger to laugh that ever was, anyway. . . .

With the money left over, she bought a new toilet seat, a teakettle, a screwdriver, and a small wooden dresser from the weekend antiques market over on Columbus. The teakettle was a sleek,
all-metal, Scandinavian design. The toilet seat she screwed on with
tremendous satisfaction while listening to Jonathan Schwartz.

Her work seemed to her more boring and inconsequential than
ever. Fax this, file this, copy this. One evening, when everyone else
had left and she was staring at the writer's number in her boss's
Rolodex, one of her colleagues poked his head into the room and
said, "Hey, Alice, *à demain*."

"Sorry?"

"*À demain*."

Alice shook her head.

"See you tomorrow?"

"Oh. Right."

It got hotter before it got cooler. Three weekends in a row she
spent lying on her bed, bedroom door closed, the Frigidaire whir-
ring and rattling away at its highest setting. She thought about the
writer, out on his island, shuttling between his pool and his studio
and his nineteenth-century farmhouse with its unobstructed harbor
views.

She could wait a very long time, if she had to.

I do not want to conceal in this journal the other reasons which made
me a thief, the simplest being the need to eat, though revolt, bitterness,
anger, or any familiar sentiment never entered into my choice. With

fanatical care, "jealous care," I prepared for my adventure as one arranges a couch or a room for love; I was hot *for crime.*

Malan had a Chinese look, with his moon face, a somewhat flattened nose, scarcely any eyebrows, a bowl-cut hairdo, and a big moustache that failed to cover his thick, sensual lips. His soft, rounded body, the fleshy hand with pudgy fingers suggested a mandarin who disapproved of traveling by foot. When he half closed his eyes while eating heartily, you could not help seeing him in a silk robe holding chopsticks between his fingers. But the expression changed all that. The feverish dark-brown eyes, restless or suddenly intent, as if the mind was focused on a very specific point, were the eyes of an Occidental of great sensitivity and culture.

The smell of rancid butter frying is not particularly appetizing, especially when the cooking is done in a room in which there is not the slightest form of ventilation. No sooner than I open the door I feel ill. But Eugene, as soon as he hears me coming, usually opens the shutters and pulls back the bedsheet which is strung up like a fishnet to keep out the sunlight. Poor Eugene! He looks about the room at the few sticks of furniture, at the dirty bedsheets and the wash basin with the dirty water still in it, and he says: "I am a slave!"

Alice picked up her phone.
NOKIA, was all it said.

But about the smell of rancid butter . . .

There was a party one night, a retirement thing for one of the editors, and afterward she slept with an assistant from the Sub-Rights Department. They did use a condom, but it stayed inside Alice when it should have come out.

"Shit," said the boy.

"Where did it go?" asked Alice, peering down the shadowy gorge between them. Her voice sounded girlish and gullible, as though this were a magic trick and any moment now he might produce a fresh prophylactic out of her ear.

Instead, it was she who completed the trick—alone in the bathroom, one foot on her new toilet seat, holding her breath. It wasn't easy, groping around with one hooked finger among the deep slippery swells. Afterward, and although she knew it couldn't prevent every dreaded outcome, she got into the tub and flushed herself out with the hottest water she could stand.

"Any plans?" she asked the boy in the morning while he belted his corduroys.

"Dunno. Might go into the office for a bit. You?"

"The Red Sox are playing the Blue Jays this afternoon."

"I hate baseball," said the boy.

We appreciate your upcoming visit to RiverMed. The following information is for your benefit. If it fails to answer any of your questions, please present them at the time of your counseling session.

The total time for the procedure is usually 5–10 minutes. Once inside the examination room you will meet your personal nurse, physician, and anesthesiologist or nurse anesthetist, who will inject a general anesthesia via an intravenous catheter inserted into an arm or hand vein. You will sit on the exam table, lie back, and place your legs in stirrups. Your physician will perform a bimanual exam (i.e., place two fingers in the vagina and feel your uterus). An instrument (a speculum) will then be placed inside the vagina and adjusted to hold the sides apart so that the doctor may see your cervix (the mouth of your uterus). Opening the cervix is necessary for the doctor to remove the pregnancy.

When the opening has been widened sufficiently using rod- or tube-shaped instruments called dilators, the physician will insert a tube or vacurette into your uterus. This tube is connected to a suctioning ma-chine. When the machine is turned on, the contents of your uterus will be drawn out through the tube and into a bottle. Then the tube will be removed and a long, thin, spoonlike instrument inserted and drawn over the inside surface of the uterus to check that nothing remains.

When the physician has finished, the speculum is removed, your legs are lowered, and you will remain lying on your back as you are wheeled to the recovery room, where your condition will be monitored. After a satisfactory recovery, which usually takes twenty minutes to an hour, you will be transferred into a room where you may rest and dress. You will be individually counseled by a nurse and given final instructions before leaving.

You may bleed off and on for three weeks.

Please let us know if we can make you more comfortable. We hope your time with us will be a positive experience.

On the second Thursday in October, while she was tugging a brush through her damp tangled hair, she heard on the radio that they'd given the Nobel Prize to Imre Kertész, "for writing that upholds the fragile experience of the individual against the barbaric arbi-trariness of history."

CALLER ID BLOCKED.

Breathlessly, as if to outrun her own advice, Alice told him about all of the things she had bought, including the toilet seat and the teakettle and the dresser that the antique dealer had described as "a vintage 1930s piece."

"Like me," he said.

"I have my period," Alice apologized.

Three nights later, as she lay with her bra around her waist and her arms around his head, she marveled at how his brain was *right there*, under her chin, and so easily contained by the narrow space between her elbows. It began as a playful thought, but suddenly she distrusted herself to resist crushing that head, turning off that brain.

To some extent, the sentiment must have been reciprocal, because a moment later he bit her abruptly through a kiss.

They saw each other less frequently now. He seemed warier of her. Also, his back was giving him trouble.

"Because of something we did?"

"No, sweetheart. You didn't do anything."

"Do you want to . . . ?"

"Not tonight darling. Tonight only *tendresse*."

Sometimes, when they lay facing each other, or when he sat across his little dining table from her, head pulsing to the side, his expression would settle into a sad sort of bewilderment, as if with the realization that she was life's greatest pleasure at the moment, and wasn't that a sorry state of affairs?

"You're the best girl, you know?"

Alice held her breath.

Sighing: "The best girl."

"Ezra," she said, clutching her stomach. "I'm so sorry, but suddenly I don't feel very well."

"What's wrong?"

"I think maybe there was something wrong with my cookie."

"Are you going to throw up?"

Alice rolled over, pulled herself up onto her hands and knees, and sank her face into his cool white duvet. She took a deep breath. "I don't know."

"Let's go to the bathroom."

"Okay." But she didn't move.

"Darling, let's go."

All at once, Alice covered her mouth and ran. Ezra got out of bed and trailed her calmly, quietly, closing the door behind her with a soft dignified click. When she was done, she flushed the toilet and rinsed her face and her mouth and leaned shivering on the vanity.

Through the door she could hear him respectfully getting on with his evening—opening the refrigerator, clinking plates in the sink, stepping on the pedal that lifted the lid to the trash. She flushed again. Then she unspooled a bit of toilet paper and wiped the bowl, the seat, the lid, the edge of the bathtub, the toilet-paper dispenser, the floor. There was blackout cookie everywhere. Alice lowered the lid to the toilet seat and sat down. In the wastepaper basket lay a galley of a novel by a boy with whom she'd gone to college, his agent's letter, requesting a blurb, still paper-clipped to its cover.

When she reappeared, Ezra was in his chair, legs crossed, holding a book about the New Deal. He watched frowning as Alice tiptoed naked across the room and slowly lowered herself onto the floor between the closet and the bed.

"Sweetheart, what are you doing?"

"I'm sorry, I need to lie down, but I don't want to ruin your duvet."

"Mary-Alice, get into the bed."

He came to sit beside her and for many minutes smoothed a hand up and down her back, like her mother used to do. Then he pulled the duvet up to her shoulders and quietly withdrew to begin his one hundred things: silencing ringers, extinguishing lights, segregating pills. In the bathroom, he turned the radio on, softly.

When he emerged, he was wearing a light-blue Calvin Klein T-shirt and shorts. He set a glass of water down on his nightstand. He fetched his book. He rearranged his pillows.

"Ninety-seven, ninety-eight, ninety-nine . . ."

He got into bed and sighed theatrically.

"One hundred!"

Alice lay silent, motionless. He opened his book.

"Sweetheart," he said finally. Bravely, brightly. "Why don't you stay here? Just this once. You can't go home like this. Okay?"

"Okay," murmured Alice. "Thank you."

"You're velcome," he said.

In the night, she awoke three times. The first time, he was lying on his back, while beyond him the skyline was still glittering and the top of the Empire State Building was floodlit in red and gold.

The second time, he was on his side, facing away from her. Alice's head hurt, so she got up and went to the bathroom to look for an aspirin. Someone had turned the Empire State Building off.

The third time she woke up, he had his arms around her from behind and was holding on to her tightly.

The fourth time, it was morning. Their faces were close, almost touching, and his eyes were already open, staring into hers.

"This," he said grimly, "was a very bad idea."

He left for his island again the following morning. When he'd called to tell her this, Alice hung up, hurled her phone into her hamper, and groaned. The same day, her father called to explain that fluoridated water is an evil propagated by the New World Order; an hour later he called again to declare that man never walked on the moon. Alice fielded such news flashes as she'd done once or twice a week every week for eight years: with an upbeat reticence that postponed her objection to a day when she'd figured out how to express it without hurting anyone's feelings. Meanwhile, she discovered her beautiful new teakettle to possess an outrageous flaw: its contiguous-metal handle could not sit thirty seconds over a flame without becoming too hot to pick up. What kind of a handle, thought Alice, can't be handled? Holding her scalded palm under the faucet, she blamed this on her writer, too. But this time, after only three days, he called. He called her from his screenhouse and described the changing trees, and the wild turkeys that hobbled along his driveway, and the tangerine glow of the sun as it sank behind his six acres of woods. Then he called her again, just *two* days later, and held the phone so that she could hear a crow cawing, and the shiver of leaves ruffled by the wind and then—nothing. "I don't hear anything," laughed Alice. "Exactly," he replied. "It's *quiet*. *Bliss*fully quiet." But it was too cold now to use the pool, and there were some disruptive plumbing repairs on the calendar, so he'd be staying only another week or so and then coming back into the city for good.

He brought with him an old Polaroid SX-70.

"Let's see," he said, turning it over in his hands, "if I can remember how to use this thing."

They took ten shots, including one of him, the only one of him, lying on his side in one of his Calvin Klein T-shirts and his own very sensible wristwatch, otherwise nothing. Fanned beside him on the bed were the nine photographs already taken, arranged for his review in two concentric arcs: murky brown forms surfacing with an edge of opalescence, as though out of a sunlit river. In fact, the more vivid the photographs became, the more the pleasure of taking them faded, and while Alice got up to go to the bathroom Ezra deposited all ten into the pocket of her purse. Then they watched *Top Hat*, with Ginger Rogers and Fred Astaire, and Ezra brushed his teeth lightly humming "Cheek to Cheek." It was not until she was back in the elevator the following morning, reaching for her keys, that she found them there: a neat square stack of herself bound tightly by one of her own hair bands.

At home, she arranged the Polaroids on her bed in several layered columns, something like the setup for Solitaire. In some, her skin looked like watered-down milk, too thin to conceal the veins running through her arms and chest. In another, a crimson flush spread across her cheeks and into her ears, while over the porcelain slope of her shoulder the Chrysler Building resembled a tiny flame in white gold. In another, her head rested against his thigh, her one visible eye closed, Ezra's fingers holding aside her hair. In another, her breasts were plumped high and smooth and round, held upward by her own hands. This one he'd taken from beneath her, so that to look at the camera she'd had to gaze down the line of her nose. Her hair, tucked behind her ears, hung forward in heavy blond curtains on either side of her jaw. Her bangs, too long, separated slightly left of center and fell thickly to her eyelashes. It was almost a beautiful photograph. Certainly the most difficult to cut up. The problem, thought Alice, was its *Alice*ness: that stubbornly juvenile quality that on film never failed to surprise and annoy her.

Tinily, like distant traffic lights, her pupils glowed red.

CALLER ID BLOCKED.

"Oh, sorry, sweetheart, I didn't mean to call you."

CALLER ID BLOCKED.
        CALLER ID BLOCKED.
        CALLER ID BLOCKED.

"Mary-Alice, I'm still looking forward to seeing you this evening, but would you mind first going to Zabar's and picking up a jar of Tiptree preserves, that's Tiptree preserves—T-I-P-T-R-E-E, preserves, as in jelly—and not just any flavor but Little Scarlet, which is the most expensive one they've got. It costs about a hundred dollars a jar and that's because they make it out of little girls like you. So: one jar of Little Scarlet Tiptree preserves, one jar of the best peanut butter you can find, and one loaf of Russian pumpernickel, unsliced. And you bring them *here!*"

"Capitana!"

More gifts:

A sheet of thirty-seven-cent stamps, one for each American state, designed to look like vintage "Greetings from" postcards.

A CD of Elgar's cello concerto, performed by Yo-Yo Ma and the London Symphony Orchestra.

A bag of Honeycrisp apples. ("You'll need a bib.")

He needed a stent. A tiny mesh tube they'd insert into a narrowing coronary artery to prop it open and restore the full flow of blood. A simple procedure. He'd already had it done seven times. They don't put you under, just sedate you, anesthetize the area around the point of insertion, wiggle it up on a catheter and pop it in. Then a little balloon is inflated, causing the stent to expand like a badminton birdie, and . . . voilà. Takes about an hour, more or less. A friend would accompany him to the hospital. If she liked, he would ask this friend, when it was over, to give her a call.

"Yes, please."

For all his assurances, he himself became gloomy. Not without pleasure, Alice felt herself being tested by these dramatic circumstances.

"Of course," she said, "we all have to worry. *I* could get cancer. Or tomorrow, in the street, you could be—"

He closed his eyes and held up a hand. "I already know about the bus."

The day of the procedure she got home from work and put the Elgar CD on. It was terribly beautiful, plaintive and urgent, and, in the beginning anyway, perfectly consonant with her mood. Twenty minutes later, however, still sawing away sublimely, the cello seemed to have moved on without her, indifferent to her suspense. Finally, at 9:40, her cell phone beeped, flashing an unfamiliar number. Businesslike, a man with an unplaceable drawl reassured her that after having been delayed the procedure had gone fine; Ezra would be staying overnight so that they could monitor a few things but otherwise everything was fine, just fine.

"Thank you so much," said Alice.

"You're velcome," said the friend.

"The Kid," he'd referred to her. As in: "I called The Kid." Ezra thought this was pretty funny. Alice shook her head.

For a while, he was in a good mood. The stent had done the

job. Paramount was going to make a movie out of one of his books. An award-winning actress had been cast in the leading role and his services had been engaged as an on-set consultant. One morning, he called her a little later than usual—Alice was already out of the shower and dressing for work—and said, "Guess who I had over last night?"

Alice did.

"How did you know?"

"Who else could it be?"

"Anyway, I didn't fuck her."

"Thank you."

"I don't think she was very impressed with my spare change dish."

"Or your humidifier."

They took more pictures.

"In this one," said Alice, "I look like my father." She laughed. "All I need is a Colt .45."

"Your father has a gun?"

"He has lots of guns."

"Why?"

"In case there's a revolution."

Ezra frowned.

"Darling," he said later, while she was slathering a slice of bread with Little Scarlet. "When you visit your father, these guns . . . Are they just lying around?"

Sucking jelly off her thumb, Alice replied, "No, he keeps them in a safe, but every now and again we get one out and practice shooting at a gourd propped up against an old dishwasher in the backyard."

She was reading some fan mail his agent had forwarded to him when he said something into the closet she couldn't hear.

"What?"

"I said," he said, turning around, "don't you have a warmer coat than this? You can't go around all winter in this thing. You need something padded, with goose down. And a hood."

A few nights later, he slid another envelope across the table. "Searle," he said. "S-E-A-R-L-E. Seventy-Ninth and Madison. They've got just the one."

The nylon made a luxurious swishing sound and the hood framed her face with a black halo of fur. It was like walking around in a sleeping bag trimmed with mink. Waiting for the crosstown bus, Alice felt pampered and invincible—also delirious with this city, which every day was like a mounting jackpot waiting to be won; then, hurrying up the steps to her building, she slipped, flailed for balance, and brought the back of her hand down on the stoop's iron railing, igniting a searing flash of pain. She went to his apartment anyway and, for the duration of the evening, hid her throbbing paw in her lap, or, when they were in bed, out to the side, as if to protect a coat of nail polish that wasn't yet dry.

In the morning, her palm was blue.

At home, she waited all day for the swelling to go down, then gave up and went downstairs to hail a cab for the nearest emergency room. The driver took her to Hell's Kitchen, where for two hours she sat in a waiting room crowded with binge drinkers and homeless people feigning psychosis in order to remain inside where it was warm. Around ten, an intern called Alice's name and led her to a gurney, where he clipped her great-grandmother's ring off her swollen middle finger and tapped each of her knuckles to ascertain where it hurt. "There." Alice hissed. *"There!"*

When the X-ray came back, the intern held it up and said, pointing: "It's broken. Your middle metacarpal—"

Alice nodded; her pupils rolled back, and, after teetering for a moment, her body pitched slowly forward and to the side, like a discarded marionette. From here she journeyed many miles to remote countries with barbarous customs and maddening logic; she made and lost companions, spoke languages previously unknown to her, learned and unlearned difficult truths. When she came to some minutes later, struggling against a nauseating undertow that seemed to want to pull her down through the center of the earth, she became remotely aware of machines beeping and tubes scraping the insides of her nostrils and too many seconds elapsing between the asking of questions and her answering them.

"Did you hit your head?"

"Did you bite your tongue?"

"Did you wet yourself?"

There was a damp spot on her sweatpants where she'd spilled the little paper cup of water someone had given her.

"You'll have to get in touch with a surgeon first thing Monday morning," the busy intern said. "Is there someone you can call to come and pick you up?"

"Yes," whispered Alice.

It was nearly midnight when she walked out into a fresh flurry, fat flakes sailing down at an urgent slant. Holding her hand as though it were made of eggshell, Alice walked to the corner and looked up and down and then up again for a cab.

CALLER ID BLOCKED.

"Hello?!"

"I just wanted you to hear what my humidifier is doing. . . ."

"Ezra, no, I broke my hand!"

"Oh my God. How? Are you in pain?"

"Yes!"

"Where are you?"

"Fifty-Ninth and Columbus."

"Can you get a cab?"

"I'm trying!"

When she arrived he was wearing black silk long underwear and had a Band-Aid on his head. "What happened?"

"I had a mole taken off. What happened to you?"

"I slipped on my stoop."

"When?"

"This morning," she lied.

"Was it icy?"

"Yes."

"So you could sue."

Alice shook her head sadly. "I don't want to sue anyone."

"Darling, the best hand guy in New York is Ira Obstbaum. O-B-S-T-B-A-U-M. He's at Mount Sinai, and, if you want, I'll call him tomorrow and ask him to see you. Okay?"

"Okay."

"Meanwhile, you're going to take this for the pain. Will you be able to sleep?"

"I think so."

"You're a brave girl. You've had a shock. Just remember: *I'm here, I'm fine, I have the warmth and comfort of my bed.*"

Alice began to cry.

"Sweetheart, you don't have to cry."

"I know."

"Why are you crying?"

"I'm sorry. You're being so nice to me."

"You'd do the same for me."

Alice nodded. "I know. I'm sorry."

"Darling, don't continually say, 'I'm sorry.' Next time you feel like saying 'I'm sorry,' instead say 'Fuck you.' Okay?"

"Okay."

"Got it?"

"Uh-huh."

"So?"

Alice sniffed. "Fuck you," she said weakly.

"Good girl."

After swallowing the pills, Alice sat down on the edge of his bed, still wearing her coat. Ezra sat in his reading chair, legs crossed and head pulsing to the side, watching her darkly. "They take about forty-five minutes to work," he said, glancing at his watch.

"Do you want me to stay?"

"Sure you can stay. Want something to eat? We've got apple-sauce, bagels, tofu-scallion cream cheese, Tropicana with Lots of Pulp."

He got up to toast her a bagel and watched her eat it with one hand. Afterward, Alice lay down to face the snow, which in the light of his balcony was falling more calmly now, stealthily and evenly, like an army of parachuting invaders. Ezra returned to his chair and picked up a book. Three times the silence was torn by a page turning; then a balmy effervescence flooded Alice's insides and her skin began to feel as though it were vibrating.

"Whoa."

Ezra checked his watch. "Is it working?"

"Mm-*hmmmmmm* . . ."

He called Obstbaum. He took her in a cab to Mount Sinai. He arranged for Zingone's to deliver groceries to her apartment twice a week for six weeks.

He took pictures of her in her cast.

"I love you," purred Alice.

"You love Vicodin is what you love. We're out of film." He went to the closet.

"What else have you got in there?"

"You don't wanna know."

"Yes I do."

"More girls. Tied up."

"How many?"

"Three."

"What are their names?"

"Katie . . ."

"No," said Alice. "Let me guess. Katie and . . . Emily? Is Emily in there?"

"Yep."

"And Miranda?"

"That's right."

"Those girls are incorrigible."

"Incorrigible," he repeated, as though she had made up the word.

Her cast was heavy. Heavier, it seemed, when she had nothing else on. Alice turned over onto her stomach and stretched like a three-legged cat. Then she pulled herself up, arched her back, her sides, rolled her head around on her neck, and grinned, wickedly.

"What?"

Walking toward him on her knees: "Let's do something *aw*ful."

It knocked him back a little. "Mary-Alice, that's the smartest thing you've ever said."

They sat in the last row, so as not to be conspicuous, also so that he could get up and stretch his back if he needed to, but he didn't. It was a Saturday matinée, and the movie theater was swarming with small children; when an especially excited one spilled popcorn on Ezra's sleeve, Alice worried he might be having second thoughts. But then Harpo lit his cigar with a blowtorch, and Groucho passed his hat through the "mirror," and it was Ezra's laugh, head-back and un-throttled, that could be heard above everyone else's. At the end, when Freedonia declares war on Sylvania and the brothers waggle their hips singing "All God's chillun' got guns," Ezra drew a plastic water pistol from his pocket and gave Alice a furtive squirt in the ribs.

"We're going to war!" they sang, walking back down Broadway, past the colored lights and tempera snowdrifts and Christmas trees bound up tightly to look like cypresses. "Hidey hidey hidey hidey hidey hidey hidey HO!" At the sturgeon shop, crowding with the others up to the sneeze-proof glass, they gazed down on the smoked fish, pickled tongue, and taramasalata as if at newborns in a maternity ward. Alice pointed at a cheese labeled FIRM SMEAR and whistled primly. When it was his turn, Ezra raised a finger and ordered "two pieces of gefilte fish, some horseradish, half a pound of kippered salmon, and—what the hell? Two ounces of your finest paddlefish roe for Miss Eileen here."

"Oops," said Alice.

Ezra turned to look at her calmly. Then, tutting and shaking his head: "I'm sorry darling. You're not Eileen."

CALLER ID BLOCKED.

"Hello?"

"Good evening. May I speak to Miranda please?"

"Miranda isn't here."

"Where is she?"

"In jail."

"Is Emily there?"

"Emily's in jail too."

"What for?"

"You don't wanna know."

"What about . . . ?"

"Katie?"

"That's right. Katie. Katharine."

"She's here. Want to speak to her?"

"Please."

. . . "Hallo?"

"Hi, Katie? It's Mr. Zipperstein, from school."

"Oh, hiya, Mr. Zipperstein."

"Hiya. How are you?"

"Fine."

"Good. Listen. I'm calling to ask whether you'd like to study at my house one night this week."

"Okay."

"You'd like that?"

"Sure."

"Tomorrow?"

"Shoot. I can't do tomorrow. I have a piano lesson tomorrow."

"Thursday?"

"Art Club."

"What about afterward? After Art Club?"

"Thursday's my night to set the table."

"I spoke to your mom about that. She said you can set the table twice on Friday instead."

"Okay."

"Thursday at six thirty then?"

"Sure."

"Which one is this again?"

"Katie."

"Stay outta jail, Katie."

"I will Mr. Zipperstein."

"Zipper*stein*."

"Zipper*stein*."

"Good girl."

"'My sweet little whorish Nora I did as you told me, you dirty little girl, and pulled myself off twice when I read your letter. . . . Yes, now I can remember that night when I fucked you for so long backwards. . . . You had an arse full of farts that night, darling, and I fucked them out of you, big fat fellows, long windy ones, quick little merry cracks and a lot of tiny little naughty farties ending in a long gush from your hole. It is wonderful to fuck a farting woman when every fuck drives one out of her. I think I would know Nora's fart anywhere.'"

"That's disgusting," said Alice.

He lowered the book and gave her a dully affronted look. Sweetly, Alice slithered under the covers and scrabbled around there until he came like a weak water bubbler.

They dozed.

When his watch beeped eight, Alice groaned and whispered, "I have to go." Ezra nodded warmly, softly, not opening his eyes.

Sitting at the table to buckle her shoes:

"You know that homeless man? The one who stands in front of Zabar's and wears a hundred coats, even in summer?"

"Mm-hmm."

"Did *you* buy him all those coats?"

"Yep."

"And do you think he went crazy before he became homeless, or the other way around?"

Ezra thought about this. "Don't sentimentalize him."

"What do you mean?"

"Don't pity him. Don't overempathize with him. He's fine."

In the bathroom, she rinsed her mouth, brushed her hair, and tied a dental-floss bow tie around the dildo standing on the vanity; then she left.

Coming down the steps of her own building:

"Good morning, dear! You look pretty today. Tell me: Do you have a boyfriend?"

"Not yet, Anna! Not yet."

FOR THE HOLIDAYS, HE went out to his island. Alice took the train up to see her mother, whom she would decide it was impossible not to sentimentalize, and returned on New Year's Eve to attend a colleague's dinner party. The eggplant was tough and the risotto too salty and afterward everyone got drunk on cheap Brut and wrote stupid things on Alice's cast. "Any resolutions?" she asked the boy slumped beside her; someone had told her he had a book of poems coming out in the spring. "Sure," he replied, straightening a leg and running a hand through his long, spiraling hair. "Quality *and* quantity."

In Union Square, a girl in gold sequins threw up in the subway trough while her friends took pictures and laughed.

When Ezra came back, they opened Champagne, real Champagne, and ate Bulgarian caviar from Murray's. He also brought her a box of jelly doughnuts from the Shelter Island Bake Shop and an eight-CD box set of Great Romantic Standards entitled *They're Playing Our Song*.

"Any you don't know?"

"'My Heart Stood Still'?"

Ezra nodded, leaned back in his chair, and took a deep breath. *"'I took one look at you, that's all I meant to do / And then my heart stood still . . .'"*

"'September Song'?"

Another deep breath. *"'For it's a long, long while from May to December / But the days grow short when you reach September . . .'"*

He had a good voice, but he distorted it, for levity's sake. Shyly,

Alice smiled down at her doughnut. Ezra chuckled softly and rubbed his jaw.

"You have jelly just here," he said.

"Ezra," she said a moment later, passing their plates to him, in the kitchen. "I don't think I can do it tonight."

"Neither can I, sweetheart. I just want to lie down with you."

On the bed she struggled to find a place for her cast.

"When does that come off?"

"Wednesday morning."

"Why don't you come here afterward and I'll give you some lunch, okay?"

"Okay. Thank you."

"How's work?"

"What?"

"I said how's work darling."

"Oh, well, you know. It's not what I want to be doing for the rest of my life, but it's fine."

"What do you want to be doing for the rest of your life?"

"I don't know." She laughed softly. "Live in Europe."

"Do they pay you well?"

"For my age."

"You have a lot of responsibility?"

"Sure. And my immediate higher-up is going on maternity leave next month, so I'll be doing some of her job soon."

"How old is she?"

"Midthirties, I guess."

"Do *you* want children?"

"Oh, I don't know. I don't know. Not now."

Ezra nodded. "My darling Eileen got to be forty and wanted a baby, with me. I didn't want to lose her so I thought about it very seriously. And I came close to doing it. I'm glad as hell I didn't."

"What happened?"

"We split up, which was very hard, and it took a while but she found someone else, Edwin Wu. And now they have little Kyle and Olivia Wu, who are four and six and pure enchantment."

They drifted toward sleep, even though he hadn't done his hundred things. Alice sniffed.

"What?"

"My grandmother, the one who likes baseball, her name is Elaine, and when my grandfather, who was an alcoholic, proposed to her, he was so drunk that he said, 'Will you marry me Eileen?'" Alice laughed.

Ezra's arm around her stiffened. "Oh, Mary-Alice. Sweet Mary-Alice! I want you to win. Do you know?"

Alice lifted her head to look at him. "Why wouldn't I?"

He ran a hand over his eyes, fingers trembling. "I'm afraid some man is going to come along and fuck you up."

The night before his birthday they shared a praline tart and watched the president announce the invasion.

In this conflict, America faces an enemy who has no regard for conventions of war, or rules of morality. . . . We come to Iraq with respect for its citizens, for their great civilization, and for the religious faiths they practice. We have no ambition in Iraq except to remove a threat and to restore control of that country to its people.

"This man is so stupid," said Alice, shaking her head.

"This is going to kill me," said Ezra, forking the tart.

She gave him a cord for his reading glasses. He gave her another thousand dollars to spend at Searle. The following evening a friend was going to throw him a party to which Alice was not invited.

"Is this the same friend who calls me The Kid?"

Ezra tried not to smile.

"Hasn't he ever heard of a kids' table?"

"Sweetheart, you don't want to be there. *I* don't want to be there.

Besides, you're the one who doesn't want people to know about us. You're the one who doesn't want to wind up on Page Six."

His back was better. His book was going well. He wanted Chinese food.

"One order of shrimp with lobster sauce, one order of broccoli with cashews, one order of hacked chicken, and—Mary-Alice, do you want a beer?—two bottles of Tsingtao. . . . Yes. Uh, no, I think it was one shrimp, one broccoli, one hacked chicken, and . . . That's right. Two sing-sow. Sing-tow. Yes. Exactly. Ching-*dow*." Helplessly, he clapped a hand to his forehead and laughed. The voice on the other end became indignant. "No!" he said. "I'm laughing at the way *I* talk!"

He hung up. "Forty minutes. What should we do?"

"Take a Vicodin?"

"We've already done that."

Alice sighed and flopped backward onto the bed. "Oh, if only there were a baseball game on!"

"Ooh, you're going to pay for that, little bitch. . . ."

He was telling her about a beautiful Palestinian journalist who'd been at the party and wanted to interview him when Alice frowned and lifted her head from his chest.

"Uh-oh."

"What?"

"Your heart is doing something funny."

"What's funny about it?"

"Shhhh."

He raised his eyebrows at her and waited. Alice lifted her head again. "It's doing three beats then a pause, four beats then a pause, three beats then a pause."

"Are you sure?"

"I think so."

"Hmm. Maybe I should call Pransky."

"Who's Pransky? The best heart guy in New York?"

"Smartass, would you get me the phone please, and my little black notebook there?"

Pransky agreed to see him the following morning and detected nothing amiss but decided he should be fitted with a defibrillator anyway. This time, while she was waiting to hear, Alice was at work, interviewing her boss's daughter's babysitter about an internship.

"So how do you know Roger?"

"He lives next to my uncle in East Hampton."

"And what does your uncle do?"

"He's in, like, securities."

"But you'd rather work in publishing."

The girl shrugged. "I like to read."

"Who do you like to read?"

CALLER ID BLOCKED.

". . . Do you want me to go outside?"

"No, no, that's okay."

"Okay. Um. Ann Beattie and . . ." CALLER ID BLOCKED. "Are you sure?"

"Don't worry. Ann Beattie and?"

"Julia Glass. I just finished *Three Junes* and it was *so* good."

"Mm-hmm. Anyone else?"

The girl turned to watch a window washer rappel down the building across the street. Several seconds went by and then she sniffed and lifted an arm laden with bangles to scratch her nose.

Beep.

"Oh!" said the girl, turning back. "And I *love* Ezra Blazer."

"What does it feel like?"

"Like I've got a cigarette lighter in my chest."

"It *looks* like you've got a cigarette lighter in your chest."

Sitting on the toilet, he watched attentively as she wrung out a washcloth and dabbed at his stitches that ended only an inch from his quintuple-bypass scar. The spiky black thread wound in and out of his skin like barbed wire. "Are you sure this is a good idea?" Alice asked. "Getting it wet so—"

"BZZZZZZZZZZT!" he said, making her jump.

On the eve of the first Boston-Yankees game they went to a restaurant called Il Bacio but which Ezra referred to as The Meatball. "The food here is shit," he said cheerfully, opening his menu. "But we can't spend all our time in that little room, do you know?" Under the table he passed her a bottle of hand sanitizer.

"I'll have the salmon," Alice said to the waiter, still rubbing her hands.

"And I'll have the spaghetti vongole without the vongole. And a Diet Coke. And—Mary-Alice, would you like a glass of wine? A glass of white wine please, for the lady."

A woman in a fuchsia pantsuit approached their booth, ecstatically wringing her hands.

"I'm so sorry. I'm embarrassing my husband, but I just had to tell you how much your books have meant to us."

"Thank you."

"I've got *two* of them on my nightstand right now."

"Good."

"And you," said the woman, turning to Alice, "are very pretty."

"Thank you," said Alice.

When she'd left, they sat looking at each other, shyly. Ezra rested his elbows on the table. He massaged his hands.

"So, Mary-Alice, I've been thinking . . ." The waiter came with their drinks. "That maybe you would like to visit me out in the country this summer."

"Really?"

"If you'd like to."

"Of course I'd like to."

He nodded. "You could take the train out to Greenport one Friday after work and then catch the ferry and Clete or I will pick you up."

"Oh, I would love that. Thank you."

"Or you could take a Friday off."

"That sounds wonderful. I will."

He nodded again, already seeming to weary of the idea. "But listen darling. We'll be out there alone, for the most part, but there *is* Clete, and a few others who come around to mow the lawn and whatnot, so I suggest we take the precaution of giving you an alias."

"What?"

"A different name."

"I know what an alias is. But why?"

"Because everyone's a gossip, you know? So we'll call you something else while you're there, and if anyone asks we'll say you're helping me with some research, and that way, if anyone talks, which of course they will, you won't have to worry about it getting back to work."

"Are you serious?"

"Deadly serious."

"Um, okay. Did you have a name in mind?"

He leaned back and folded his hands on the table. "Samantha Bargeman."

Alice laughed so suddenly she had to put down her wine. "And *where*," she said, "did you get *that* name?"

"I made it up." He wiped his hands on his napkin and pulled a business card from the pocket of his shirt:

SAMANTHA BARGEMAN
Editorial and Research Assistant to Ezra Blazer

"But there's no number on it. What kind of a business card doesn't have a number on it?"

"Sweetheart, you don't want anyone to actually *call* you."

"I know, but . . . for credibility's sake. Who's going to believe this is really my card?"

Unfazed, he sat back to make room for his spaghetti. He picked up his fork.

"Fine," laughed Alice. "Did you . . . ? When were you . . . ?"

"Maybe in July. Maybe Fourth of July weekend. We'll see."

That night, in addition to the rest of the cards—two hundred cards, printed on butter-colored cardstock and packed tightly into a heather-gray box—he gave her:

Six green peaches.

A Vermont Country Store catalogue, from which he said she should order some Walnettos, plus whatever else she wanted, and charge it to his account.

Fifteen one-hundred-dollar bills wrapped in a notebook-lined piece of paper on which he'd written, in red marker: YOU KNOW WHERE TO GO WITH THIS.

"This week the United States Congress passed historic legislation to strengthen and modernize Medicare. Under the House and Senate bills, American seniors would for the first time in Medicare's thirty-eight-year history receive prescription drug coverage. We're taking action because Medicare has not kept up with the advances of modern medicine. The program was designed in the 1960s, a time when hospital stays were common and drug therapies were rare. Now drugs and other treatments can reduce hospital stays while dramatically improving the quality of care. Because Medicare does not provide coverage to pay for these drugs, many seniors have to pay for prescriptions out of pocket, which often forces them to make the difficult choice of paying for medicine or meeting other expenses. In January, I submitted to Congress a framework for Medicare reform that insisted on giving seniors access to prescription drug coverage, and offering more choices under Medicare. The centerpiece of this approach is choice. Seniors should be allowed to choose the health-care plans that suit their needs. When health-care plans compete for their business, seniors will have better, more affordable options for their health coverage. Members of Congress and other federal employees already have the ability to choose among health-care plans. If choice is good enough for lawmakers, it is good enough for American seniors—"

"Oh shut up," muttered Alice, getting up to change the station before resuming cutting the tags off her new clothing from Searle.

At her door:

Shave and a haircut, two bits.

It was Anna, wearing a misbuttoned robe and tremulously extending a jar of sauerkraut. "Dear, can you open this?"

"... There you go."

"Thank you. What's your name?"

"Alice."

"That's a pretty name. Are you married?"

"Nope."

"I thought I heard someone. Do you have a boyfriend?"

"No, no boyfriend, I'm afraid ..."

In addition to the Walnettos, Alice put a checkmark next to Coconut Watermelon Slices, Mary Janes, Turkish Taffy, and Toy Army Men Gummy Candy ("A Salute to Your Sweet Tooth"). Then she got into bed and fell asleep with the radio on, Camus listing off her knees and the pen she'd been using to underline certain passages blotting her pajama sleeve with ink.

"... I love you," Cormery said quietly.

Malan pulled the bowl of chilled fruit toward him. He said nothing.

"Because," Cormery went on, "when I was very young, very foolish, and very much alone ... you paid attention to me and, without seeming to, you opened for me the door to everything I love in the world."

Her back hurt. Her breasts were swollen. At work, she snapped at the new girl for unloading the office dishwasher too slowly.

From under her bathroom sink, she pulled out a pink plastic clamshell graying with dust. TUE read the last blister no longer containing a pill. White tells your body you're pregnant; blue says just kidding. Three years earlier, six weeks of this had made her weepy and irascible to the point of lunacy, and she'd quit. But she was older now, older and more alert to the probability of hormonal ambush; this time, she'd be ready for the hysterical thoughts, and outthink them.

So: one white pill tonight, one white pill tomorrow, one white pill on Friday, plus a fourth on Saturday, after lunch. That, she reckoned, should get her through the weekend blood-free. . . .

CALLER ID BLOCKED.

"Hello?"

"All packed?"

"Just about."

"What time's your train?"

"Nine twelve."

"You won't believe this, but I'm rereading *David Copperfield*, for my book, and four lines down on page one hundred and twelve I've just come across the word 'bargeman.'"

"No."

"Yes! Listen to this: 'He informed me that his father was a barge-man, and walked, in a black-velvet head-dress, in the Lord Mayor's Show. He also informed me that our principal associate would be another boy whom he introduced by the—to me—extraordinary name of Mealy Potatoes.' That's what I'm going to call you from now on, Mary-Alice. Mealy Potatoes."

"Good."

"Can you imagine? That I should read *bargeman* the night before you come? How often does one see that word?"

"Hardly ever."

"Hardly ever. That's right."

Alice took a sip of Luxardo.

"Fucky fuck?"

"If you want."

"No, I guess we shouldn't. It's late."

She waited.

"Darling."

"What."

"Tell me something."

"Okay."

"Do you ever think this isn't good for you?"

"On the contrary," Alice said a little too loudly. "I think it's *very* good for me."

Ezra laughed softly. "You're a funny girl, Mary-Alice."

"I'm sure there are funnier."

"You're probably right."

"Anyway," she said. "You make me happy."

"Oh, sweetheart. You make me happy, too."

LIGHT SHIMMERED IN THE trees, whose leaves, when the wind ran through them, sighed like the gods after a long and boozy lunch. The air was balmy and brackish and here and there carried a whiff of pinesap bubbling under the sun. Alice dove into water that he kept heated to a temperature approaching that of blood and after torpedoing half a length surfaced to settle into thirty laps of an unhurried breaststroke: legs froglike, hands coming almost together before swiveling away again and again, always the right reaching forward to touch down between the insects that crawled along the flagstone edge, always the left folding close to wipe her nose before the next lap commenced. Some days, it could even seem to her that she was making a kind of progress with this routine—as though the laps she swam were not the selfsame distance traveled and untraveled over and over, but lengths laid like pipe end-to-end and that would someday deliver her to a destination as far away as their great sum. Coming almost together and then pulling apart, her hands looked to her like the hands of someone once tempted by prayer but who had since renounced it for other means of mollifying herself: someone learned, someone liberal, someone literate. Someone *enlightened*. The pumphouse hummed.

In the evenings, they listened to *Music for A Weekend to Remember*, which was like Jonathan only cornier, and took their plates out to the screenhouse, or, if there was a game on, into the pink-glowing den. On the mantelpiece, next to a glass pyramid that threw quivering rainbows onto the wall, sat an antique wooden calendar with

three windows in its face and dowels that rolled the linen scrolls
inside ahead to the correct weekday, date, and month:

SATURDAY

2

AUGUST

The dowels were pale and smooth and whenever passing Alice
could not resist twisting one ever so slightly . . . although she never
dared shift SATURDAY all the way to SUNDAY, or 2 to 3, or AUGUST to
SEPTEMBER, for fear of not being able to shift them back.

Behind the sofa stood a narrow marble console stacked to her elbows' height with books. Many were by prominent writers, others
by names she knew as friends. The friend who called her The Kid,
for example, had written a book about Auschwitz that Ezra had
given a guardedly favorable quote. There were also several galleys,
including one of a biography of Arthur Miller and another of a
novel scheduled for publication that fall by Alice's own employer, a
letter from her boss tucked crisply inside:

> Dear Mr. Blazer,
>
> As you'll see in my introduction, Allatoona! is a very special
> novel, not to mention a subtle, respectful, and ultimately trium-
> phant tribute to your influence. I'm not asking for an endorse-
> ment, only that you might enjoy the book as much as all of us here
> at Gryphon have done, with surprise and delight at its confidence,
> its exquisite calibration, its searing wit—

Alice shut the galley and took the Auschwitz book out to the
porch.

Some dinnertimes, an elderly neighbor would drop by, bearing
eggs from his henhouse along with the local hearsay. Other nights
she and Ezra played cards, or read, or took a flashlight down to his
dock to look up at the stars. One Saturday they walked all the way

to the Ram's Head, where a wedding party was still going strong: men wielding croquet mallets chased barefoot bridesmaids around the lawn while a jazz quintet rolled out big band standards in the bar. "No," Ezra said firmly, when Alice pulled teasingly on his arms. But then the tribal rat-a-rat of "Sing Sing Sing" started up and a moment later he was percussing the air as if possessed by Lionel Hampton. A bit of finger snapping here, heel swiveling there; at one point he even got up on his toes and dared a brief accordioning of the knees. He'd taken Alice's hand and was spinning her through Spirograph designs that became longer and looser with each rotation when a woman wearing an upside-down corsage shimmied over to announce: "You know, everyone says you look *just* like my husband." "I *am* your husband," replied Ezra, before proceeding to dip Alice almost horizontal and leading her up toward the band.

His bedroom was at the top of the house, where the floors creaked sedately and the gnarled branches of an old oak tree filled the windows with undulating green. In the mornings, as she lay facing him, staring into the radiating brown of his irises and marveling at how unworn they looked, how limpid and alert, even after so many birthdays and wars and marriages and presidents and assassinations and operations and prizes and books, Alice sighed. Ninety-seven years they'd lived between them, and the longer it went on the more she confused his for her own. Outside, the birds gossiped blithely. When the sun reached her face, Alice sat up and tucked a piece of hair behind her ear. Her cheek was still creased with the pillowcase's wrinkles. Solemnly, she touched a finger to her nose, then her chin, then her elbow, the tip of her nose again, and tugged on one ear. "Bunt," Ezra said hoarsely. Yes! Nose, chin, elbow, thigh, earlobe, earlobe, tip of her nose again, three quick claps. "Steal." Good! Chin, thigh, earlobe, earlobe, elbow, elbow, imaginary visor. "Hit and run." When it was his turn, Ezra mirrored what she had done, but in double time, and with a deadpan face, and every sequence ended with him pointing at her belly button. Laughing, Alice fell back to the pillow. Ezra gathered her in and kissed her hair. "Sweetest girl. You are the sweetest girl." The words were like a hot feather in her ear. In her other ear, with a tone that sounded almost apologetic for having to remind them, his watch beeped noon.

"I follow my course with the precision and security of a sleepwalker." And yet a sleepwalker's course is anything but precise and secure. It is the uncertain leader who strains to reassure his subjects and perhaps above all himself that his objectives are sound and pure. Of only one thing does he feel certain: that he would like to lead. He would like to have power; he would like to be worshipped; he would like to be obeyed. To an extent these desires are felt by all politicians, or else they would have chosen another, less authoritarian profession. But in some cases the desires are extreme, borne of a compulsion to compensate for past humiliations— an illegitimate father, maybe, or rejection by an academic institution one aspired to attend. There chafes a sense that the world does not understand him, does not appreciate him, and so he must remake it into a world that does. Domination is not merely a fantasy but also a form of revenge for his status as a failure, a subordinate, "an outcast among outcasts"—as The New York Times *would put it in an obituary of the Führer running to no fewer than thirteen thousand words.*

In the kitchen stood three half bottles of Pinot Noir, a jug of Stolichnaya, and an unopened bottle of Knob Creek. Looking out the window down to the pool, where Clete was skimming impurities off the surface with a long-handled net, Alice uncapped the vodka, tipped it up for a swig, and returned to the porch.

But megalomania is not the word. Both suffix and prefix imply an excess, an incongruent sense of one's own influence, delusion. Yet Hitler was not deluded as to the magnitude of his power. He was deluded as to the worthiness of his objectives, yes, but it does not seem possible that he

*could have overestimated his impact on the history of humanity. When,
then, does one man's delusion become the world's reality? Is it every
generation's destiny to contend with a dictator's whims?* "*By shrewd and
constant application of propaganda,*" *we read in* Mein Kampf, "*heaven
can be presented to the people as hell and, vice versa, the wretchedest
experience as a paradise.*" *But only when the people in question fail in
their duty toward vigilance. Only when through inaction we are complicit. Only when we are sleepwalking ourselves.*

Another swig.

"Baby? Baby, where are you?"

A radio came on. A toilet flushed. Feet crossed the old floorboards
and treaded boyishly down the stairs. Alice watched through the porch
window as he went over to what looked like an old wooden munitions
box, selected an album from the stack inside, and slid it ceremoniously
from its sheath. A moment later there was an abrupt, furry blurting
sound, followed by the tropical strains of what sounded like a luau.

*Beyond the blue horizon
Waits a beautiful day
Goodbye to things that bore me
Joy is waiting for me!*

Between verses he shouted through the window: "Want a
drink?"

They were in the screenhouse, licking barbecue sauce from their
fingers and watching a canoe glide across the glassy harbor, when
a figure appeared on the lawn, approaching unsteadily through the
dusk. "Virgil!" Ezra called out. "What's the good word?"

"Mole got under my toolshed this morning but I took care of
him."

"You took care of him?"

"I took care of him." The old man coughed, lifted the screenhouse's door, and stooped warily to enter.

"Listen, Virgil; I've got a favor to ask. You know this lot over the road? The one that goes down to North Cartwright?"

"Yup."

"Do you know who owns it?"

"Lady down in Cape Coral's had it for years."

"What sort of a lady?"

"My age about. Stokes, her name is. Uncle used to live in that little gray clapboard over on Williette. When he died his kids sold it to those musical fellows."

"Well, I'd like to get in touch with Miss Stokes, if I can, because I've been thinking I'd like to buy that lot before someone else comes along and puts up a car wash."

Virgil nodded, coughing again, his shoulders convulsing and the skin around his liver spots flushing a vivid shade of plum. "Darling," Ezra said quietly. Alice nodded and went into the house; when she'd returned and handed Virgil a glass of water, Virgil said, "Thanks, Samantha."

Later, she and Ezra were in the kitchen playing gin rummy when Alice inquired casually what one "should do out here, in case of an emergency."

Calmly reordering his hand, Ezra replied, "You mean what should you do if we're in the middle of doing it and my cigarette lighter goes off?"

"That sort of a thing, yes."

"Call Virgil."

"Ha."

"I'm serious. Virgil's the local EMT."

"The local EMT is a hundred years old?"

"He's seventy-nine years old, and he was an ambulance medic in World War Two. He was there when Patton said, 'We're training you bastards to kick the butts of the Japanese.' Not that *you* should know who Patton was. Gin."

He got up to go to the bathroom and came back looking impressed. "I'd almost forgotten we had asparagus."

"So . . . there's no hospital on the island?"

"There's a hospital in Greenport. And another one in South-ampton. But don't worry. Virgil knows what he's doing. And anyway"—he flung out a hand—"look at me. I'm fine." After blinking at her thoughtfully for a moment, he brought his hand back in to look at his watch.

"Have you read this?" She held up the Auschwitz book.

Ezra shook his head. "It's no good."

"What do you mean?"

"Too much toilet training."

"Excuse me?"

"Hitler was toilet-trained too early, Mussolini was left on the pot too long. It's all Freudian speculation that has nothing to do with anything. If you want to learn about the Holocaust I'll show you what to read."

On Sundays, she brooded. How dreary it would be, back in the city, five more days of answering phones, hustling blurbs, unjamming staplers. When Ezra went down to the pool for his Aqua Fitness, Alice stood by the window and watched as he descended to wade back and forth across the sun-dappled shallow end, savoring its resistance. Then the wind picked up, erasing him from view, and the rest of the morning she spent drifting from room to room, picking up books and putting them down again, pouring glasses of lemonade and sitting at the kitchen table to drink them, listening to the bees. The clock over the sink ticked loudly.

He came in a little after two to find her lying on the sofa, a forearm over her eyes.

"Sweetheart, what's wrong?"

"Nothing. Just thinking."

"Don't you want to use the pool?"

"I will, in a bit."

"What time's your train?"

"Six eleven."

"What time do you get in?"

"I should be home by nine thirty."

"Clete'll take you to the ferry. As for me . . ." He looked around, as though the room were a mess and he didn't know where to start. "I'm going to stay out here for a while. At least until the end of September. I've got to finish this draft."

"Okay."

"It's giving me trouble."

"Mm-hmm."

"I have something for you." From his shirt pocket he pulled a sheet of paper with three ring holes in it, folded neatly into fourths:

GITTA SERENY, INTO THAT DARKNESS
PRIMO LEVI, SURVIVAL IN AUSCHWITZ
HANNAH ARENDT, EICHMANN IN JERUSALEM

"Thank you," said Alice.

"You're velcome," he said.

He was born in Altmünster, a small town in Austria, on March 26, 1908. His only sister was then ten, his mother still young and pretty, but his father was already an ageing man.

"He was a nightwatchman by the time I was born, but all he could ever think or talk about were his days in the Dragoons [one of the Austro-Hungarian Imperial élite regiments]. His dragoon uniform, always carefully brushed and pressed, hung in the wardrobe. I was so sick of it, I got to hate uniforms. I knew since I was very small, I don't remember exactly when, that my father hadn't really wanted me. I heard them talk. He thought I wasn't really his. He thought my mother . . . you know. . . ."

"Even so, was he kind to you?"

He laughed without mirth. "He was a Dragoon. Our lives were run on regimental lines. I was scared to death of him. I remember one day—I was about four or five and I'd just been given new slippers. It was a cold winter morning. The people next door to us were moving. The moving van had come—a horse-drawn carriage then, of course. The driver had gone into the house to help get the furniture and there was this wonderful carriage and no one about.

"I ran out through the snow, new slippers and all. The snow came half-way up my legs but I didn't care. I climbed up and I sat in the driver's seat, high above the ground. Everything as far as I could see was quiet and white and still. Only far in the distance there was a black spot moving in the whiteness of the new snow. I watched it but I couldn't recognize what it was until suddenly I realized it was my father coming home. I got down as fast as I could and raced back through the deep snow into the kitchen and hid behind my mother. But he got there almost as fast as I. 'Where is the boy?' he asked, and I had to come out. He put me over his knees and leathered me. He had cut his finger some days before and wore a bandage. He thrashed me so hard, his cut opened and blood poured out. I heard my mother scream, 'Stop it, you are splashing blood all over the clean walls.' "

Her boss was on the phone, feet on his desk, rolling a piece of Scotch tape between his fingers.

"What about Blazer? Why don't we publish Ezra Blazer anymore? Hilly wouldn't know literature if it went down on him."

Alice dropped a file into the wire tray outside his door and kneeled to fiddle with the strap on her shoe.

"No. No! I didn't say that. Hilly's full of shit. I said we'd do a million for the new book *plus* two-fifty for the backlist, even though it's unearned by more than the value of your house in fucking Montauk. Does that sound 'prudent' to you?"

In Germany today, this notion of "prominent" Jews has not yet been forgotten. While the veterans and other privileged groups are no longer mentioned, the fate of "famous" Jews is still deplored at the expense of all others. There are more than a few people, especially among the cultural élite, who still publicly regret the fact that Germany sent Einstein packing, without realizing that it was a much greater crime to kill little Hans Cohn from around the corner, even though he was no genius.

CALLER ID BLOCKED.

"Hello."

"How are you, Mary-Alice?"

"I'm all right. You?"

"I'm fine. I just wanted to check on you."

"Mm-hmm."

"You sure you're all right? You sound a little blue."

"I am a little blue. But it's nothing. Don't worry. How's your book?"

"Oh, I don't know. Who knows if it's any good. It's a funny business, this. Making things up. Describing things. Describing the door someone just walked through. It's brown, the hinges are squeaky . . . Who gives a shit? It's a door."

"'Endeavors in art require a lot of patience,'" Alice said finally. She could hear the frogs croaking.

"Memory like a steel trap, Mealy Potatoes."

The camp was between forty and fifty acres (six hundred metres by four hundred) and was divided into two main sections and four sub-sections. The "upper camp"—or Camp II—included the gas chambers, the installations for the disposal of the corpses (lime-pits at first, then huge iron racks for burning, known as "roasts"), and the barracks for the Totenjuden, *the Jewish work-groups. One of the barracks was for*

*males, another, later, for females. The men carried and burned the bod-
ies; the twelve girls cooked and washed.*

*The "lower camp" or Camp I was subdivided into three sections,
rigidly separated by barbed-wire fences, which, like the outer fences,
were interwoven with pine branches for camouflage. The first section
contained the unloading ramp and the square—Sortierungsplatz—
where the first selections were made; the fake hospital (the Lazarett)
where the old and sick were shot instead of gassed; the undressing barracks where the victims stripped, left their clothes, had their hair cut off
if they were women, and were internally searched for hidden valuables;
and finally the "Road to Heaven". This, starting at the exit from the
women's and children's undressing barrack, was a path ten-feet wide
with ten-foot fences of barbed wire on each side (again thickly cam-
ouflaged with branches, constantly renewed, through which one could
neither see out nor in), through which the naked prisoners, in rows of
five, had to run the hundred metres up the hill to the "baths"—the
gas chambers—and where, when, as happened frequently, the gassing
mechanism broke down, they had to stand waiting their turn for hours
at a time.*

She was about to send off an email rejecting another novel written in the second person when her screen went black and the air-
conditioning sputtered out, leaving behind a dim, primordial
silence.

"Fuck," said her boss, down the hall.

An hour later she and her colleagues were still bent over stalled
paperwork in the dank-growing air when he came around scowl-
ing and told them all that they could go home, if they could get
there.

Twenty-one flights down in the lobby, firefighters milled around
the sealed elevator bank, eyes raised to the halted dials. On Fifty-
Seventh Street, cars jockeyed for a path through the lightless inter-
sections while the number of pedestrians seemed to have quadrupled

since morning. Just north of Columbus Circle, where a self-appointed traffic conductor worked in mirrored sunglasses and shirtsleeves rolled up to his biceps, the line for Mister Softee ran the length of the block. Longer still were the lines to use the old-fashioned phone booths earning another stay of execution: people approached them warily, even sheepishly, as if entering confessionals right there on the street. At Sixty-Eighth and Seventy-Second shuffling throngs pushed onto buses already sagging from the load. At Seventy-Eighth World of Nuts and Ice Cream was giving cones away. Another block up, the neon harp outside the Dublin House appeared drained of all its color, and heat that was only average began to feel, under these mysterious circumstances, extraordinary: seeping and sinister and ineludible, like gas filling a cell. Outside Filene's Basement two women with four bags and five children between them haggled with the driver of a limousine pointed uptown. On the opposite corner, looking more hunchbacked than ever under his hundred coats, the homeless man rested his elbows on a newspaper dispenser and, taking it all in, yawned.

At Anna's door there was no answer. Inside her own apartment Alice shed her shoes, her blouse, her three-hundred-dollar skirt, poured herself a glass of Luxardo, and slept. When she awoke it was to a fathomless blackness and the plaintive beeping of her phone. Immediately outside her front door a fifth flight of stairs led up to the roof, or rather to a door bearing warning of an alarm that in two years she'd never heard go off; ignoring it now she ascended through the purple rhomboid of sky and in the relief of a feeble breeze walked across the ceiling of her own apartment to stand at the building's prow and look down into the street. A car turning off Amsterdam accelerated west, its headlights pushing through the dark with a new and precious intensity. Candlelight flickered on a fire escape two facades away. To the right, beyond the ribbon of river black as ink, the shore of New Jersey was illuminated as sparsely as if by campfires in the wild. "Cold beer here," a man's voice floated up from Broadway. "Still got some cold beer here. Three dollars."

Her phone sounded another dire beep. Without the subway rumbling, without trains hurtling up the Hudson and the hum of air conditioners and refrigerators and Laundromats three to a block, it was as though a mammoth heartbeat had ceased. Alice sat down and a moment later looked up to confront the stars. They seemed much brighter without the usual competition from below— brighter and more triumphant now, their supremacy in the cosmos reaffirmed. From the direction of the flickering fire escape came a few noncommittal chords on a guitar. The beer seller gave up or ran out. The moon, too, looked sharper and more luminous than usual, such that all at once it was no longer Céline's moon, nor Hemingway's, nor Genet's, but *Alice's*, which she vowed to describe one day as all it really was: the received light of the sun. A fire engine Dopplered north. A helicopter changed its direction like a locust shooed by giant fingers slicing through the sky. In her own hand Alice's phone sounded three final exasperated beeps and died.

. . . *there comes to light the existence of two particularly well differentiated categories among men—the saved and the drowned. Other pairs of opposites (the good and the bad, the wise and the foolish, the cowards and the courageous, the unlucky and the fortunate) are considerably less distinct, they seem less essential, and above all they allow for more numerous and complex intermediary gradations.*

This division is much less evident in ordinary life; for there it rarely happens that a man loses himself. A man is normally not alone, and in his rise or fall is tied to the destinies of his neighbors; so that it is exceptional for anyone to acquire unlimited power, or to fall by a succession of defeats into utter ruin. Moreover, everyone is normally in possession of such spiritual, physical and even financial resources that the probabilities of a shipwreck, of total inadequacy in the face of life, are relatively small. And one must take into account a definite cushioning effect exercised both by the law, and by the moral sense which constitutes a self-imposed law; for a country is considered the more civilized the more the wisdom and efficiency of its laws hinder a weak man from becoming too weak or a powerful one too powerful.

"The Nobel Prize in Literature for 2003 has been awarded to the South African writer John Maxwell Coetzee, who, in the committee's words, 'in innumerable guises portrays the surprising involvement of the outsider.'"

Alice turned off the radio and went back to bed.

CALLER ID BLOCKED.
    CALLER ID BLOCKED.
    CALLER ID BLOCKED.
    Beep.
    He hung up.

At her door again:
    Shave and a haircut, two bits.
    Sighing, Alice picked up her keys and her phone and followed the old woman shuffling eagerly down the hall. The vacuum cleaner stood agape in a large dining room with floor-to-ceiling curios and a fireplace whose delicate molding had not yet been smothered over by their landlord's indiscriminate brush. Behind them stretched a shadowy maze of yet more rooms, one after another all the way to the street, and in the air hung a stale, savory smell—half a century's worth of latkes and sauerkraut, Alice guessed. On the mantelpiece lay a rent slip gritting its teeth for $728.69.
    "Have you changed your clocks yet, Anna?"

"What?"

"Have you changed your—"

CALLER ID BLOCKED.

The words flashed like a heartbeat resuscitated in her hand. "I'll be right back, Anna, okay?"

He sounded woozy, as if he'd recently woken up from a long nap, and in the background she could hear an aria diminuendoing. "What are you doing, Mary-Alice?"

"I was just helping the old lady on my floor replace the bag in her vacuum cleaner."

"How old?"

"Old. Older than you. And her apartment is bigger than both of ours combined."

"Maybe you should be fucking *her*."

"Maybe I am."

Back down the hall Anna was trying to wedge the vacuum's bag out of its recess with a carving fork. "I'll do it," offered Alice.

"What?"

"I said I'll do it for you."

"Oh, thank you dear. My granddaughter gave it to me. I don't know what for."

"Have you changed your clocks yet?" Alice asked, standing.

"What?"

"I said did you remember to change your clocks back this morning?"

Anna's eyes watered. "My clocks?"

"Daylight Saving Time," Alice said loudly.

Culled from the mail:

A Symphony Space flyer on which he'd circled the Kurosawa films he thought she should see, specifically *Rashomon* and, if she were able to stay for the double bill, *Sanjuro*.

A Film Forum postcard on which he'd circled the Charlie Chaplin films he thought she would enjoy: *The Great Dictator*, *City Lights*, and *Modern Times*.

A MoMA Film brochure featuring a photograph of an actress drinking from a coupe glass in *Rosenstrasse* and whose hairstyle he suggested she try, should she ever decide to cut hers short.

His back was bothering him again, so she went to the Film Forum alone.

"When he twists the lady's nipples with his wrenches!"—and she ran around the room, tightening the air with invisible wrenches. "And when he salts his prison food with cocaine!"—and she bugged her eyes and put up her dukes. "And when he roller-skates in the department store! . . . And when he runs down the up escalator! . . . And when he gets drunk on the shot-up barrel of rum!" Flinging out her arms, so that an imaginary pair of shirt cuffs flew off, Alice did a sort of slow-motion moonwalk around him in his reading chair, and sang:

Se bella giu satore
Je notre so cafore
Je notre si cavore
Je la tu la ti la twaaaaah!

"*Señora?*"
"*Pilasina!*"
"*Voulez-vous?*"
"*Le taximeter!*"
"Eat your tart."
"*Tu la tu la tu la waaaaaaaah!*"

"Oh, Mary-Alice," he laughed, wiping an eye and reeling her in to kiss her fingers. "My darling, funny, cuckoo Mary-Alice! I'm afraid you're going to be very lonely in life."

NOW THAT HIS BOOK was done, a number of deferred medical matters could be addressed, including a colonoscopy, a prostate screening, and some tests a pulmonologist had recommended to investigate a recent shortness of breath. He didn't have cancer, and a steroid inhaler did away with the wheezing inside an afternoon, but it was also decided, at the urging of a new orthopedic surgeon, that his spinal stenosis be treated with a laminectomy. The surgery was scheduled for late March and a rotation of private nurses arranged to be on hand for two weeks, which stretched into three. One Saturday, shortly after he'd started another novel and gotten back on his feet, he and Alice and Gabriela, the day nurse, went out for a walk.

"Four pages," he announced.

"Already?" said Alice. "Wow."

Ezra shrugged. "I don't know if it's any good."

They sat down to rest on a stoop on Eighty-Fourth Street and watched as a man with a toddler leashed to his wrist paused to frown at his phone.

"You want children, Samantha?" asked Gabriela, who was Romanian.

"I don't know. One day maybe. Not now."

"That's okay. You have time."

Alice nodded.

"How old are you?"

"Twenty-seven."

"Oh, I didn't know. You look sixteen."

"She gets that a lot," said Ezra.

"Anyway, you still have time."

"Thanks."

". . . It's when you are thirty-five, thirty-six, you need to worry."

"Mm-hmm."

"So when do you want to have children?"

"Well, as I said, Gabriela, I'm not sure I do want to have them, but if it were up to me I'd wait until the last possible moment. Like when I'm forty."

Gabriela frowned. "Forty is too old. Forty things don't work right. Forty you are too tired."

"When do you think I should do it?"

"Thirty."

"No way."

"Thirty-two?"

Alice shook her head.

"Thirty-seven. You can't wait longer than thirty-seven."

"I'll think about it."

A long-legged redhead in spandex jogged past. Ezra watched her all the way to the corner.

"I know," said Gabriela. "Let's ask Francine."

"Who's Francine?"

"The night nurse," said Ezra. "She doesn't have kids."

On Columbus, they stopped again so that Ezra could chat with the hot dog vendor. "How's business, my friend?" The vendor made an exasperated gesture up and down the block, as though his truck were parked in a ghost town. "Terrible. No one want hot dog. Everyone want smoothie."

"Is that right?"

The vendor nodded glumly.

Ezra turned to Alice. "Want a hot dog?"

"Okay."

"Gabriela?"

"I like hot dogs."

"Two hot dogs, sir."

"What does 'halal' mean?" asked Gabriela.

"Good for Muslims!" the vendor called down proudly.

While Gabriela took a call on her phone, Alice and Ezra sat on the bench where they'd met. They rested quietly for a moment, until Ezra said something about the plane trees that Alice didn't hear for her thoughts—about where she'd been in her life, where she was going, and how she might get there without too much difficulty from here. Considerations complicated by this maddening habit of wanting something only until she'd got it, at which point she wanted something else. Then a pigeon swooped in and Ezra shooed it away with his cane; the way he did this, with a debonair little flick, reminded Alice of Fred Astaire.

"Sweetheart," he said, watching her eat. "This summer, why don't you take two weeks off and come out to visit me? Would you be bored?"

"Not at all. I'd love that."

He nodded. Licking mustard off her palm, Alice asked, "What did Adam say about your book?"

"'Ezra, I—I don't know what to say. It's genius. A masterpiece. I mean, Jesus Christ it's good. Every *word* . . . Every *single fucking word* . . .'"

"Is spelled correctly."

Ezra blew his nose. "Is spelled correctly."

"When's he going to submit it?"

"He's going to wait until the fall. Have you finished?"

"I'm up to page one sixty-three."

"And?"

"I like it."

"What."

"What?"

"What's that tone?"

"Well . . . Who's speaking? Who's telling the story?"

"What do you mean? The narrator's telling the story."

"I know but—"

"Finish it first. Then we can talk about point of view. Anything else?"

"The girl in the bagel shop. Who talks like that, these days? So carefully? So formally?"

"You do."

"I know but I'm—"

"What? Special?"

Alice raised her eyebrows at him but kept chewing.

"Mary-Alice," he said tenderly, a moment later. "I know what you're up to."

"What?"

"I know what you do when you're alone."

"What?"

"You're writing. Aren't you?"

Alice shrugged. "A little."

"Do you write about this? About us?"

"No."

"Is that true?"

Alice shook her head hopelessly. "It's impossible."

He nodded. "Then what do you write about?"

"Other people. People more interesting than I am." She laughed softly, lifting her chin toward the street. "Muslim hot dog sellers."

Ezra looked skeptical. "Do you write about your father?"

"No."

"You should. It's a gift."

"I know. But writing about myself doesn't seem important enough."

"As opposed to?"

"War. Dictatorships. World affairs."

"Forget about world affairs. World affairs can take care of themselves."

"They're not doing a very good job of it."

A woman from Ezra's building came down the path wearing a Gore 2000 cap and power walking a shih tzu. "Hello," Ezra said as she passed. "Hello, Chaucer," he added to the dog. For her part, Alice was starting to consider really rather seriously whether a former choirgirl from Massachusetts might be capable of conjuring the consciousness of a Muslim man, when Ezra turned back to her and said: "Don't worry about importance. Importance comes from doing it well. Just remember what Chekhov said: 'If there's a gun hanging on the wall in the first chapter, in a later chapter it must go off.'"

Alice wiped her hands and stood to throw her napkin away. "If there's a defibrillator hanging on the wall in the first chapter, in a later chapter must it go off?"

When she'd returned to him, Gabriela was there, holding his scarf and helping him to his feet; the sun had disappeared behind the high-rises on Columbus and all around them paces quickened in the sudden shade. Back to the wind, Ezra lodged his cane in the groin of his corduroys and struggled with his jacket's zipper. "No no," he said quietly, when Gabriela moved to help. "I can do it." Dwarfed by the plane trees, he looked smaller and frailer than he did in the close refuge of his apartment, and for a moment Alice saw what she supposed other people would see: a healthy young woman losing time with a decrepit old man. Or were other people more imaginative and sympathetic than she thought? Might they acknowledge that everything was still more interesting with him than without, and perhaps even that her gameness and devotion were qualities the world needed more of, not less? Behind them, the planetarium came aglow in violet. The halal hot dog seller began shuttering his truck. While Ezra adjusted his gloves, Gabriela gave Alice a sisterly wink and came to stand beside her, bouncing in the cold. "Samantha!" she said in a stage whisper. "Francine says freeze an egg."

With a change at Ronkonkoma, the train took a little under three hours. Alice passed the journey drinking a bottle of hard lemonade and watching the rusted chicken wire and psychedelic graffiti of Queens give way to daffodils and doghouses, dogwoods and vines.

At Yaphank, there was a smattering of chicory flowers along the tracks, quivering like tiny well-wishers. At the other end of her car sat an old woman who rested her hands on her purse and her purse in her lap, staring out the window at the scenery spooling by while a group of teenagers whooped and hollered all around her. Every now and again their horseplay spilled into the aisle, or bumped into the woman's seat, or, in one instant, sent a baseball cap sailing into the arm of her periwinkle blazer. Even with the conductor bearing down on them, the kids carried on—hurling bananas, snatching phones—until, standing over them, the conductor cleared his throat and said:

"Excuse me. Is this lady bothering you?"

Like gophers into holes, the teenagers dropped into their seats and remained there for the rest of the ride, communicating in monkish whispers.

"Hi Samantha."

"Hi Clete. How's it goin'?"

"Not bad. Nice weather for a visit to the country."

"It sure is."

When they pulled into the driveway, Ezra was just emerging from his studio. "Sorry, miss!" he called out across the lawn. "Your reservation isn't until tomorrow." He came closer. "How are you, Mary-Alice?"

Alice widened her eyes.

"I mean Samantha-Mary. Samantha Mary-Alice. Mary-Alice is your middle name, isn't it? But you prefer Samantha, don't you, Samantha Mary-Alice?"

"That's right," said Alice.

"Anyhow." Clete grinned. "See you Sunday, boss."

As they approached the house, Ezra put an arm around her. "Ninety-three pages."

"That's great."

"I don't know if it's any good."

The cleaning lady worked around them while they ate lunch. Alice began to tell him about the old woman on the train, but as

soon as she said "periwinkle" Ezra lowered his ginger ale and
shook his head.

"Don't sentimentalize her."

"You always say that. Don't sentimentalize people. As though I
have a choice."

"*Sentiments* are okay. Not sentimentality."

The cleaning lady winked. "He is so funny."

"Who?"

"*You*, Mister Blazer."

"He certainly is," said Alice, getting up. "Hey, the Yankees are
playing the Red Sox tonight."

"Hey, I'm going to take a nap. And then I'll be in my studio. I've
got some boxes to go through."

"What boxes?"

"For my biographer."

"What biographer?"

"My eventual biographer." In the living room there was a thump.
"Janice," Ezra called over his shoulder. "Is everything all right?"

"I just killed the biggest wasp."

"I thought George Plimpton was the biggest wasp."

"I'm going for a swim," said Alice.

"Wait, darling. What time's your train?"

Alice looked at him.

"I mean," he said, shaking his head, "what time's the baseball
on?"

It was cool for June; steam rose from the water as though a river
of magma flowed only a fathom below. Rustling trees cast trembling shadows on the basin, whose layers had chipped away over
the years to leave swirls of old grays, greens, and aquamarines, like
an antique sea chart. Beneath the surface, Alice's hands, still coming
together and swiveling apart, began to look less like instruments
of propulsion than like confused magnets, or hands trying to find
their way out of a dark room. But still, she swam. She swam until
the wind whistled and the sun sank pink behind the redbuds. She

swam until her lips turned blue and her nipples knotted. She swam until a series of lights came on in the house and Ezra's silhouette could be seen at the kitchen door, calling for her with the worried singsong of any homesteader calling for his dog.

Still dripping, she found on the bed:

A commemorative issue of *Life* magazine, FDR 60th Anniversary Edition.

A porn magazine from 1978, the entire issue comprising a story about a tailor named Jordy who the local community believes is a homosexual and thus is trusted to accompany young women into the fitting room. ("The most sexually conservative woman has no qualms about stripping for her doctor—or her tailor. Jordy was, so far as older or less desirable customers were concerned, an inanimate fixture who adjusted the clothes he sold to their bare or relatively bare bodies like an emotionless automaton . . .")

A souvenir program from the 33rd Annual Allegheny County Fair, featuring The Doodletown Pipers, Arthur Godfrey and His Famous Horse Goldie, and the Banana Splits. On the back, in black marker and his singularly mesmerizing slant, he had written: HEY, DOODLE. I DO LOVE YOU, YOU KNOW.

In the shallow end she popped up beside him.

He said, "You're like a little boat."

Alice shook the water from one ear and pushed off for another lap. When she'd swum back to him, he said, "Remember Nayla?"

"The Palestinian?"

"Yep. She came out to interview me last week, and Mary-Alice, I'm telling you, she has the most beautiful skin you've ever seen. It's like . . ." He smoothed a hand down his cheek. *"Chocolate milk."*

"Chocolate soymilk."

"That's right."

"So it went well." Alice floated onto her back.

"I invited her to have lunch with me when I get back to the city. She said she'd call. Darling, it doesn't matter to me, not in the slightest, but are your tits getting smaller?"

Alice sank herself bending to look. "I think so. I have this sinus problem, and my doctor prescribed a steroid that I'm supposed to spray up my nostrils, and it works but I think it's also causing my breasts to shrink."

Ezra nodded reasonably. "What do you want to do tonight?"

"Are there options?"

"Gin rummy. Or there's a concert at the Perlman school."

"Perlman school."

"Don't you want to know what they're playing?"

"It doesn't matter," said Alice, diving under again.

The drive took them past the country club, where golfers loped after balls rolled into the long shadows, and up Sunset Beach, where Ezra slowed for some girls carrying daiquiris over the road and Alice lowered her window to feel the wind with her hand. From here, you could see all the way across the water to the North Fork, where the train from the city came to its slow, inexorable halt— its tracks ending abruptly, surrounded on three sides by grass, as though the men whose job it was to lay them down a century and a half earlier had looked up one day and saw they could go no far- ther: a bay lay in their way. It gave the land beyond it a wilder feel, uncharted and unreachable by the steel veins of the metropolis— whose relentless intensity had lately seemed increasingly at odds with Alice's dream of a more contemplative life. A life of seeing, *really* seeing the world, and of having something novel to say about the view. On the other hand: Could all the rural quietude on earth cure the anxiety of self-doubt? Was she even capable of being alone for as long as it took? Would it make her life any less inconsequen- tial than it was now? And, hadn't he already said everything she wanted to say?

Ezra parked in a lot facing the water and with the sunset at their backs they headed for a marquee whose scalloped edges snapped and fluttered in the breeze. "Mary-Alice," he said, as they crossed the lush green grass stride for stride. "I have a proposal for you."

"Uh-oh."

"I want to pay off your college loans."

"Oh my gosh. Why?"

"Because you're a smart girl, a remarkable girl really, and I think it's time you should be doing whatever it is you want to be doing in life. Wouldn't it be easier if you didn't have all that debt hanging over your head?"

"Yes. Although it's not that much. I've already paid off most of it."

"Even better. What's left?"

"About six thousand, I think."

"So I'll give you six thousand, and you can get rid of the rest of it all at once, and maybe then you'll be able to see your way in life a little more clearly. More freely. What do you say?"

"May I think about it?"

"Of course you should think about it. Think about it forever if you like. And whatever you decide, we don't ever have to talk about it again. I'll just give you the money, or not, and that'll be the end of it. Okay?"

"Okay. Thank you, Ezra."

"You're velcome," they said simultaneously.

The concert was a special guest piano performance by a young Japanese woman who'd already played auditoriums in London, Paris, Vienna, and Milan—although from where they sat now she looked like a child of nine approaching an instrument large enough to be a baby giraffe's coffin. The first three notes sounded like day dawning, day or time itself; then the music exploded into the battering wind and rain of a violent squall, the girl's fingers darting and leaping and trilling at implausible speeds even as her face remained smooth and neutral as a mask. This was followed by two brief Stockhausen pieces, which by contrast sounded to Alice like a cat walking around on the keyboard; between them,

during the stern lull in which everyone knows not to clap, a spate
of coughs rippled through the audience, as though the dissonant
tones still hanging in the air were not what remained of the music
but an irritating gas.

During intermission, Ezra was greeted by a friend, a man with
white leonine hair and a turquoise handkerchief sprouting from his
seersucker pocket. "Ezra my dear. What do you think?"

"She's wonderful. Though perhaps a little aloof."

"Stockhausen is aloof. How's your book?"

Alice hung back, sipping white wine and gazing coolly out toward the bay; behind her, two female students were discussing tri-
ads, and fermatas, and then, a touch more cagily, who might be
chosen to solo in the benefit concert the following month. Alice
finished her wine and was about to move off altogether when Ezra
touched her elbow and said, "Cal, this is Mary-Alice."

"Oh," said Alice. "Hi."

"Hello."

"I was just telling Cal about how I heard Maurizio Pollini play
The Tempest a hundred years ago, at the Louvre. His tails were as
long as a freight train. Darling, you really must try to see Pollini
one day."

"You like music?" Cal asked.

"Oh yes," said Alice.

"Mary-Alice is an editor," said Ezra.

"Well," said Alice, "an associate editor."

"How fine," said Cal. "For which house?"

"Excuse me," said Ezra. "I'm just going to get a Diet Coke."

"Gryphon," said Alice, stepping closer to make room for the
people filing behind her.

"You must be very clever then. Roger doesn't hire dummies."

"You know Roger?"

"Of course. Brilliant man. Brilliant editor. Is that what you want
to do? Edit?"

A woman carrying a baby excused herself to squeeze between

them. Recognizing her, Cal leaned in for a kiss. "Felicity! This is Mary-Alice. Ezra's friend. And this?"

"Justine."

"*Justine . . .*"

Alice found Ezra outside, sitting on a bench under a maple's canopy, his freshly shaven face looking drawn and gray in the dying light. "Sorry honey. I suddenly felt a little light-headed."

"Do you want to go home?"

"No, I'll be all right. I want us to have a nice night out together. We can stay."

Sitting beside him, Alice said, "Cal knows Roger. My boss."

"Oops. Oh well."

Alice nodded. "Oh well."

A few yards away an elegantly dressed couple passed a cigarette between them. The woman said something in French that made Ezra look over and the man smoking with her laugh.

"What are you thinking?" asked Alice.

Ezra turned back to her, surprised. "I was thinking about my book. About a scene I haven't got right. Not that you ever get them right, mind you. You might as well write about the Hutus for all you're going to get right about them."

When they'd thrown their plastic cups away and pushed politely past the others back to their seats, the pianist returned to her bench and stared at the keys reflected there in the high ebony gloss with what seemed a superhuman concentration. Then she flung up her wrists, flared her nostrils, and the Hammerklavier was sprung from its cage: a great rumbling rigorous pounding that was anything but aloof; on the contrary, the woman's shoulders rocked forward and back, her foot pumped the damper pedal so emphatically that even her heel cleared the floor, and her head jerked wincingly up and to the side as if sparks were flying off the keyboard and threatening to enter her eyes. The effect, on Alice, was dazzling and demoralizing all at once: reverberating in her sternum, the music made her more desperate than ever to *do, invent, create*—to channel all her own energies into the making of something beautiful and unique to herself—but it also made her want to love. To submit to the loving of someone so deeply and well that there could be no question as to whether she were squandering her life, for what could be nobler than dedicating it to the happiness and fulfillment of another? At a certain point the pianist was leaning back slightly, hands working opposite ends of the keyboard as though one had to be kept from popping up while the other was held down, and here Alice turned to look at Ezra, who was watching with his mouth open; beyond him the fermata girls sat frozen in their own poses of wonder and humility: whatever they could do, it wasn't this, would never be this, or would only become this once a great many more hours had been sacrificed to the ambition. Meanwhile, their hourglasses were running down. Everyone's hourglass was running down. Everyone's but Beethoven's. As soon as you are born the sand starts falling and only by demanding to be remembered do you stand a chance of it being upturned again and again. Alice took Ezra's long cool fingers into her own hand and squeezed. This time, between movements, no one coughed.

The following afternoon, he drove her to the ferry himself. They were early, and while they sat in the car watching the barge turn ponderously into its berth, he said, without looking at her:

"Is this relationship a little bit heartbreaking?"

The glare off the harbor hurt her eyes. "I don't think so. Maybe around the edges."

From the top of the ferry ramp flowed a stream of people laughing, waving, hoisting duffel bags onto their shoulders and shielding their eyes from the sun. A young male couple held hands, while in his free arm the taller man cradled a beribboned houseplant.

"And do you ever worry about the consequences?"

"What consequences?"

Now he looked at her sternly.

"Are *you* worried?" asked Alice.

"No. But that's because I'm at the end of my life, and you . . ."—he laughed softly, at the neatness of it—"you're at the beginning of yours."

Shave and a haircut, two bits.

"Oh, hello dear. Have you got any toilet paper?"

"But Anna, you're holding a roll in your hand!"

Stumped, the old woman turned back to the hall.

"Is something wrong, Anna?"

Turning around again eagerly: "No dear. Nothing's wrong. Why?"

"Do you need something?"

"I don't think so. Tell me dear. Do you have a boyfriend?"

Shave and a haircut, two bits.

"Dear . . . What's your—?"

"Alice."

"Alice. Can you tell me what time it is?"

"Almost four."

"Four what?"

"Four nothing. It's almost four, five minutes before four. Anna, why are you carrying that roll of toilet paper around?"

Shave and a haircut—

It had been fewer than ten minutes since their last conversation, but when Alice opened the door again Anna clutched her bosom and recoiled, as if she hadn't expected to find anyone at home. "Oh! Dear. Hello. I wonder whether . . . Could you help me . . . change a . . ."

". . . bulb?"

It was in the kitchen, where Alice had not yet been, a room easily accommodating of a large rust-mottled table and six vinyl-padded chairs. A weak, cloudy-afternoon light struggled through the filth-glazed windows, the lower panes of which had been papered over with yellowing pages from the *Times*. *REAGAN NOSTALGIC FOR G.O.P. SENATE. RIFKA ROSENWEIN WED TO BARRY LICHTENBERG. IRMGARD SEEFRIED IS DEAD AT 69.* The defunct bulb hung spiderlike from a wire over the stove, whose burners had been unaccountably patched up in places with aluminum foil. Alice pulled a chair out from under the table and stepped onto its seat. When she'd unscrewed the dead bulb and went to step down again for its replacement, she put a hand on the cooktop to steady herself and reflexively snatched it back.

"Oh! Anna, your stove is hot!"

"Is it?"

"Yes! Are you cooking something?"

"I don't think so, dear."

"But were you just using it? Did you cook something today?"

"I don't know, dear. I don't know."

Back in her own apartment Alice dialed the number on her rent slip and paced impatiently waiting for the recorded menu to end. She pressed zero. Then she pressed zero again. ". . . At the tone, please say your name and the number of your unit. *Beep.*"

"Mary-Alice Dodge, Two-Oh-Nine West Eighty-Fifth Street, Five-C."

". . . Yeah?"

"Hi, this is Alice, in Two-Oh-Nine Five-C, and I'm calling because Anna, down the hall, keeps knocking on my door, and she's been doing it for a while, and I really don't mind helping her out every now and again, or even keeping her company, because she's a nice woman and I think sometimes she knocks just because she's lonely, but today she's knocked three times already, and I think maybe she doesn't even remember from one time to the next; first it was something about toilet paper, then she wanted to know the time, then she said she needed help changing a light bulb, which I did, and while I was there I noticed that her stove, which looks really old by the way, was extremely hot. I don't know if it's supposed to be like that, but it seemed much too hot to me, even though it wasn't on. And look, as I said, it's not that I'm not willing to lend her a hand from time to time, or even to keep an eye on her, in an unofficial sort of way, but there's only so much that I can do. And if she's becoming forgetful, or if there's something wrong with her stove and she doesn't know it, or if she were to leave it on and go out for a while, or fall asleep—"

"Okay. Hold on a minute, okay?"

She waited two minutes at least.

"Mary-Alice?" His voice was much changed from before—higher-pitched and almost musical in its politeness. "I've got Anna's granddaughter Rachel here on the line with us. Do you want to tell her what you were just telling me?"

"I'm so sorry, Mary-Alice," Rachel hurried to put in. "I'm so sorry it's been a bother. Thank you so much for your help."

"The Nobel Prize in Literature for 2004 has been awarded to Elfriede Jelinek, for her musical flow of voices and counter-voices in novels and plays that with extraordinary linguistic zeal reveal the absurdity of society's clichés and their subjugating power."

"I'll have the salmon."

"And I'll have the fusilli salsiccia without the salsiccia."

"Twelve pages," he said gravely, when the waiter walked away.

"Oh," said Alice. "I thought—"

He shook his head. "It wasn't any good."

Alice nodded. "What about your back?"

"My back is bad, darling. This thing didn't work."

"What thing?"

"The denervation I had last week."

"Oh, I didn't . . . What's denervation?"

He nodded. "Denervation is when they use radio frequency

to destroy a nerve so that it no longer sends a pain message to the brain. I've had it done before and it worked, but for some reason it didn't work this time." Their drinks arrived. "The good news," he added, removing the wrapper end from his straw, "is that now I can listen to Jonathan Schwartz without having to turn the radio on."

Walking back to his apartment they were halted by a young man in a trench coat swerving amiably into their path.

"Blazer! You were robbed!"

Wild with excitement, the fan even dared to extend his hand. Warily, Ezra drew his own from his pocket and accepted it. On the shake, the younger man gave a deferential little bow; as he did, the wind lifted a yarmulke from his head, tilting it through the air and setting it down in the middle of Amsterdam. The man put a hand on the back of his head and laughed. Then, pointing at Ezra, as though Ezra had conjured the wind:

"Next year man! Next year!"

They walked the rest of the block in silence. In the elevator, Ezra extracted a leaf from Alice's hair and let it flutter to the floor. "What's going on with the Sox?"

"They're up two games on Anaheim."

"Good darling."

"What's going on with your Palestinian?"

His head jerked back, freshly incredulous. "Nayla? She *still* hasn't called." His gaze down at Alice hardened, as though she might somehow be complicit in this offense. When the elevator *ping*ed and its doors opened, Alice stepped out while Ezra stayed put. "I mean," he said, lifting a palm, "how are we supposed to get along with these people?"

Boston beat Anaheim three games to zero. The next night, the Yankees won their series against the Twins three games to one. Alice waited hopefully, but when he called her it was to say, "Sixteen pages."

"Wow. How's your back?"

"It hurts."

"Are you taking something?"

"Am I taking something. Of course I'm taking something. The problem is, I can only take it every other day. Otherwise, you get hooked, and getting off it is hell."

She watched Game One of the ALCS at her bar. The Sox blew it in the ninth, failing to score off Rivera after the Yankees raised their lead from one run to three.

CALLER ID BLOCKED.

"I'm worried about your grandmother."

"So am I. She's been wearing her lucky robe since July."

"I suppose you'd like to watch the game here tomorrow night."

"I suppose I would."

Again, Boston lost. Three nights later, when they lost *again*, nineteen to eight, he switched off the television and tossed her the phone. "You'd better call her."

"Hi, Nana. It's Alice. . . . I know. . . . I know. . . . It's terrible. . . . I'm sorry. . . . No, I watched it at a friend's house actually. . . . No, no one you know. . . . Mm-hmm. . . . Oh really? . . . That's weird. . . . Was Doreen with him? . . . Yeah, he's a Shriner, too. . . . Okay. . . . I should go. . . . I should go now, Nana. . . . I love you too. . . . Okay. . . . Good night. . . . Good night."

"What'd she say?"

"That Francona's in a coma."

"That's good. What else?"

"That she ran into my father's brother at the supermarket and he said I gave a nice trilogy at my grandfather's funeral. I think he meant a eulogy."

The following afternoon he left a message on her voice mail asking if she wouldn't mind stopping in Duane Reade on the way over and picking up one jar of folic acid, one Mylanta cherry flavor with calcium, and ten bottles of Purell, two-ounce size. When she arrived, he was pacing the rug in his socks, hands on his back, grimacing. Alice handed him the bag.

Peering into it: "Hmm."

"What's wrong?"

"Nothing darling. It's not your fault. Never mind."

At midnight, bottom of the ninth, the Yankees were up by one and Boston fans stood in the bleachers and prayed. Feebly, someone raised a sign that read 4 MORE GAMES. Alice watched from between her fingers while Ezra got up and began to do his one hundred things.

"The party's over . . ."

Millar walked. The Sox replaced him with Roberts, who stole second. Then Bill Mueller hit a single straight down the middle and Roberts rounded third and slid home.

"Yesss!"

Holding his toothbrush, Ezra came out of the bathroom and sat down.

The score stayed the same for the next two innings. Alice watched from the floor, a knuckle between her teeth; then Big Papi hit a two-run homer and in an instant she was on her feet, making a running jump onto the bed. "We did it! We won! The Red Sox won! We won we won we won we won we WON!"

"You did darling. Fair and square."

"Now the party's over!"

For Game Five she arrived wearing one of her Searle skirts and a cap with a B on it. Ezra intercepted her in the communal hallway and looked both ways before yanking her out of the elevator by the arm. "Are you *crazy?* In *this* town?" The television was already on and an industrious desk clearing appeared to be in progress: after handing her her drink and the delivery menu for Pig Heaven he resumed licking envelopes, tearing up faxes, tossing old magazines into the wastepaper basket and stepping over miniature ziggurats of foreign editions accumulated on the floor, whistling as he went.

"Hey Mealy," he said, looking up from a bank statement. "Have I ever told you my Glow-Worm story?"

Alice put a check mark next to Pork Soong. "Nope."

"In the 1950s there was a popular song called 'Glow Worm,'

recorded by the Mills Brothers. And in the early sixties, when I was at Altoona teaching *creative writing*"—he shook his head—"I advised one of my students that he needed more detail in his fiction. It's detail, I explained, that brings fiction to life. He'd written a short story whose first sentence read: 'Danny came into the room whistling.' Then we had this little chat and he went home to revise it and when he came back the following week the first sentence read: 'Danny came into the room whistling "Glow Worm."' That was the only thing new in the entire story."

Alice giggled.

"Easiest white girl to laugh there ever was, Mary-Alice."

"What happened to him?"

"Who."

"Your student!"

"He won the Nobel Prize."

"Come on."

"He played for the Washington Senators for a while, actually. Back when there were only eight teams to a league."

"There were only eight teams to a league?"

"Oh, Mary-Alice, this is hopeless! There were eight teams to a league beginning in the Mesozoic Era all the way up to 1961, when they introduced the expansion teams, who got all the guys the other teams didn't want, like Hobie Landrith and Choo-Choo Coleman— Choo-Choo Coleman! How'd you like *that* for a name?—and the Mets were so inept that Casey Stengel, the old Yankees manager who'd been dragged out of retirement to manage them, went into the dugout one day and said, 'Can't anybody here play this game?'"

It was still four–four in the bottom of the ninth when he muted a Viagra ad and swiveled brightly to face her. "Darling, in the cooler in the back of the deli here on the corner they have Häagen-Dazs bars. Do *you* want one?"

"Now?"

"Sure. You'll be right back. But listen. I want vanilla on the inside, chocolate on the outside, nuts. If they don't have that I want chocolate on the inside, chocolate on the outside, no nuts. And if they don't have that I want vanilla on the inside, chocolate on the outside, no nuts. Plus whatever you want darling. My wallet's right on the table there. Go!"

At the deli they only had raspberry. And in the convenience store one block up they had only chocolate on the inside, chocolate on the outside, nuts. Alice picked one up and stared at it for a faintly agonizing moment—it wasn't even the right brand—before putting it back again and running the long block over to Amsterdam, where, in the narrow all-sorts shop that sold pornography next to Caramel Creams, she found, in the back, a freezer stocked almost exclusively with vanilla on the inside, chocolate on the outside, nuts.

"Sí!"

The cashier was eating takeout and watching a television stashed under the counter. "What happened?" Alice asked.

"Ortiz struck out." Fork aloft, he continued watching for a moment before lifting his other hand to take Ezra's money. When at last he looked up and saw the B on Alice's hat, he inhaled sharply. "Ah, la enemiga."

"Where have you been?" Ezra asked her when she got back.

In the twelfth inning, Ortiz tried to steal second but was called out after Jeter, legs spread, sprung vertically into the air to catch a high throw from Posada. He snagged it and, after seeming to hang in space for an impossibly long moment, returned to the ground and tagged Papi on the back.

"My God," said Ezra, pointing his ice-cream stick at the screen. "For a moment I thought I was watching Nijinsky."

"Ugh. I can't stand him. Look how smug he looks."

"Remember when we used to have sex, Mary-Alice?"

"He was safe!"

"No he wasn't darling."

"Yes he was!"

In the thirteenth, Varitek dropped three knuckleballs, letting Yankees advance to second and third. Alice groaned. Another sign went up in the stands: BELIEVE.

"In what?" said Ezra. "The tooth fairy?"

With two outs in the bottom of the fourteenth, Ortiz fouled right, then left, plus two more fouls up and over the backstop, then hit a fair ball that dropped down in centerfield, driving Johnny Damon home.

"Hoooraaaaaaaayy!"

"All right, Choo. That's it. Time for bed."

"Uh, Mary-Alice," he said to her voice mail the following morning, less than an hour after she'd left. "I'm sorry to ask you this, but before you come over here this evening—I assume you are coming over here this evening—would you mind first going to Zabar's and picking up some applesauce? The chunky kind? I'll pay you back." His voice sounded flat and irritable, drained of the previous evening's garrulousness, and when Alice arrived after an emergency ebook meeting that had run the full length of the afternoon he was holding his back, pacing and grimacing again, the television on mute and an electric heating pad warming the empty seat of his chair. As quietly as she could Alice put the applesauce into the refrigerator, got a tumbler down from the cupboard, and unwound the wax on a new bottle of Knob Creek. CALL MEL RE: WILL read a Post-it note stuck to the counter. A second note next to it read Q-TIPS!!! Even the way this looked in his incontrovertible hand made her feel a fool for ever thinking she could write. When she looked up again he was in his chair, neck stoically erect, the back of his head like a wax copy of itself if not for its infinitesimal pulsing.

She carried her drink to the bed and lay across it. In the flickering silence they watched the pregame graphics as intently as if any moment now their own life expectancies would be posted there. GAME 3. LONGEST 9 INN. GAME IN POSTSEASON HISTORY (4:20). GAME 5: LONGEST GAME IN POSTSEASON HISTORY (5:49). 21 HOURS,

46 MINUTES TOTAL OF 1ST 5 GAMES. 1,864 PITCHES. Alice memorized each lineup, briefly contemplated life in the Dominican Republic, and wondered about dinner. Her instinct, if not innate then informed by old childhood fears, was to ride out and perhaps even allay such moods by being as still and quiet as possible. But the bourbon had different ideas.

"I love that color," she said when the screen cut to a wide shot of Yankee Stadium with its grass mown into stripes that were actually two slightly different shades of emerald.

Several seconds later, Ezra replied in a low and even voice: "Yes. Night-game green."

When Jon Lieber took to the mound, Alice got up again to refresh her drink. "Would it be all right if we turned the sound on now?"

It was too loud, as though the night before they'd been watching with a dozen friends all laughing and chatting at once, and one of the announcers had a slight Southern accent that sounded almost stoned in its serenity, the other a rich, reassuring baritone not dissimilar to the one that narrated the Viagra ads. Babbling away about the bullpen, Curt Schilling's tendon, and the "difficult conditions" presented by the weather, their voices filled the little room like disembodied dinner guests trying to ignore the tension mounting between their hosts. Forecast: Drizzle. Wind speed: 14 mph, left to right. Superimposed against the misty skyline, her and Ezra's reflections in the yellow glow of his reading lamp had the trapped and inanimate look of dollhouse detainees. Alone together, together alone . . . Except of course they weren't alone. Ezra's pain was with them. Ezra, his pain, and Alice, barely tolerable envoy from the enraging world of the healthy.

"Red Sox on top here, four—nothing, and due to a technical error tonight's game is being brought to you by AFN: the American Forces Network. Our friends at AFN are delivering coverage to the US Armed Forces serving in one hundred seventy-six countries and US territories and of course aboard navy ships at sea. We say welcome to our men and women in uniform, serving so far from our shores, and thank you for everything you do."

In the stands, three men with their hoods pulled up against the rain juggled plastic cups of beer and hand-painted signs: ON LEAVE FROM IRAQ. 31ST CSH HOLLA: GO YANKS!

"Not a city in this country," the Southern voice mused, "that reminds me more of the sacrifice and freedom that we enjoy because of our men and women . . ." Jason Varitek adjusted his chest protector. ". . . What a—What a guy. What a leader, man. He hit that fly ball . . . Take a look at this. Look at this guy, if you think of all the innings he's caught, all that he's done . . . Now watch what happens: he *continues* to hustle, into the dugout, so that he can get the gear on, and get back out, and catch as many pitches from Curt Schilling as he can, to get him comfortable for the bottom of the sixth . . ."

"On very tired legs . . ."

"Just makes you think he mighta made a pretty good soldier . . ."

Ezra pressed mute.

Alice stared at the screen a moment longer before finishing what was left in her glass. "Are you hungry? Do you want to order something?"

"No, darling."

"I'll get you some Q-tips tomorrow if you want."

He leaned over to look for something on the floor. "Thank you, dear."

"I wish they would stop showing that."

"What."

"His sock. It's making me queasy."

Ezra took a pill.

"I thought you weren't supposed to take it every day."

"Thank you, Little Miss Elephant Brain."

"Whoa! Did you see that?"

"What?"

"A-Rod slapped him!"

They watched as the ball dribbled over the foul line and Jeter sprinted home. "He was running to first and Arroyo went to tag him and A-Rod slapped the ball out of his glove!"

Francona came out to complain. The umpires huddled. When they reversed the call, New York fans booed and pelted the grass with trash.

"I can't believe it," said Alice. "That was *incredibly* childish." She looked at Ezra, but Ezra was looking at the screen. "If *I* were a Yankee I'd be ashamed, trying to get ahead like that."

"If you were a Yankee," Ezra said quietly, "they wouldn't be in the playoffs."

Alice laughed. "Can we turn the sound back on now?"

Slowly, he rotated to face her. "Mary-*Alice* . . ."

"What?"

"I *hurt*."

"I know you do. But what am I—"

Ezra flinched. "But what are you supposed to do about it?"

Uncertainly, Alice nodded.

"Wait a minute," she said then. "I do a lot actually. I go to Zabar's for you, and to Duane Reade, and to the deli to get you Häagen-Dazs during extra innings—"

"Darling, you offered to do those things. Remember? You offered to help me out when I'm unwell. You said, 'Whatever you need, I'm right around the corner.' I would not have asked you otherwise."

"I know, but—"

"Do you think I like being like this? Do you think I enjoy being old and crippled by pain and dependent on other people?" His head was pulsing more obviously now, as though it might explode.

"Fuck you," said Alice.

For a while the only sound was the changing frequency of the static on the television screen as it flickered from dark to light and back again. Alice covered her face with her hands and left them there for a long moment, as if to be transported—or as if she were counting, giving one or both of them a chance to hide—but when at last she took them away again Ezra was still there, exactly as he'd been: legs crossed, eyes black with anguish, waiting. His face blurred through the glaze of her tears.

"What should I do with you, Mary-Alice? What would you like me to do? What would *you* do, if you were me?"

Alice covered her face again. "Treat me like shit," she said into her hands.

When she got home, there was a letter from the Harvard Student Loan Office in her mailbox, thanking her for paying off her Federal Perkins debt in full.

The Red Sox won.

Without being asked, the bartender poured what remained of the bottle into Alice's glass.

Alice moved the glass one inch to the side, then replaced her hand in her lap.

"Do you play chess?" the man beside her asked, in a British accent.

Alice turned to him. "I have a board."

"Do you speak French?"

"No. Why?"

"There's an expression chess players use to clarify that a piece is only being adjusted in its place, not yet moved to another square."

"Oh really? What's that?"

"*J'adoube.*"

Alice nodded and, looking up at the television, lifted her glass and this time drank from it.

"Hi," she said, knocking on her boss's door. "Here's that—"

He slammed down the phone.

"Sorry," said Alice, "I didn't—"

"Fucking Blazer is staying with Hilly."

Furiously he massaged his forehead with his fingers. Alice laid the file on his desk and left.

"The thing is," she said to the British man, whose name was Julian, "they haven't been in the World Series since 1986. And they haven't *won* a World Series since 1918. And some people attribute this to the Curse of the Bambino: they think the Red Sox are being punished for selling Babe Ruth to New York."

"To the Yankees."

"Yes. Although these days there are also the Mets, but they didn't exist until the sixties." Alice took a sip. "Before that there were only eight teams to a league."

Pujols took second on ball one inside.

When Renteria hit it back to Foulke, Foulke threw him out at first, and the dugout emptied onto the field, where the men ran to join a celebratory huddle, leaping onto one another's backs and into one another's arms and punching the air and pointing gratefully to the heavens. In the stands, camera flashes pop-pop-popped like muzzle fire. There was a brief satellite image of soldiers in Baghdad celebrating in their sand fatigues and then the picture cut back to the Bank of America Postgame Show and Bud Selig handed Manny Ramirez the MVP trophy. A reporter asked him how it felt.

"First, you know, it was a lot of negative stuff, you know, I was gonna get traded, but, you know, I keep my confidence on myself and I believe in me and I did it, you know, I'm just blessed, and, you know, I prove a lot of people wrong, you know, I knew I could do this and thanks God I did it."

"Do you believe in curses, sir?"

"I don't believe in curse. I think you make your own destination, and we did it, you know, we believe in each other. We went out there, we play relaxed, and we ground it out and we did it."

Alice looked at her phone. The bartender bought them a round.

"Every man makes his own destination," Alice said wryly, putting her phone back into her purse.

"He's right," said Julian, pulling her toward him for a kiss.

Shave and a haircut, two bits.

She stood in Alice's doorway holding a bottle of wine, which was dusty and had no name except for a dense parade of Hebrew lettering, the old woman's head wobbling faintly as if attached to the rest of her by a spring. "Can you open this for me, dear?"

The cork came out black.

"Here you go," said Alice.

"Would *you* like some?"

Alice returned to her counter, filled two jam jars halfway, and brought them back to where Anna continued to stand faintly quivering just inside her door. Her robe, made of a faded daisy print, had a brown stain shaped like Florida on its lapel. Anna accepted the glass of wine warily, with both hands, suggesting it had been some time since she'd drunk anything standing up.

"My nephew killed himself today."

Alice lowered her glass.

". . . So I needed some wine."

"I don't blame you," Alice said softly. "How old was he?"

"What?"

"How—"

"Fifty."

"Was he sick?"

"No."

"Did he have any children?"

"What?"

"Did he have any—"

"No."

Neither of them had taken a sip, but even so Anna was looking down at her drink as if wondering when it was going to work.

"Did you vote today?" Alice asked.

"What?"

"Did you vote? For the president?"

"Did I float?"

Alice shook her head.

"Tell me . . . ," Anna began.

"Alice."

"I know. Do you live here alone?"

Alice nodded.

"And you don't get lonely?"

Alice shrugged. "Sometimes."

Anna peered past her now, down the hall to where Alice's reading light was on and *The Fall of Baghdad* lay facedown on her bed. The radio on her dresser could be heard quietly calling New York for Kerry and Nebraska for Bush. "But you have a boyfriend, don't you dear? Someone special in your life?" Her jam jar of wine, which she continued to hold in two hands like a priest's chalice, tipped another degree toward the floor.

Alice smiled a little sadly. "I might."

CALLER ID BLOCKED.

SATURDAY
21
MAY

SATURDAY
18
JUNE

SATURDAY
2
JULY

A car door slammed.

"Sorry folks!" he called out from the kitchen window. "Your reservation is for tomorrow!"

Ignoring him, the children hopped jauntily up the flagstone path, the boy weaving a toy police boat through the air and the girl trailing fairy wings that glittered amethyst under the high summer sun. Holding the screen door open for them, Ezra resembled a butler to elves. "Olivia! You've grown wings!" Kyle's hopping continued all the way up the steps and into the living room, where he collapsed upside down on Ezra's ottoman and, hair sweeping the floorboards, announced, "Olivia has a loose tooth!"

"Is that right, Olivia?"

Sitting on the very edge of the sofa cushion so as not to crush her wings, Olivia nodded.

"How loose?"

"Weally loose!" said Kyle.

Sneaking a look at Ezra, Olivia blushed.

Over lunch:

"Ezra?"

"Yes sweetheart."

"How'd you get to be so sophisticated?"

Ezra lowered his pickle. "How am I sophisticated?"

Olivia shrugged. "You wear nice shirts. And you know the president."

A grape rolled off Kyle's plate toward the edge of the table. "Uh-oh!" said Alice, lunging to catch it. "Runaway grape."

"Wunaway gwape!"

"I'm not *that* sophisticated," concluded Ezra.

"Ezra works hard," said Edwin, pulling a shard of potato chip out of his daughter's hair. "If *you* work hard and do well in school then maybe one day *you'll* be able to afford nice shirts, too."

"And meet the president?"

"And *become* the president," said Eileen.

"That's right," said Ezra. "President Wu. Madam President Wu. You'd already be better than the one we've got now."

Olivia spooned mint-chocolate-chip ice cream into her mouth and worked her jaw slowly, meditatively, as though it contained a foreign object. Sitting on Alice's lap, Kyle farted.

"Whoops," said Alice.

"Whoops," said Kyle, giggling into his spoon.

In the pool, he wore lobster-print swimming trunks and his sister a too-big one-piece that drooped to reveal her pale, penny-flat nipples. "Look," Olivia commanded, while her mother vigorously rubbed sunblock into her arms; flanked by four chocolate-filled molars, the loose tooth teetered steeply back and forth under her finger like a drunk.

"Wow," said Alice. "That *is* loose."

It was a warm day, cloudy but close, yet Ezra sat in his deck chair wearing trousers, a long-sleeved button-down shirt, and laced-up Oxfords tied in double bows. *The Perpetual Orgy* lay bookmarked in his lap and his Penn State Altoona cap was perched so lightly on his head its letters caved in a little. "Now, remember, boys and girls. I have this chemical I put in the pool that makes urine turn red. Bright red! The second someone pees in the pool, it's going to turn bright red." Kyle shot a furtive, furrowed glance to his wake.

"Marco," said Alice.

"Polo!" screamed the children.

"Marco."

"Polo!"

"Marco!"

"POLO!"

"MARCO!"

"POLOAAAAAAAAAAHHHHHHHHH!"

Ezra put up a hand. "Excuse me, but does anyone here actually know who Marco Polo was?"

Kyle and Olivia halted, bobbing in place and blowing water from their noses and lips; then Olivia turned to Alice and asked sweetly, "Will you take me to the deep end?"

Alice crouched while the little girl half climbed, half floated onto her hip; then she waded until she could no longer touch the pool's bottom and had to pull one hand over the other on the long side of its flagstone edge. The deeper she went, the tighter Olivia clung, peering over her shoulder and shuddering as though having caught sight of a grisly shipwreck below. "Mayday, Mayday!" laughed Alice when Kyle's remote-control police boat caught up with them and butted her in the breast.

"Don't let go Olivia," her mother called.

When they reached the far corner, the girl's limbs were as tight around Alice as a vise. "How's this?" Alice asked.

"Good," Olivia murmured, teeth chattering.

Bouncing his foot and looking a little bored, Ezra asked if anyone knew any jokes.

Edwin lowered his BlackBerry. "What do you call twins before they're born?"

"Wombmates!" Olivia shrieked in Alice's ear.

"That's good," said Ezra. "What else?"

Kyle tried to stand on a kickboard. "What do you get when you cwoss a Tywannosauwus wex with a . . . with uh . . ."

"With a what?"

The kickboard popped up. "I forget."

Ezra shook his head. "Needs work."

"Why did the cookie go to the hospital?" said Olivia.

"Why?"

"Because he felt crummy!"

Kyle cackled; Ezra groaned. Still barnacled to Alice, Olivia turned to her and wrinkled her nose. "Needs work?"

"I've got one," said Ezra. "A guy flying into Honolulu turns to the guy sitting next to him and says, 'Say, how do you pronounce it? Hawaii or Havaii?' 'Havaii,' says the other guy. 'Thanks,' says the first guy. And the other guy says, 'You're velcome.'"

The little ones stared at him.

"I don't get it," said Kyle.

"He talks funny," said Olivia. "Right?"

"Right."

"But what's funny about it?" said Kyle.

"Nothing," said Ezra. "Never mind."

"Needs verk," suggested Eileen.

The wind picked up, shuffling the leaves. Undeterred, the children taught Alice Sharks and Minnows, then Monkey in the Middle, then a made-up game that involved one and then the other of them climbing onto her back and pretending to whip her hindquarters with a foam-noodle riding crop.

"Do you want children, Mary-Alice?" Eileen asked.

Kyle waved the noodle above his head like a lasso, flicking water into her eyes. "Maybe," said Alice. "When I'm forty."

Lifting her sunglasses, Eileen shook her head. "Forty's too old."

"So I've heard. But I'm afraid to do it sooner. I'm afraid it will . . . consume me."

"Mary-Alice is a very tender person," explained Ezra.

Eileen nodded, squinting at the sky. "I take it back. Forty isn't too old to have a child. *Fifty* is too old to have a *ten*-year-old child."

When a light rain began to stipple the flagstones, Ezra pushed himself up and clapped his hands. "Who vants a jelly doughnut?" While Alice and Eileen helped them into socks that in theory would keep the ticks at bay, the children shivered, whined, whimpered, cajoled, and threw tragic glances over their shoulders at the departed water, still oscillating and densely pockmarked now with rain. The remote-control police boat bumped up against the aluminum ladder. Foam noodles lay on the surface like snakes sprung from a can. When all the remaining towels, tote bags, tubes of Coppertone and miniature goggles had been gathered up, Alice fell in line behind the others trudging in the manner of weary seafarers up the lawn: Ezra, making his long solitary strides past the redbuds no longer in bloom; Edwin and Kyle, pointing scientifically at something in the harbor; and Olivia and Eileen, on legs identically proportioned and knock-kneed. "See those trees?" Eileen was saying to her daughter, while all around them the rain made a racket like oil frying. "When Mommy was a little girl she helped Ezra plant those trees . . ."

After dinner they played Scrabble.

Kneeling on her chair, wearing a nightgown that had the Little Mermaid on it, Olivia considered her options for a long, tooth-worrying moment before at last extending an arm across the table and laying out, with maximum suspense: BURD.

"No sweetie," said Edwin. "It's B-*I*-R-D."

"Oh," said Olivia, slumping. "I forgot."

"That's okay, honey," said Ezra. "You just had a junior moment."

Edwin put down FRISBEE. "Sixteen points."

"No proper names," said Eileen.

Edwin took back FRISBEE and put down RISIBLE. "Good one," said Alice. "Thirteen points."

"What does it say?" asked Kyle.

"It says 'risible,'" said Eileen.

"What's 'risible'?" asked Olivia.

"Something funny," said Alice. "Something silly, or ridiculous, that makes you laugh." She put down PEONY. "Twelve points."

Ezra put down CLIT.

Alice covered her mouth with the scorepad. Over her wineglass, Eileen widened her eyes.

Screwing his lips to one side, Ezra consulted his letters again and then shook his head ruefully. "That's all I got." Looking up from his BlackBerry, Edwin grinned.

"What?" said Kyle. "What does it say?"

"It says '*clit*,'" Eileen said clearly.

"That's not a word," said Olivia.

"Yes it is!" said Kyle. "Clift is a word!"

"That's right," said Ezra, looking relieved. "Clift *is* a word."

"What does it mean?" asked Alice.

"It's another word for 'cliff.'"

"There's also Montgomery Clift," said Edwin.

"No proper names," Eileen repeated. "Anyway, that's not what it says."

"Never mind," laughed Alice. "Twelve points for Ezra."

Olivia took a finger out of her mouth and turned to stare at her. "Why do you laugh after everything?"

"Who?" said Alice. "Me?"

Olivia nodded. "You laugh after everything."

"Oh," said Alice. "I hadn't realized I was doing it. I have no idea why."

"I have a theory," said Ezra, rearranging his tiles.

"You do?"

"I think you laugh to keep things light. To defang the situation."

"What's defang?" asked Olivia.

"It's what's going to happen to you soon," said Edwin, tickling her in the ribs.

"It was *his* idea," Eileen said the following morning, back down at the pool. "*He* was raised Catholic and thinks everyone should have some sort of religious education. But when it came time to explain to them how Mary became pregnant with Jesus, I could hardly keep a straight face."

"Mom! Mom look!"

"Olivia, socks!"

Still wearing her nightgown, Olivia rounded the pumphouse like a wind-filled sail and arrived breathlessly on the flagstone deck, waving a bill. "Look! Look what the tooth fairy brought me!"

"Wow!" said Ezra. "Fifty smackers."

"That's very generous," said Eileen.

"Can I keep it?"

"Give it to your father please. And put some socks on." When she'd gone, Eileen looked pointedly at Ezra. "*Fifty* dollars?"

"What? It's nothing compared to what I gave the hot dog guy."

Alice looked up from her book. "You gave money to the hot dog guy?"

"Sure."

"How much?"

He waved a fly away. "Seven hundred."

"Seven hundred dollars!"

"You don't even like hot dogs," said Eileen.

Ezra shrugged. "I wanted to help him out. I wanted to help out a friend. He'd been telling me about how he's had a tough time lately; the cost of his permit's going up and his landlord keeps raising the rent on his apartment and he's got a wife and three kids to take care of. He told me he wasn't going to be able to pay his bills next month unless he found a way to come up with some extra cash. So the next day I went back to him and I said, 'What's your name?' And he told me his name, and I got out my checkbook, and he said, 'Wait! That's not my real name.'"

Alice groaned.

"So already I was out of my depth, see. But what the hell. I wrote him a check. I wrote him a check for seven hundred and fifty dollars."

"I thought you said seven hundred," said Eileen.

"No darling. Seven hundred and fifty."

"You said seven hundred," said Alice.

Ezra shook his head. "I'm getting a little forgetful."

"Anyway," said Alice.

Ezra held up his hands. "I haven't seen him since."

"May I ask," said Eileen, "the provenance of this hot dog man?"

"He's Yemeni, I think." They watched as Kyle came swaggering down the lawn carrying a pair of flippers and the remote control to his boat. Ezra looked worried. "I probably just gave seven hundred and fifty bucks to al-Qaeda."

"En garde!" said Kyle, dropping the flippers and swinging the remote control's antennae toward them in an arc.

Like a shot, Ezra flipped backward onto the lawn, plastic deck chair and all, his head barely missing the root of an old spruce stump. Delighted, Kyle dropped the remote control to the ground and joined him on the grass with a bumbling pratfall.

"I'm serious," said Ezra, still lying on his back. "My defibrillator just went off."

"Oh my God," said Eileen.

"Are you okay?" asked Alice.

"It's okay. I'm okay. I think I'm okay. It's just . . . It was just . . . a bit of a shock." He laughed shakily. "Literally."

Eileen picked the remote control up by its antennae and tossed it like a dead animal into the woods. "But we should call a doctor, don't you think? Just to be sure?"

When Virgil arrived, it was Olivia who ran to meet him in the driveway, fairy wings flouncing. "Whoa!" she said. "How old are *you*?"

In Alice's mailbox when she got home:

A jury summons.

An invitation to the Third Annual Fire Island Black Out beach weekend, addressed to the man who'd lived in her apartment before her.

A notice from the NYC Department of Buildings, a copy of which had also been taped to the lobby door: *WORK PERMIT: PLUMBING – ALTERATION TYPE 1 APPLICATION FILED TO PERFORM SUBDIVISION OF EXISTING SIX (6) ROOM RAILROAD ON 5TH FLOOR INTO TWO SEPARATE ONE (1) BEDROOM APARTMENTS. GENERAL CONSTRUCTION, PLUMBING, GAS AND INTERIOR FINISHES AS REQUIRED. EXISTING APARTMENT DOORS TO REMAIN. NO CHANGE TO EGRESS FROM APARTMENT TO HALL.*

In the jury assembly room she sat next to a man wearing a T-shirt that read IT'S NOT THAT I'M ANTISOCIAL, I JUST DON'T LIKE YOU. In front of her, another man was eating a blueberry scone and explaining to the woman next to him why some Muslims do their best to avoid most musical genres. He'd been to MoMA the day before, and there had overheard a docent speaking to a group of schoolchildren about the "musicality" of Kandinsky's work; this had struck him as an especially interesting point of comparison, "because the Muslims you'd expect to prefer Kandinsky over figural artists would almost certainly be the same ones who live in suspicion of music, whose sensuality and purposelessness, they believe, encourage humans' baser tendencies."

"What tendencies?" the woman beside him asked.

"Promiscuity," said the man, chewing. "Lust. Immodesty. Violence. To my very conservative uncle, for example"—he brushed some crumbs off his lap and onto the floor—"Britney Spears and Beethoven are the same thing. Music is offensive because it appeals to our more animalistic passions, detracting from our more intelligent pursuits."

"So if your uncle were in a restaurant and they started playing classical music, would he put his hands over his ears? Would he get up and leave?"

"No. But he would probably find the playing of any music at all extremely silly."

The more you learn, thought Alice, the more you realize how little you know.

At 9:20, a short bald man stepped onto a box at the front of the room and introduced himself as Clerk Willoughby. "My fellow Americans. Good morning. Everyone please look at your summons. We want to make sure you're all in the right place on the right day. Your summons should read July fourteenth, Sixty Centre Street. If anyone is holding a summons that says something different, please take your things down the hall to the main office here and they'll get it cleared up."

A woman behind Alice sighed loudly and began gathering her things.

"Now. In order to be a juror in this court, you must be a citizen of the United States, you must be over eighteen years old, you must understand English, you must live in Manhattan, Roosevelt Island, or Marble Hill; and you must not be a convicted felon. If anyone does not meet those requirements, you too should pick up your things and take them to the administration office."

The man in the antisocial T-shirt got up and walked out.

"Jury duty hours are from nine a.m. to five p.m. with a lunch break from one to two p.m. Jurors not involved in a trial and thus still here in the assembly room at four thirty will in all likelihood be allowed to leave at that time. If a judge is making use of you, however, it's out of my hands and you will have to stay until you are dismissed by the judge. The average length of a trial is seven days. Some are longer, some are shorter. At this point we'll be showing you a short orientation film, and I would be grateful if everyone would please remove your headphones and close your books and newspapers and give it your full attention."

The movie began with a fade-in on a lake. Led by a burly guard, a herd of medieval villagers trooped down to the water's edge.

In olden times, said a voice-over, *in Europe, if you were accused of a crime or misdemeanor, you had to go through what they called trial by ordeal. This was an idea that first surfaced some three thousand years ago, in the time of Hammurabi.*

The herd of villagers parted to make way for a man whose wrists had been bound tightly with rope. Two guards pushed him toward the water.

One of these ordeals called for you to plunge your hand into boiling water. Three days later, if the hand healed, you were pronounced innocent. Another trial by ordeal was even more extreme. It demanded that you be tightly bound and thrown into the water. If you floated, you were guilty. If you sank, you were innocent.

Now the guards were tying the prisoner's feet while a pair of officials stood by, watching impassively. The villagers were hushed, apprehensive. Then the guards heaved the prisoner into the water. The prisoner sank. Bubbles rose in his stead. The officials watched for a moment before signaling to the guards to pull him out. The villagers cheered.

Was this fair and impartial justice? They *thought* so. . . .

Despite her mood, which was restless and premenstrual, Alice enjoyed the film. It reminded her of social studies and in the end did not really ask of her very much—only that she not take her civil liberties for granted, and when had she ever done that? With the credits rolling behind him, Willoughby mounted his wooden box again and, like a magician demonstrating the integrity of his materials, held up a sample summons and instructed everyone to tear off a perforated portion that would have to be handed in. "Not *this* piece," he said at least twice, once to each side of the room. "*This* one." But each time either his knuckles or his pointing hand had obstructed Alice's line of vision, so that when it came time for her to turn her own piece in the officer receiving it tutted direly and said, handing it back, "This is the wrong piece."

"Oh, sorry. What should I do?"

Seizing the summons again, the clerk removed a Scotch-tape dispenser from her desk, taped the pieces together and thrust them back. "Sit down." Then, shaking her head, and already gesturing to the next person in line, she added, "Very poor."

At 10:35, Clerk Willoughby began reading names.

"Patrick Dwyer."

"José Cardozo."

"Bonnie Slotnick."

"Hermann Walz."

"Rafael Moreno."

"Helen Pincus."

"Lauren Unger."

"Marcel Lewinski."

"Sarah Smith."

In front of Alice, the man whose Muslim uncle did not like music for its animalistic passions was reading *The Economist*. Alice took out her Discman, untangled its cord, and pressed PLAY.

"Bruce Beck."

"Argentina Cabrera."

"Donna Krauss."

"Mary-Ann Travaglione."

"Laura Barth."

"Caroline Koo."

"William Bialosky."

"Craig Koestler."

"Clara Pierce."

It was a Janáček CD, whose first track she listened to three times, and with each playing felt herself less, rather than more, capable of comprehending its complexity. But violence? Lust? A low-grade, objectless lust seemed to be her default state; perhaps music, like alcohol, could give it a reckless vector . . .

"Alma Castro."

"Sheri Bloomberg."

"Jordan Levi."

"Sabrina Truong."

"Timothy O'Halloran."

"Patrick Philpott."

"Ryan McGillicuddy."

"Adrian Sanchez."

"Angela Ng."

A little after four those whose names had not been called were dismissed with orders to return in the morning. Alice went back to the pub where she'd spent her lunch hour and ordered a glass of wine, followed by a second glass of wine, then laid her money down next to a section of newspaper containing the headline *Baghdad Bomb Kills Up to 27, Most Children,* and at the first subway stop she came to descended unsteadily underground. It was rush hour now, and instead of changing via the long airless stampede at Times Square she got out at Fifty-Seventh Street and decided to walk. Her eyes felt overexposed and she wove a faint zigzag down the block, as if unaccustomed to the third dimension. A rumbling blast from a sidewalk grate suggested an underworld riled by her escape. Overhead, the forest of glass and steel swayed vertiginously against the sky. A man following close behind her whistled tunelessly, the sound thin and snatched away from them by the great static city din that was like two giant seashells against the ears: the undulating drone of wind and wheels rushing to make the light, taxis honking, buses groaning and sighing, hoses spraying the pavement, crates being stacked and van doors trundling shut. Wooden heels. A pan flute. Petitioners' spurious salutations. It was eighty-three degrees, but many of the stores had propped open their doors—you could almost see the expensive air gusting out and withering on the street—from which truncated melodies blared like a radio set to scan: Muzak Bach, Muzak Beatles, "Ipanema," Billy Joel, Joni Mitchell, "What a Wonderful World." Even from the entrance to the 1/9 there seemed to emanate the muffled bebop of a swing band. . . . But then Alice passed the stairs down into the ground and still the music became louder and clearer, and developed a kind of height, a floating-up quality, the unique reverberation of brass and drums in the open air. Then she saw the dancers.

It was as if a present-day *Rigoletto* had overflowed the stage of the opera house and spilled out into the square. Under a wide white sky the sea of bouncing arms and swinging hips rocked metronomically; every now and again a limb was flung with such enthusiasm it looked liable to dislodge. A few bodies moved sluggishly, with concentration, irony, or age, but a gritty determination to keep moving at all costs appeared to be unanimous. Tall men danced with short women, tall women with short men, old men with young women and old ladies with old ladies; near the bag check three children skipped around their maypole of a mother on red-blinking heels. Some dancers danced alone, or with invisible partners, or, in a few rogue cases, in a well-sealed zone of avant-gardist expression. Teenage girls rolled themselves easily under bridges made by their own arms while less elastic bodies snagged halfway and let go in favor of a baggy Charleston. Others ignored the tempo entirely, including an elderly couple who danced so slowly they might as well have been in their own living room. A hot summer night, "Stompin' at the Savoy," five thousand civilians gathered peaceably under clouds kindly withholding their rain, and clinging to each other this oblivious pair seemed the key to it all, the sanity that enabled the delirium, the eye of the rapture. The only interruption to their reverie came when a jitterbugger passing by tripped, colliding softly with the old woman's backside, and her reaction was the merest glance down and behind her, as if to avoid stepping on a dog.

When "Sing Sing Sing" started up, Alice turned and walked the remaining twenty blocks uptown.

At Ezra's, she let herself in and went to the bed. Ezra opened his eyes. "Darling. What's wrong?"

Alice shook her head. Ezra observed her concernedly for a moment before lifting a hand to her cheek. "Are you sick?"

Again Alice shook her head no, and for many seconds sat staring at a book review that lay open on the duvet beside him. Staring back at her was a cheap caricature of him in which his eyes were too close together and his chin resembled a turkey's wattle. She slid the paper away, undid her sandals, and drew her legs up to lie as close beside him as she could. She put an arm around his chest and hid her face in his ribs. He smelled, as ever, like chlorine, Aveda, and Tide.

The sky bled pink, then violet. Ezra reached up to turn on the light.

"Mary-Alice," he said, with the gentlest forbearance conceivable. "Your silences are very effective. Do you know?"

Alice rolled onto her back. Her eyes filled with tears.

"I've spent a lot of time here," she said finally.

"Yes," he replied, after another long moment. "I expect this room will be imprinted on your brain always."

Alice closed her eyes.

"Alejandro Juarez."

"Kristine Crowley."

"Nigel Pugh."

"Ajay Kundra."

"Robert Thirwell."

"Arlene Lester."

"Catherine Flaherty."

"Brenda Kahn."

Alice was not the only one who'd sought out the same seat she'd sat in the day before, as though if they started over elsewhere the long wait of yesterday wouldn't count. The man with the Muslim uncle had exchanged his *Economist* for a laptop whose screen saver was a photograph of himself with someone of identical complexion; they also had the same eyebrows, the same angle to their jawlines, the same brand of windbreaker in which they stood with their arms around each other against a dramatically marbled sky. Behind them, brown mountains stretched into the distance, triangular summits intricately veined at the top with snow. Then an Excel document poured up from the bottom of the screen, replacing nature with a blinding blizzard of cells.

"Devon Flowers."

"Elizabeth Hamersley."

"Kanchan Khemhandani."

"Cynthia Wolf."

"Orlanda Olsen."

"Natasha Stowe."

"Ashley Brownstein."

"Hannah Filkins."

"Zachary Jump."

Sometimes, a name had to be repeated, and its owner discovered to have been in the men's room, or stretching his legs in the atrium, or asleep. Only once did someone fail to materialize at all, and the effect on the room was a kind of jarring collective consternation. Who was this AWOL Amar Jamali and what reason could he have for standing up the American judiciary? And yet, Alice envied Amar Jamali a little, desperate as she was to be somewhere else herself. Someone else herself.

"Emanuel Gat."

"Conor Fleming."

"Pilar Brown."

"Michael Firestone."

"Kiril Dobrovolsky."

"Abigail Cohen."

"Jennifer Vanderhoven."

"Lottie Simms."

"Samantha Bargeman."

Alice looked up. The woman beside her yawned.

"Samantha Bargeman?"

A few others lifted their heads and looked around. Alice turned her summons over in her lap and frowned.

"Samantha Bargeman . . ."

The man in front of her, recently reappeared, rubbed an eye with the heel of his hand. Willoughby scanned the room witheringly, then shook his head and wrote something down.

". . . Purva Singh."

"Barry Featherman."

"Felicia Porges."

"Leonard Yates."

"Kendra Fitzpatrick."

"Mary-Alice Dodge."

Still stunned, Alice stood and followed the others down a windowless corridor into a room where copies of a questionnaire were passed around and filled out in a near silence syncopated by sneaker squeaks, sniffs, throat clearings and coughs. A clerk rubbed his chin as he read over everyone's answers; then a couple of unsuitables were dismissed and those remaining led into an adjacent room for questioning by an attorney alone.

"Have you ever been sued?"

"No."

"Have you ever sued anyone?"

"No."

"Have you ever been a victim of a crime?"

"I don't think so."

"You don't know?"

"I'm not sure."

"Malpractice?"

"No."

"Rape?"

"No."

"Theft?"

"Well, maybe. But nothing important."

"It says here you're an editor."

"Yes."

"What kind of an editor?"

"Fiction mainly. But I'm planning to give my notice next week."

The attorney glanced at his watch. "This is a drug case. Do you use drugs?"

"No."

"Does anyone you know use drugs?"

"No."

"No one?"

Alice shifted in her seat. "My stepfather did cocaine when I was little."

The attorney looked up. "He did?"

Alice nodded.

"At home?"

She nodded again.

"Was he ever violent with you?"

"Not with me, no."

"But with someone else?"

Alice blinked at the attorney for a moment and then replied, "He's not a bad person. He's just had a hard life."

"And what about your father?"

"What about my father?"

"Did he use drugs?"

"I don't know. I don't think so. We didn't live with him." Her voice wavered. "I couldn't say."

"I'm sorry, I—"

"It's okay."

"I didn't mean to—"

"You didn't."

"I wasn't—"

"I know. You didn't. It's not—It's not that. I'm just . . . tired.
And sort of going through a difficult time."

"Choo?"
   "Mmm?"
   "Where are you?"
   "At home."
   "What are you doing?"
   "I was sleeping. Are you all right?"
   "I'm having chest pains."
   "Oh, no. Did you call Pransky?"
   "He's in Saint Lucia. His secretary said I should go up to Pres-
byterian."
   "She's right."
   "Darling, you can't be serious."
   "Of course I'm serious!"
   "You want me to go to an emergency room in Washington
Heights at eight o'clock on a Saturday night?"
   Through the taxicab's windows the Upper West Side became
Harlem and Harlem a neighborhood whose name she didn't know,
a wide-avenued wasteland of delis and beauty salons, dollar stores
and African hair braiding, *iglesias* and a sky almost Midwestern in
its sweeping pastel striations. At 153rd their driver braked suddenly
to avoid a plastic bag swirling in the road between Trinity Ceme-
tery and Jenkins Funeral Chapel. When they'd recovered from the
jolt, Ezra leaned forward politely while Alice righted his cane. "Excuse me, sir! Would you mind slowing down a little please? I'd like
to get to the hospital and *then* die."
   They sat for over an hour in the lobby watching two girls color
butterflies on the floor while a third slumped motionless against
a heavily pregnant woman's arm. Then a young Korean woman
in green clogs and burgundy scrubs summoned Ezra for an EKG
and afterward stationed him to wait in a long room with too few

partitions for the dozens of men and women lying on gurneys or sitting in wheelchairs, most of them old and black or old and Hispanic and still dressed in their pajamas or robes and slippers from home. Some were asleep, and in this position looked as though they were trying to decide whether death might be preferable to another hour in this fluorescent beeping limbo. Others watched the young orderlies to-ing and fro-ing with a dazed, even wondrous expression that suggested it was not the worst Saturday night they'd ever had. A few feet away from where Ezra had been moored to an IV dripping liquid sugar into his arm an odorous man with soiled trousers and bloodshot eyes wandered sociably up and down the aisle. "Sit down Clarence," a nurse said to him as she passed.

"I knew this would happen," said Ezra.

A little after ten, their nurse returned to say that she'd spoken with Pransky's office and his EKG had indicated nothing out of the ordinary but they wanted to keep him overnight anyway just to be sure. Previously perfunctory, her manner had become girlish, flirty even; clutching her clipboard to her chest she fluttered her eyelashes and said, "By the way, my mother is a huge fan. She'd kill me if I didn't tell you *The Running Gag* is her favorite book."

"Good."

"How are you feeling now? Any pain?"

"Yep."

"The same? Worse?"

"Same."

"What does it feel like?"

Ezra levitated a hand.

"It's radiating?" said Alice.

"That's right. Radiating. Into my neck."

The nurse frowned. "Okay. Let me see if I can get you something for that. Anything else?"

"Can I have my own room?"

"You'd have to pay."

"That's fine."

In the cubicle across from theirs a woman produced a rosary from her purse and began working her fingers along it while the man lying beside her squirmed and moaned. Another couple, in matching Mets sweatshirts, prayed in tandem, their hands clasped to their foreheads with such assiduous concentration that even Clarence stumbling to within an inch of their toes failed to break the spell. "Jesus!" said the man, laying his hands on his partner's abdomen. "Let this pain cease and desist!" Ezra watched spellbound, eyes bright and jaw slack; he could never get enough of humanity, so long as it slept in another room.

"Your mouth is open," said Alice.

He shut it, shaking his head. "I hate that. My brother started doing it about a year before he died. It looks terrible. Whenever you catch me doing it, darling, tell me to stop."

"No!"

"You don't have to make a big deal of it. Just say 'Mouth.' "

Alice got up and went to the parting in the curtain. Ezra checked his watch.

"Did I tell you the apartment next to mine is for sale?" he asked.

"How much?"

"Guess."

"I don't know. Four hundred thousand?"

Ezra shook his head. "A million."

"You're joking."

"I'm not."

"For a studio?"

"It's a small two-bedroom. But still."

Alice nodded and turned back to the curtain. She looked both ways.

"I've never seen you wear jeans before."

"Oh? What do you think?"

"Walk a little."

Alice slid the curtain to one side and went as far as a cart of bedpans before turning around. Clarence appeared outside his own

cubicle and clapped. "Doesn't she look great?" Ezra called. When
Alice had got back, he said, reaching for her arm, "So what should
I do?"

"About what?"

"The apartment."

"What about the apartment?"

"Should I buy it?"

"Why?"

"So someone with a baby doesn't move in. And so I could knock
down that middle wall and turn it into one big room, and then we'd
have so much more space here, darling. We need more space in the
city, we really do."

The man in the Mets sweatshirt pointed at something in the
Post. The woman beside him laughed. "Don't," she said, holding
her stomach. "It hurts."

"Mouth," said Alice.

Ezra snapped it shut, like a ventriloquist's doll, and a moment
later squeezed Alice's hand. "Sweetheart, I hate asking you this, but
I've just remembered something. I'm going to need my pills."

At 125th, a pair of black men with saxophones boarded the car and
faced off in the aisle. Their duet began slowly, with the men tiptoe-
ing toward and away from each other like a lone man in a mirror;
then it accelerated, becoming louder and more chaotic, and the other
people in the car began to nod and clap, whoop and whistle; a man
with a bleeding-rose tattoo on his bicep sprung to his feet and started
to dance. *There are some men who buy diverting talk to lead astray from
the word of God*, cautioned a pamphlet by Alice's foot. On the other
hand: *Who takes the greatest pleasure in leading the other one astray?* In
his bathtub the night before a clot of her own blood had escaped and
unfurled like watercolor. Ezra had put a Bach partita on—its case still
lay open on the ottoman—and brought her a glass of Knob Creek.
Applying a new fentanyl patch to the skin just above his defibrillator

he'd left his hand in place long enough to recite the Pledge of Allegiance. Alice watched him shave. His ophthalmologist had prescribed some drops to regulate the pressure in his eyes but he'd developed an allergy to them and the skin around his lashes had turned papery and chapped. In bed, they'd read, Ezra Keats and Alice an article about the previous week's Tube bombings in the *Times*; by 11:10 the light was off, the elevator still, the glittering skyline dimmed by a scrim he'd had installed to temper the morning sun. To mitigate his back pain, he slept with a foam pillow under his knees. To dull cramps that by four in the morning had become severe to the point of nauseating her, Alice got up and went into the bathroom to take one of his pills. ONE TABLET BY MOUTH EVERY 4–6 HOURS OR AS NEEDED FOR PAIN read the cylinder in her palm. WATSON 387 a machine had imprinted on the smooth oval tablet swallowed a moment before. If there were a pill that would make her a writer living in Europe and another that would keep him alive and in love with her until the day she died, which would she choose? She had once counted twenty-seven different pill dispensers in that bathroom, vials with science-fiction names from Atropine to Zantac and a barrage of exclamatory imperatives: TAKE ONE TABLET DAILY OR EVERY SIX TO EIGHT HOURS AS NEEDED. TAKE 1 TABLET BY MOUTH AT BEDTIME FOR ONE MONTH THEN INCREASE BY 1 TABLET EACH MONTH UNTIL TAKING 4 TABLETS. TAKE 2 CAPSULES NOW THEN 1 CAPSULE EVERY 8 HOURS TILL GONE. ONE TABLET WITH A GLASS OF WATER ONCE A DAY. TAKE WITH FOOD. AVOID EATING GRAPEFRUIT OR DRINKING GRAPEFRUIT JUICE WITH THIS MEDICINE. DO NOT TAKE ASPIRIN OR PRODUCTS CONTAINING ASPIRIN WITHOUT THE KNOWLEDGE AND CONSENT OF YOUR PHYSICIAN. KEEP IN THE REFRIGERATOR AND SHAKE WELL BEFORE USING. USE CAUTION WHEN OPERATING A CAR. AVOID THE USE OF A SUNLAMP. DO NOT FREEZE. PROTECT FROM LIGHT. PROTECT FROM LIGHT AND MOISTURE. DISPENSE IN A TIGHT, LIGHT-RESISTANT CONTAINER. DRINK PLENTY OF WATER. SWALLOW WHOLE. DO NOT SHARE WITH ANYONE FOR WHOM THIS MEDICINE IS NOT PRESCRIBED. DO NOT CHEW OR CRUSH . . . and so on, ad nauseam, especially if you contemplated the mounting sum of so many laboratory-spun chemicals commingling in your gut—words reducing a not insignificant portion of life's remainder to standing in pharmacy lines and looking at your watch and pouring glasses of water and waiting and counting and eating pills.

An old woman lay where she'd left him, muttering Spanglish. A receptionist directed Alice up to the inpatient unit, where she found Ezra reclining in a softly lit room with a twinkling river view, his clothes folded into a pile on the radiator and the strings of a crisp baby-blue hospital gown tied in a bow behind his neck. His hands were clasped on the turned-down edge of the bedsheet and his eyebrows were raised delightedly at a woman with a white lab coat and a platinum ponytail running down the length of her back. His chest pain, she was reassuring him, was probably just a bit of gas. But his blood pressure was up and she was glad he was staying the night anyway, so that they could keep an eye on him. Ezra beamed.

"Mary-Alice! Genevieve here is going to order me some chicken. Would *you* like something to eat?"

When Genevieve had gone, Alice put his pill bag on the bed and sat in a chair by the window while he inventoried its contents. The light of a plane entered the lower left-hand corner of the window's frame and climbed its flight path slowly, steadily, like a roller-coaster ascending. Alice watched until it had exited the top-right corner of the window; as soon as it did another winking beacon appeared bottom left and began its identical climb along the same invisible track.

Ezra swallowed a pill. "Go, little Uroxatral, far and near, to all my friends I hold so dear . . ."

When a third plane appeared, Alice turned away from the window. "Your eye is bleeding."

"That's okay. The ophthalmologist said this would happen. Don't worry darling. It's getting better, not worse."

A small Chinese woman entered holding a clipboard. "I have some questions for you."

"Shoot."

"When did you last urinate?"

"About half an hour ago."

"Last bowel movement?"

Ezra nodded. "This morning."

"Defibrillator?"

"Medtronic."

"Allergies?"

"Yes."

"To what?"

"Morphine."

"What happens?"

"I have paranoid hallucinations."

"Diseases?"

"Heart disease. Degenerative joint disease of the spine. Glaucoma. Osteoporosis."

"Is that it?"

Ezra smiled. "For now."

"Your eye is bleeding."

"I know; don't worry about that."

"Emergency contact?"

"Dick Hillier."

"Health-care proxy?"

"Also Dick Hillier."

"Who's this?"

"Mary-Alice. My goddaughter."

"Will she be staying with you tonight?"

"That's right."

"Religion?"

"None."

The nurse looked up. "Religion?" she repeated.

"No religion," said Ezra. "Atheist."

The nurse studied him for a moment before turning to Alice. "Is he serious?"

Alice nodded. "I think so."

Turning back to Ezra: "Are you *sure?*"

Ezra flexed his toes under the covers. "Yep."

"*Okaaaaay*," said the nurse, cocking her head and writing it down, this terrible mistake. When she'd left, Alice asked, "Why do they ask that?"

"Well, if you say you're Catholic and it looks like you're getting close to the end, they send a priest around. If you're Jewish, they send a rabbi around."

"And if you're atheist?"

"They send Christopher Hitchens around."

Alice covered her face with her hands.

"Easiest white girl—"

"Ezra!"

"What!"

"I can't . . ."

"You can't what?"

She took her hands away. "This!"

"I don't follow you, darling."

"It's just . . . so . . . *hard.*"

"And you're telling me this now?"

"No! I wouldn't do that. I wouldn't leave you here. I *love* you." That much was true. "You've taught me so much, and you're the best friend I have. I just can't . . . It's so not . . . *normal.*"

"Who wants to be normal? Not you."

"No, I don't mean normal. I mean . . . good for me. Right now." She took a deep breath. "If I'm with *you* . . ."

Ezra shook his head neatly, as if she'd been misinformed about who he was. "Sweetheart, you're tired."

Alice nodded. "I know."

"And shaken up I think. But we're going to be fine."

Sniffling, Alice nodded again and said, "I know. I know."

He watched her thoughtfully for a moment, the spot of blood under his eye like a stopped tear. Then he grimaced good-naturedly and leaned forward a little to adjust his pillows. Wiping her cheeks,

Alice hurried to help, and in the process extracted a handset from where it had slipped down behind his shoulder. "Oh!" Ezra said brightly, taking the control. "There's a television." Turning the handset around, he aimed it at the screen, switched the power on, and surfed until he came to highlights of the game. New York was up by three in the bottom of the ninth.

They watched as Renteria struck out.

"Mouth."

When Ortiz popped one up to Jeter, Ezra turned a hand over on the bed, inviting Alice to rest her own in his palm. He was still looking at the screen. "*Alice*," he said rationally. "Don't leave me. Don't go. I want a partner in life. Do you know? We're just getting started. No one could love you as much as I do. Choose *this*. Choose the adventure, Alice. *This* is the adventure. This is the *mis*adventure. This is living."

Shave and a haircut, two bits.

The nurse came in with their hospital chicken.

II
MADNESS

Our ideas about the war *were* the war.

—WILL MACKIN, Kattekoppen

WHERE ARE YOU COMING from?
  Los Angeles.
  Traveling alone?
  Yes.
  Purpose of your trip?
  To see my brother.
  Your brother is British?
  No.
  Whose address is this then?
  Alastair Blunt's.
  Alastair Blunt is British?
  Yes.
  And how long do you plan to stay in the UK?
  Until Sunday morning.
  What will you be doing here?
  Seeing friends.
  For only two nights?
  Yes.
  And then?
  I fly to Istanbul.
  Your brother lives in Istanbul?
  No.
  Where does he live?
  In Iraq.
  And you're going to visit him in Iraq?
  Yes.

When?
On Monday.
How?
By car from Diyarbakir.
And how long will you be there?
In Diyarbakir?
No, in Iraq.
Until the fifteenth.
And then?
I fly back to the States.
What is it that you do there?
In the States?
Yes.
I've just finished my dissertation.
In?
Economics.
And now you're looking for a job?
Yes.
In the States?
Yes.
What does Mr. Blunt do?
He's a journalist.
What sort of a journalist?
A foreign correspondent.
And you'll be staying with him?
Yes.
At this address?
Yes.
For only two nights?
Yes.
Have you ever been to the United Kingdom?
Yes.
Your passport doesn't have any stamps in it.
It's new.

What happened to your old one?

The lamination became unglued.

Sorry?

This part peeled up.

When were you last here?

Ten years ago.

What were you doing here?

I had an internship at a bioethics council.

You had a visa?

Yes.

A work visa?

Yes.

Do you have it with you?

No.

Do you have your ticket to Istanbul with you?

No.

Why not?

It's electronic.

Itinerary?

I didn't print it out.

All right then, Mr. Jaafari. Could I ask you please to take a seat?

I WAS CONCEIVED IN Karrada but born high over the elbow of Cape Cod. The only doctor on board was my father, a hematologist-oncologist whose last delivery had been at Baghdad Medical School, in 1959. To sterilize the umbilical scissors, he'd used a slug of flask whiskey. To get me breathing, he'd slapped the soles of my feet. Alhamdulillah! cried one of the stewardesses, upon seeing that I was a boy. May he be one of seven!

At this point in the story, my mother will usually roll her eyes. For many years, I took this as disdain for the male favoritism of her homeland, if not merely relief at having been spared five additional children, whatever the gender. Then my brother, who was nine at the time, suggested a different theory: She rolls her eyes because those stewardesses spent the entire flight leaning over her to light Baba's cigarettes. In Sami's version, the whiskey belonged to our father, too.

As to the question of my nationality, immigration officials scratched their heads for three weeks. Both of my parents were born in Baghdad. (So was Sami, on the same day as Qusay Hussein.) The plane in question belonged to Iraqi Airways, and, in the United Nations' opinion, an in-flight birth was to be considered a birth in the aircraft's registered country. On the other hand, we were moving to America at a relatively sympathetic time, and even today a baby born in American airspace is entitled to American citizenship, no matter who owns the vehicle. In the end, I was granted both: two passports with two colors and three languages between them, although my Arabic is barely serviceable and I didn't learn a word of Kurdish until I was almost twenty-nine.

So: two passports, two nationalities, no native soil. I once heard that, perhaps as compensation for their rootlessness, babies born on planes are granted free flights on the parturitive airline for life. And it's a winsome idea: the stork that delivers you remains yours to ride here and there and everywhere, until it's time for you to return to the great salt marsh in the sky. But, as far as I know, I was never offered such a bonus. Not that it would have done me much good. Initially, we did all our sneaking back on the ground, via Amman. Then Iraq invaded Kuwait and all American passport holders were grounded from riding Iraqi storks for what would amount to thirteen years.

MR. JAAFARI?

I went to her.

I'd just like to run through your itinerary with you again. You've come from Los Angeles, yes?

Yes.

And you're booked on a flight to Istanbul on Sunday. Is that correct?

Yes.

And do you know which airline you're flying?

Turkish Airlines.

And do you know what time your flight departs?

Seven fifty-five in the morning.

And what happens when you arrive in Istanbul?

I have a layover of about five hours.

And then?

I fly to Diyarbakir.

On which airline?

Also Turkish Airlines.

What time?

I don't know exactly. I think it leaves around six.

And then?

I arrive in Diyarbakir and a driver picks me up.

Who is this driver?

Someone my brother knows.

From Iraq?

From Kurdistan, yes.

And where does the driver take you?
To Sulaymaniyah.
Where your brother lives.
That's right.
How long is that drive?
About thirteen hours.
But you've never met this man before?
The driver? No.
Is that dangerous?
Potentially.
You must really want to see your brother.
I laughed.
What's so funny? asked the officer.
Nothing, I said. I do.

OUR FIRST HOME IN America was on the Upper East Side, a one-bedroom fifth-floor walk-up in an old tenement building owned by Cornell Medical College, my father's new employer. Sami slept on the sofa. I slept in an incubator at New York Hospital. When I had amassed five pounds and my mother became intractable in her opinion that the swarming verticality of Manhattan was no place for child-rearing, we moved out to Bay Ridge, where my father's housing stipend was good for the entire second floor of a two-story house with gardenias in the window boxes and a long sunny terrace freshly sodded with AstroTurf. My earliest memory takes place on this terrace, where, having just woken up from a nap, I reached up to touch a cat performing high-wire stunts on the iron railing and was rewarded with a hissing swipe to the face. No fewer than seven Polaroids of my serrated cheek attest to that part of the memory, although I do occasionally wonder whether I have confused waking up from a nap with merely surfacing from four years of infantile amnesia. My mother says this was the same day that she and Sami took me into the city to see *Peter Pan*. All I remember of *that* is Sandy Duncan hurtling toward us, looking crucified on her wires—but that's it, just a single mental slide, and certainly I would not have linked it to the scar on my cheek without prompting.

All of which raises the question: Why was my mother taking me to a Broadway show I was nearly too young to remember?

The last time I saw my brother, in early 2005, he said that parents have no way of knowing when their children's memories will wake up. He also said that the oblivion of our first few years is never entirely cured. Plenty of life is memorable only in flashes, if at all.

What don't you remember? I asked.

What *do* I remember? What do *you* remember of last year? Of 2002? Of 1994? I don't mean the headlines. We all remember milestones, jobs. The name of your freshman English teacher. Your first kiss. But what did you *think*, from day to day? What were you conscious of? What did you say? Whom did you run into, on the street or in the gym, and how did these encounters reinforce or interfere with the idea of yourself that you carry around? In 1994, when I was still in Hayy al-Jihad, I was lonely, although I'm not sure I was aware of it at the time. I bought a notebook and I started a journal, in which a typical early entry went something like this: 'School. Kabobs with Nawfal. Bingo at the HC. Bed.' No impressions. No emotions. No ideas. Every day ended with 'bed,' as though I might have pursued some other conclusion to the cycle. Then I must have said to myself, Look. If you're going to spend time on this, do it right. Write down what you're feeling, what you're thinking, what truly distinguishes the day, or what's the point? I must have had this conversation with myself because after a while the entries became longer, more detailed and analytical. The longest was about an argument I'd evidently had with Zaid about Claudia Schiffer. And at least once I wrote some ponderous lines about what life might have been like had I not come back to Iraq. But even these later passages have a wooden quality, as though I wrote them preoccupied with how they would look to someone else. And after six weeks or so, I quit—put the notebook into a box and didn't go back to it for twenty years. When I did, I had to force myself to read it. My handwriting looked so childish, so stupid. My 'ideas' were embarrassing. Most unnerving was how much of what I'd written was unrecognizable. I don't remember arguing with Zaid. I don't remember spending so many Friday evenings at the Hunting Club. I don't remember ever desiring, never mind contemplating, an alternative life back in America. And who is this Leila, who had tea with me on a 'coolish' Tuesday in April? It's as if I blacked out for entire weeks at a time.

I asked why he'd started a journal in the first place.

Maybe, he said, I was feeling my solitude too keenly. Maybe I thought that by writing things down, inking out a record of my existence, I was counteracting my . . . my disappearance. My erasure. You know what they say: Make your mark on the world. But I'm telling you, little brother, this notebook is a very sorry mark.

Anyway, you've made other marks since then.

Sami nodded. Small marks, yes.

And you have Zahra now.

This was four years ago, in my brother's backyard in Sulaymaniyah, where although it was early January it was nearly sixty degrees. We ate dates from a bowl passed between us and tossed the pits into crocus beds just sprouting. Two weeks later, Sami and Zahra got married. They have a little girl now, Yasmine, who in Zahra's opinion has Sami's mouth but my eyes. I agree about the mouth. It's a wide mouth that turns up a little at the edges even when she's not smiling. Our eyes, however, share little but a capricious shade of green. Mine tend to be set in a furrowed, doubtful expression, whereas Yasmine's seem forever suspended in wondrous melancholy. Between the upturned mouth and the plaintive eye lift it can look as though she is wearing both of the drama masks at once. I recently made a photograph of her the new screen saver on my laptop, and every morning when I sit down to open it up I think I detect a slight overnight adjustment to the ratio between comedy and tragedy in my little niece's face. Such a wide spectrum of emotions it seems capable of expressing, emotions you might think impossible if not for many years of observation and experience—and yet, she is only three, which makes you wonder whether every now and again one of us is born with a memory already switched on and never unremembers a thing.

What don't I remember? Lots. Contemplating the blackouts in their aggregate makes my breath come short. But in my experience,

too, writing things down does not work—except maybe in the sense
that the more time you spend writing things down the less time you
spend doing things you don't want to forget.

You would have thought there was no one less erasable than my
brother. A tall and solid man who looks even taller and sturdier
in his white laboratory coat, he speaks in a sonorous voice, voices
vigorous opinions, and requires an average of four round meals a
day. When he said this thing about forestalling his disappearance,
I laughed. I said it reminded me of *The Incredible Shrinking Man*,
when Grant Williams climbs through one of the holes in a window
screen and delivers his closing monologue to a slowly encroaching
still of the Milky Way: *So close, the infinitesimal and the infinite . . .
smaller than the smallest . . . To God there is no zero! I still exist!* But
who disappears? Not a man with a belly laugh. Not a man whose
hands, when he plays a piano, make an octave look like an inch.
The last time I saw my brother, leaning gigantically back in his
plastic garden chair, he grinned and brushed unseen particles from
his biceps, then lifted his face to scan the clouds fleeting west like an
exodus across the Kurdish sky. He looked, in this moment, so much
like a creature that exerts its own forces on the world, and not the
other way around, that it seemed to me a ludicrous idea, that should
he fail to jot down his bedtimes and Bingo winnings, he might disappear. But then he disappeared.

WHEN I'D BEEN SITTING another twenty-five minutes, I got up and asked one of the other officers if I might go to the bathroom. She was a young woman with a lavender hijab and thick black mascara that gave her otherwise sympathetic eyes a spidery look. Skeptically, she fetched a male officer to accompany me. This man was several inches shorter than I and, for some reason, chose to follow a yard or so behind me as we walked, so that I felt as if I were taking a small child to the toilet rather than being chaperoned myself.

Only when we passed an unmanned checkpoint did my minder quicken his pace. Of course, one would have to be very desperate indeed to try to jump passport control without a passport. And even if you were to slip through unapprehended, what then do you do, trapped in England without one? Peddle contraband or pull pints in the hinterland, until you die? Mine had been taken from me in exchange for a half sheet of paper confirming my detainee status. This slip of paper I was now carrying into the men's room with two hands, as though it bore the instructions I needed to urinate and flush. Rather than wait outside, my minder followed me in and, having offered to hold my slip, stood by the sinks jingling the coins in his pocket while I drained my bladder and then took my time soaping and rinsing and drying my hands. It was something to do. Checking my cell phone messages would have been another thing to do, but I didn't have a signal. When we'd returned to my seat, my minder nodded without a word and resumed his post by the line for EU nationals. In front of me, time and again, a passport was presented, fanned, examined, stamped, and returned, its integrity verified and its owner already turning his mind toward the logistics of Baggage Reclaim and Onward Travel. Whereas the woman who'd taken my passport remained nowhere to be seen.

TO ACCESS THE ASTROTURFED terrace, you had to squeeze through a narrow hallway of a room containing a single twin bed and an upright piano. The bed was Sami's. The piano was there when we moved in. The space in between was so tight that my brother could reach up and trill the keyboard's topmost octave even while he was lying down.

The piano had a plain boxy shape and was made of a dark wood that was nicked all over and turned reddish in the midmorning sun. It was an old Weser Bros., revamped during the Second World War, when the construction of new pianos could not meet the demand, inspiring manufacturers to rehabilitate used models with new arms, new legs, new key tops and new scrolls; they also hid the tuning pins on top with a long mirrored casing designed to make the instrument look smaller than it was. The mirror on ours had a diagonal crack across one corner and much of its surface had become mottled with age. I think it was Saul Bellow who said that death is the dark backing a mirror needs if we are to see anything; what, then, does one make of so much darkness already showing through?

I call it Sami's piano but technically it belonged to our landlords, Marty Fish and Max Fischer, who lived downstairs.

Fischer played first violin for the New York Philharmonic. Fish played piano in a West Village piano bar popular with people who like their show tunes mangled by drunken sing-alongs. We Jaafaris referred to these two men jointly as the Fishes and Marty in the singular as Shabboot, because his extraordinary ovoid shape

reminded my brother of the carp Baghdadi fishermen used to but-
terfly and grill on the Tigris. Maxwell Fischer, on the other hand,
was too unassailably debonair for a nickname. A Bavarian graduate of the Paris Conservatoire, he was a devoutly trim man who
took his early-morning constitutionals in paisley cravats that on the
pavements of Bay Ridge looked as exotic as if he'd wound an Indian cobra around his neck. Fischer had a soft high voice and crisp
German diction that lent all conversations with him an aura of the
philosophical. We always knew when he was home, because instead of the muffled Sondheim or Hamlisch that signaled Shabboot
battling a funk, floating up came the virtuous strains of Elgar, or
Janáček, played if not on a cherished pair of hi-fi speakers then on
Fischer's Stradivarius by Fischer himself. The violin he flossed and
buffed as if it were a surgical instrument. He swept the communal
foyer once a day and on Saturdays vacuumed so protractedly that
for half an hour afterward the silence rang in your ears. It became
second nature for me to remove my shoes whenever entering the
Fishes' apartment, long before I no longer had to be told to take
them off on going into a mosque. But all this domestic pulchritude
was Fischer's doing. Left to himself, Shabboot would have let the
dust form drifts and the ironing a pastel hillock on the bedroom
floor. The only thing Shabboot cleaned voluntarily was his answer
to Fischer's violin: a Macassar Ebony Steinway that, at nearly seven
feet long, dwarfed the living room around it and was the reason the
old Weser Bros. had been relegated upstairs.

Our mother's tendency to mythologize our childhoods would
have you believe that Sami, who had never touched a musical instrument before, sat down at that piano for the first time and was
rolling out bagatelles by sundown. I don't think it was quite like
this. A more accurate version surely begins with a fact that has long
confounded my parents, and me to a degree as well, and that is that
my brother did not like living in America. Almost from the beginning he complained of missing his Baghdadi friends and pointedly
lagged behind in school, although he was no less clever than his

classmates and had spoken English as well as Arabic since he was three. At home, he became mopey and shiftless, getting off the sofa only for meals or to smoke marijuana in the basketball courts in the park with a Trinidadian girl who lived behind the synagogue on the next block. Then one afternoon Shabboot, who'd come upstairs to address a glitch in the plumbing, lingered over the Weser Bros. long enough to pluck out the opening measures of Bohemian Rhapsody and Sami got up from the sofa and asked him to do it again. Half an hour later the drainpipe in the kitchen was still leaking and Sami and Shabboot were sitting hip to hip at the piano, Sami chewing his lip and Shabboot humming corrections, rearranging Sami's fingers, and jabbing indignantly at the keyboard's sticky middle D. This is how one would find them nearly every Wednesday afternoon thereafter: in summer silhouetted against the terrace, in winter with mugs of tea steaming up the mottled mirror. In theory, there was no practicing allowed after ten thirty at night, but often Sami would wait until all was dark at the other end of the apartment and then resume his playing with one foot on the damper pedal and his head cocked so low to the keyboard you'd think his ear could vacuum up the sound. Of course, one can play a piano only so quietly. About as well as you can whisper a tune. But no one dared discourage my brother; he was unhappy and my parents blamed themselves. At least when he was playing the piano he was not shiftless.

Nor was he ambitious, in any conventional sense. He did not give recitals. He did not *perform*. For Sami, the aim in playing was simply to play: to match finger to key, one after the other or in their cherrylike clusters, and to enjoy the result as one enjoys listening to a story unfold. In his tiny bedroom that was more a corridor than a destination, my brother hunched over his piano with something like the charged necessity that grips chain smokers, or binge eaters, or people who bounce their knees. Maybe it absorbed a nervous energy. Maybe it blunted a pain; I don't know. It could even seem wasteful, the way he went through sheet music, rarely playing a piece more than twice in favor of moving on: to another sonata, another concerto, another mazurka, nocturne, or waltz. As though their notes were part of an infinite current and Sami the copper wire through which they wanted to flow. Of course, every now and again he would stumble over a difficult passage and back up to play it again, but this was rarer than you'd expect. And never, not once—I cannot even imagine it—did he growl or drive his fists into the keys with impatience. I have always envied my brother his affair with that piano. You can tell when someone is unbedeviled by time.

WHEN I'D SAT HOLDING my half sheet of paper for a full forty minutes more I stood up and asked the woman in the lavender hijab whether I might be allowed to make a call.

Who's dealing with you?

I didn't catch her name. She has blond hair, down to here. . . .

Denise. Let me see if I can find her.

My seat was still warm.

I had some extracurricular reading on post-Keynesian price theory with me, but instead of opening it I was watching the other arrivals as they reached the end of the metal maze. A man wearing a turban and a badge on a ribbon around his neck stood at the terminus and directed each new group or solitary traveler to a desk. People shuffled forward in suits and saris, stilettos and sweatpants, pushing strollers or carrying neck pillows or briefcases or teddy bears or shopping bags festooned with two-dimensional bows and holly. Sometimes only one passport would be stamped; other times you heard two or three or four stamped in quick succession—like library books, once upon a time. And the overall rhythm of people advancing and stamps stamping had a kind of prolonged regularity to it, like a jazz improvisation that, for all its deviations, never loses its beat.

Then a small, unaccompanied woman failed to move on. She had dark shoulder-length hair and stood at the desk she'd been shunted to shyly, as though trying to become invisible. She nodded at everything the immigration officer said. She nodded even when it looked from the officer's face that maybe she had not understood the question. She did not have any luggage with her, only a small satin-embroidered purse that she held with both hands in front of her hips like a fig leaf. The officer frowned at her kindly, but also intently, as if he were trying to prop her up with his eyes.

When the officer handed the girl a half sheet of paper like mine the girl turned around to sit down and I saw that she was Chinese.

Not five minutes later her officer returned. It piqued me that this should happen so quickly, while my own officer took her time.

To a second officer the first officer said: Tell her that you are here to translate.

The translator tugged up her trousers and crouched down to speak to the girl in short twanging sounds that to my ears could have been the same language played backward. The girl nodded.

Tell her that she's not in trouble, we're just concerned about her welfare and need to ask her some additional questions before we can let her through.

Again the second officer spoke and the girl nodded.

What is the name of her school here in the UK?

The girl took a piece of paper out of her purse.

Pointing, the first officer said: Whose number is this?

Her professor's.

Who is her professor?

'Professor Ken.'

Professor Ken helped her arrange this visa?

Yes.

But she doesn't know the name of Professor Ken's school?

'Ken School.'

How long is she planning on staying?

Six months.

Does she have a return flight?

No, but she'll buy one.

Where will she live?

Professor Ken has a house.

Where?

She doesn't know.

How much money does she have?

Professor Ken has given her a scholarship.

Do her parents know she's here?

The girl nodded.

Does she have a phone number for them? A number we could call?

The girl produced a pink Nokia and showed it to the second officer, who wrote something down.

Tell her she's not in trouble; we're just concerned that she seems to be here without a place to stay and hardly any English skills.

When the second officer had translated, the girl spoke at length for the first time, in a high-pitched rush that seemed to strain against panic. Then abruptly she stopped talking and both officers looked uncertain as to whether she was done.

She says she's here to learn English, the second officer said. Her family knows she's here. She got a scholarship from Professor Ken, who arranged for the visa, and when she's collected her luggage she's supposed to call this number and Professor Ken will come and pick her up.

The first officer frowned. Tell her she's going to be waiting here just a little bit longer. Tell her she has nothing to worry about. Tell her she's not in trouble. It's just that we're concerned for her safety and need to make some general inquiries. We need to ensure she's in good hands.

When the second officer had translated this, the girl sniffed.

Tell her she's not in trouble, the first officer said again, more kindly than before, but this time the girl, still sniffling, did not seem to hear.

ACCORDING TO CALVIN COOLIDGE, economy is the only method by which we prepare today to afford the improvements of tomorrow. Whatever else you think about Coolidge, the statement does seem more or less correct, and when I came across it for the first time shortly after starting graduate school I thought: At last, I'm pursuing a profession befitting of my neuroses.

This is because my mind is always turning over this question of how I'm going to feel later, based on what I'm doing now. Later in the day. Later in the week. Later in a life starting to look like a series of activities designed to make me feel good later, but not now. Knowing I'll feel good later makes me feel good enough now. Calvin Coolidge would approve, but according to my mother there is another term for such super-modulated living, and it translates roughly into not being able to live like a dog.

You would be happier, she has been heard to say, if you were more like your brother. Sami lives in the moment, like a dog.

For the record, my brother's name means *high*, *lofty*, or *elevated*— not traits you'd readily associate with an animal that sniffs assholes and shits in plain sight. But I suppose my parents could not have predicted his canine spontaneity when they named him; nor could they have known that the one they named *making a home* would grow up to have nothing in his refrigerator but seven packets of soy sauce and an expired carton of eggs.

In December of 1988, on the flight to Baghdad from Amman, our parents forbade us from bringing up two subjects with our Iraqi interlocutors: Saddam Hussein and Sami's piano, never mind

the ten years of music lessons he'd taken from our homosexual
landlord downstairs. At any rate, what most of my aunts and uncles wanted to discuss around my grandmother's kitchen table was
the exotic extent of my Americanness: my Brooklyn accent, my
Don Mattingly jersey, my pristine navy-blue passport and my em-
bossed City of New York Certification of Birth. This last, of course,
meant that I would be entitled to run for the American presidency
one day, and while Sami and I practiced juggling oranges with our
cousins in the back garden our elder relatives discussed this prospect with all the sobriety and momentousness of a G7 convention.
President Jaafari. President Amar Ala Jaafari. President Barack
Hussein Obama. I suppose one does not sound so very much more
unlikely than the other. And yet, at twelve years old, I knew perfectly well that my parents' truer hope was that I too would do
as they had done, and as my brother looked all but certain to do,
and that was to become a doctor. A doctor is respected. A doctor
is never out of work. Being a doctor opens doors. Economics my
parents also consider respectable, but reliable? No. Ungraspable
(my father's word). And even if one is more likely to ascend to the
office of the presidency with a doctorate in economics than with a
medical degree under his belt, my mother no longer mentions my
eligibility these days, maybe because she thinks the position does
not befit a man largely incapable of escaping, except infrequently
and accidentally, a consciousness trained on how every action un-
dertaken is later going to make him feel.

On Christmas, my uncle Zaid and aunt Alia came over with
their four girls, who, lined up in their matching red hijabs, looked
like a set of Russian dolls. Ten years earlier, the oldest, Rania, had
held my diapered bottom in her lap and fed me one by one the ruby-
like seeds of a pomegranate. She was older now, too pretty to look
at directly, as one strains to look at the sun. On entering the kitchen
she went straight over to my brother and said: BeAmrika el dunya
maqluba! Amrika is America. Maqluba means upside down, and
for this reason is also the name of a meat-and-rice dish that's baked

in a pan and upended before serving. El dunya maqluba means the world is upside down, an expression typically employed to describe people or places in a state of high excitement verging on mayhem. My brother laughed. America on Christmas indeed. The world is upside down in America today!: what it brought to mind was one of those illustrations of world peace, or harmony in spite of diversity—people with different-colored faces holding hands like a chain of paper dolls stretching all the way around the world. Only in this instance for once the ones standing on America were the ones with the blood going to their heads.

According to modern cartography, the antipode of my bedroom in Bay Ridge is a wave in the Indian Ocean, several miles southwest of Perth. But to a twelve-year-old boy traveling abroad for the first time since he was a toddler, it might as well have been my bedroom in my grandparents' house in Hayy al-Jihad. I shared this room with three other cousins whose parents had emigrated soon after their children were born. (My father and Zaid were the oldest of twelve siblings, five of whom have left Iraq; four remain and three are dead.) To listen to us boys as we lay in our bunks and complained about what we were missing back home was to think we were high-rolling lady-killers serving ten years' hard time. Ali and Sabah, who lived in London, worried that their girlfriends would be usurped by men of legal driving age. Hussein, who lived in Columbus, was tormented over not being able to watch the Bengals play the 49ers in the Super Bowl, the result of which it would take us ten days to learn. (The Bengals lost.) Today, you could stand in Firdos Square and Google how the Bengals or the 49ers or the Red Sox or the Yankees or Manchester United or the Mongolia Blue Wolves are doing *right now*; you could check out the temperature in Bay Ridge or Helsinki; you could find out when the tide will next be high in Santa Monica or Swaziland, or when the sun is due to set on Poggibonsi. There is always something happening, always something to be apprised of, never enough hours to feel sufficiently apprised. Certainly not if you are also nursing some nobler

ambition. Twenty years ago, however, in incommunicado Baghdad, time crept.

I once heard a filmmaker say that in order to be truly creative
a person must be in possession of four things: irony, melancholy, a
sense of competition, and boredom. Whatever my deficiencies in
the first three areas, I enjoyed such an abundance of the fourth that
winter in Iraq that by the time we returned to New York I had
eked out my first and only poetry cycle. What else did I do? Spent
hours upon hours juggling, which is to say dropping and picking
up oranges in the backyard until I could no longer see them for the
dusk. With my father and Zaid I visited our relatives buried outside
Najaf, and in the evenings sat at the kitchen table, doodling in the
margins of my homework—an inordinate amount of homework,
to make up for all the school I was missing—while my grandfather
sat beside me, slowly rotating the pages of *Al-Thawra*. One evening,
he looked over to see me adding a few details to a sinking warship.
If you're going to be the president of Amrika, he said, you're going
to have to do better than that.

With Sami, I went to the Zawraa Park Zoo, where we tossed
lit cigarettes to the chimpanzees and laughed at how human they
looked when they smoked them. My brother had just graduated
from Georgetown, where he'd been president of the Pre-Med Society and wrote a thesis on curbing tuberculosis in homeless popula-
tions. Somewhat contrary to this foundation, within a week of our
arrival in Baghdad he'd taken up, without any apparent compunc-
tion, the unofficial Iraqi national pastime of chain-smoking Marlboro Reds. Our grandmother's roof had a distant view of the Tigris,
and as he stood beside me up there, smoking and squinting toward
Karrada, my brother told me about how, on hot summer nights in
the seventies, he and our parents would carry mattresses up to the
roof in order to sleep in the relief of the river's breeze. It was not
warm the night I heard this story; nor was there a mattress to hand,
only an old afghan blanket that Sami had slung over his shoulder
and carried up from the den. Still, in the moonlight, my brother lay

down, patted the space beside him, and as we stared up at the stars together Sami predicted it would not be long before Iraq was glorious again. Pothole-free roads, glittering suspension bridges, five-star hotels; the ruins of Babylon, Hatra, and the stelae of Nineveh all restored to their majesty and made visitable without the supervision of armed guards. Instead of Hawaii, honeymooners would fly to Basra. Instead of gelato, they would swoon over dolma and chai. Schoolchildren would pose in front of the Ur ziggurat, backpackers would send home postcards of al-Askari, retirees would Bubble Wrap into their luggage jars of honey from Yusufiyah. Baghdad would host the Olympics. The Lions of Mesopotamia would win the World Cup. Just you wait, little brother. Just you wait. Forget Disney World. Forget Venice. Forget Big Ben pencil sharpeners and overpriced café crèmes on the Seine. It's Iraq's turn now. Iraq is done with wars, and people are going to come from all over to see its beauty and history for themselves.

I once fell in love with a girl whose parents had divorced when she was very young. She told me about how, having learned from her mother what was going to happen—that the two of them and her baby sister were going to move into a new house, across town— she became preoccupied with questions of what you can and cannot take with you when you move. Repeatedly, she went back to her mother for clarification. Can I take my desk? My dog? My books? My crayons? Years later, a psychologist would suggest that perhaps this fixation on what she could and could not take had arisen because she had already been told what they were *not* going to take: her father. And, if not a father, what should a little girl be allowed to hold on to? At the time, I felt ill-equipped to judge this hypothesis, but I did have my doubts about the validity of the memory itself. I asked Maddie whether it wasn't possible that she did not, in fact, recall the actual moment in which she asked these questions, but rather whether her mother had told her the story so many times that it had retroactively acquired the status of a memory in her mind. Eventually, Maddie would concede that maybe the memory had, in fact, been born in her mother's telling. But she also said that she did not see what difference this made, if either way it was part of her story and she was not going out of her way to delude herself. She also remarked that it surprised her not to remember anything at all about the actual moment of separation from her father, despite it being one of her life's most critical developments. I asked how old she'd been at the time. Four, she said. Four going on five. Being under the impression that my own superior memory would never have excised such an event, I suggested that maybe Maddie was one of those people who don't remember anything from before they were, say, six. I was very arrogant then. It would not surprise me to learn that when Maddie thinks of our time together she does not remember loving me at all.

Home from graduate school years later, I was having dinner with my parents in Bay Ridge when my father started talking about Schiphol, the airport just outside Amsterdam. Specifically, he was telling us about how, in Dutch, schiphol means ship grave, because the airport had been built on land reclaimed from a shallow lake notorious for its many shipwrecks. Dad, I said. I already know this. You told me this when I was twelve. You told me this when we were *there*, waiting for our flight to Amman. That can't be right, he said. I only just read it this afternoon. Well, maybe you'd forgotten that you knew it, I said, because I can clearly remember sitting in the terminal, waiting to board, and looking out across the tarmac and thinking about the boats buried underneath. I remember picturing ships like skeletons, with bones like human bones—femurs and fibulae and giant rib cages for hulls.

Huh, said my father.

A moment later I added:

Or maybe it was Sami. Maybe Sami told me about the ships.

At this point my mother held up a hand and said that this was the first she had ever heard about any ship grave. She also reminded us that that December, of 1988, when I was twelve, was the same December in which Sami was recovering from mono and spent our layovers en route to Baghdad slumped over our luggage or prostrate on a bench. Well, I said. He still could have said it to me. Or maybe he said it on the way back, when we passed through Schiphol again on the way home. Now my mother gave me a wounded look that a moment later softened into something like pity for me and my selective amnesia. Amar, she said quietly, your brother was not with us on the way home.

AS IT GOES, DENISE'S hair is more of a walnut color. She's also wider in the hips than I'd remembered, and in the crook of one elbow was carrying a manila folder so thick you would have thought I was Alger Hiss. I made a show of sitting up straighter, bookmarking the book I hadn't been reading, and raising my eyebrows in the manner of someone cooperative yet bemused. I *was* bemused, but my inclinations toward cooperation were waning.

Denise sat down beside me and spoke quietly, discreetly, while I detected in her eyes a certain frisson. As though she'd been waiting a long time for a case like mine. Maybe I was even her first.

Mr. Jaafari. Apart from your American passport, do you have any other nationality passport or identification document?

Yes.

You do?

Yes.

What?

An Iraqi passport.

(Again the frisson.) How is that?

My parents are Iraqi. They applied for one after I was born.

Do you have it with you?

I bent down to unzip my backpack. When I'd pulled it out and handed it to her Denise began turning the pages of my second passport slowly, by the edges, like you handle a postcard whose ink isn't yet dry. When do you use this?

Very rarely.

But under what circumstances?

Whenever I enter or leave Iraq.

And does that give you an advantage?

What sort of an advantage?

You tell me.

If *you* had two passports, I said evenly, wouldn't you use your British one whenever entering or leaving the UK?

Of course, said Denise. That's the law. But I don't know what the law is in Iraq, now do I?

I didn't mean to, but I smiled. And faintly, Denise flinched. Then, still holding my second passport—which is to say the only passport I had left—she nodded slowly, comprehendingly, tapped it lightly once on her knee, and stood up and walked away.

SOMETIMES I THINK I remember the pomegranate. Its tannic sweetness, the sticky juice running down my chin. But to this day there is an instant Polaroid of the moment taped to our refrigerator in Bay Ridge and again I cannot be certain whether if there were no photograph there would be no memory.

In both, Rania is wearing a blue hijab. The way she's holding me, the way the fabric flows down over her shoulders and around my diaper and into her blouse, make it look like we are posing for a Maestà. How many times does a boy open the refrigerator of his youth? Six thousand times? Nine thousand? Whatever the number, it was plenty to make an indelible impression. Every glass of milk, every swig of juice, every leftover slice of maqluba . . . And of course my brother would have seen it every day for a good many formative years as well.

The following December, my parents returned to Baghdad on their own. I stayed in Bay Ridge, under the pretense that I did not want to miss Junior Varsity Swimming tryouts, and was supervised by the parents of a classmate whose bedroom contained a lumpy trundle bed and a life-sized poster of Paulina Porizkova. I did not try out for the swim team and when my parents returned at the end of January they did not ask me how it had gone. They were preoccupied with the news that my brother wanted to marry Rania.

He had also mentioned wanting to move to Najaf in order to study at an Islamic seminary there. When my father told me that, my mother covered her face with her hands.

That Rania was our first cousin was not inherently the problem.

Nor was the problem the heightened risk of offspring with a recessive gene disorder—although my parents had long made clear
their opinion that clan fidelity is not worth burdening a child with
something that might be avoided with a little genetic testing. The
problem was that marrying Rania clearly indicated a broader intention to resettle in Iraq, whose values my brother had claimed
to prefer over the rather less decorous ones on display in America.
And yet, to be valid in Sami's own mind—to accord with the more
decorous values he claimed to prefer—the engagement required
our parents' blessing. Rania's parents had already given theirs; they
had even waived a dowry. But my mother and father were not so
ready to sanction Sami's rejection of the life they had strenuously
uprooted themselves to grant us. What they decided was that their
blessing would be contingent on Sami and Rania marrying in New
York *and* Sami earning his graduate degree from an American university. He could study religion instead of medicine if he wanted.
He could return to Iraq afterward if he wanted. But if he wanted to
marry Rania with full parental endorsement, these were the conditions, and my brother agreed.

We expected him to arrive in New York with Rania and our
grandmother the following July. At the airport, however, we found
my father's mother waiting outside the Arrivals gate alone. She had
flown with them as far as Amman, where they were to catch a con-
necting flight to Cairo, but the Jordanian authorities had stopped
Sami and Rania on the basis that they did not believe they were
going to America in order to be married. What is your *real* reason for traveling to America? To get married, said Sami. That is a
lie! said the authorities. You would not be traveling together if you
were not already married. No, Sami insisted. Really. We are not yet
married; we are going to be married in the States, where my parents
live and are expecting us. Then you must be a whore, one of the
officers said to Rania. A *slut*. How else do you explain this traveling
with a man who is not your husband?

At this, Rania had fainted, which the officers gladly took as con-firmation of their suspicions.

As a result Sami and Rania returned to Iraq while our grand-mother flew alone on to Cairo, London, and New York. She was meant to visit us for seven weeks, my grandfather having stayed behind in order to recuperate from a hip operation. But then Iraq invaded Kuwait and seven weeks became seven months. My grand-mother was not the only one displaced: I had moved into Sami's bedroom and given her mine, owing to my mother's concern that Sami's room was *too drafty*, by which I think she meant *contains a piano*, which my grandmother had been raised to regard as a frivo-lous invention, although apparently not so frivolous as to be resisted when she thought no one else was home.

From time to time, Zaid would call to tell us that everyone was fine. Jiddo's hip was getting better. Alia was taking care of the fruit trees. There was no mention of air-raid sirens, or cruise missiles whistling across the sky, for life in a panopticon had long condi-tioned Iraqis to believe that the walls have ears and the windows have eyes and you never know when the watchmen are off duty so you assume they are always on. Less convincingly, the panopti-con was also blamed for my brother's long silences. Sami had never been a letter writer, so I had no right to expect in-kind replies to the loquacious novellas I typed up and mailed off to him roughly once a month. However my brother did not even acknowledge those let-ters, not in his breezy *Greetings from Baghdad!* postcards and not when he called, which I seem to remember him doing only twice. The first time was on New Year's Eve, when our parents would have been back in Iraq themselves had there not been a war on. Ostensibly, the call was to wish us a Happy 1991, inshallah, but then Sami went on to say that he and Rania were not going to be mar-ried, after all. He did not sound disappointed. Instead, he sounded perfectly sanguine: sanguine and maybe even a little relieved. Rania was going to study art history in Paris and he too had reconsidered

his plans to move to Najaf and was looking into applying to Baghdad Medical School instead. What's wrong with the medical schools
in America? I asked when it was my turn on the phone. Nothing,
Sami said blithely. What's wrong with the medical schools in Iraq?

The second call came about three months later, by which time
America had begun to withdraw its troops and my grandmother
was packing up to go home. This time, Sami spoke only to our father, who, after hanging up, immediately took his jacket off the
coatrack and went out for a walk. When he got home he went into
my bedroom, where my grandmother's suitcase was three-quarters
full and her boarding passes to London, Cairo, and Amman were
propped up against my fishbowl of dice. He sat her down on my
bed and took her hands in his. Then he told her that Ahmed, her
husband of fifty-seven years, had had an embolism that morning,
and died.

MR. JAAFARI?

I looked up to see her standing on the other side of the immigration desks, evidently refusing to complete the distance between us.

We'd like to ask you a few more questions. Do you want to come through?

We rode an escalator together down to the baggage claim, where Denise consulted the overhead monitors. Then we walked the full length of the vast hall to locate my suitcase standing in solitude beside a stopped carousel. Extending its handle I tipped it into its wheeling position and followed Denise most of the way back to the escalator followed by a left into Goods to Declare. A male customs officer awaited us there, and while I hoisted my case onto a metal examination table he snapped on a pair of purple rubber gloves.

Pack the bag yourself?

Yes.

Anybody help you pack?

No.

Are you aware of all of the contents of your bag?

Yes.

While he poked around among my socks and underwear, Denise resumed her own questioning, thinly disguised as small talk.

So. What's the temperature like in Iraq this time of year?

Well, it depends on where you are, of course. In Sulaymaniyah it should be pretty mild, like in the fifties.

What's that? Denise said to the customs officer. Ten? Twelve?

Got me.

So when did you last see your brother? She opened my Iraqi passport again.

In January of 2005.

In Iraq?

Yes.

Is he an economist too?

No, he's a doctor.

The customs officer held up a package wrapped in pink-and-yellow gift paper. What's this?

An abacus, I said.

An abacus like for counting?

That's right.

Why do you have an abacus?

It's a present, for my niece.

How old is your niece? asked Denise.

Three.

And you think she'd like an abacus? the customs officer asked.

I shrugged. The customs officer and Denise both pondered my face for a moment and then the officer began prying at a piece of tape. The paper underneath was thin and as the tape peeled away it took some of the color with it, leaving behind a white gash. Peering into the open end, the officer gave the package a little shake; we all could hear the wooden beads clacking together as they slid back and forth on their thin metal rods. An abacus, the customs officer repeated incredulously, before feebly attempting to rewrap it.

I followed Denise back up the escalator and down a narrow hallway into a room where she gestured toward a chair facing a desk. Sitting on the other side of the desk, she began jiggling a mouse. Several seconds passed, and then I asked whether if this was going to take quite a bit longer I might make a call.

To Mr. Blunt?

Yes.

We've already called him.

Eventually Denise found what she was looking for and stood

up to cross the room and jiggle another mouse attached to another computer. This monitor looked newer than the first and was rigged up to an elaborate array of auxiliary equipment including a glowing glass slide and a camera that looked like a tiny Cyclops. A photograph of my most neutral expression was taken, followed by my fingerprints, all digitally. In order to get a complete and acceptable set Denise had to squeeze each of my fingers between her own forefinger and thumb and roll the tip over the glowing slide at least twice, sometimes three times; with one of my thumbs, four. I did not find Denise attractive. Nor was there anything suggestive to the way she manipulated my fingers, so it was a surprise when our prolonged physical contact began faintly to arouse me. Cooperating as we were, united by our desire to appease her hard-to-please computer with its red Xs and supercilious little *pings*, gave me the feeling that we were merely *playing* border control, and that any moment now Denise's mother would call her in for supper and I would be freed.

Instead, when the fingerprinting was done, we progressed to a second room, this one containing a small square table and three metal chairs. The upper half of one of the walls was composed of a dimmed glass in which my reflection was less a mirror image than a silhouette. Running horizontally under the glass was a long strip of red plastic, or rubber, like the tape you press on a bus to request a stop. A notice had been taped to the glass: PLEASE DO NOT LEAN ON THE RED STRIP AS IT SETS OFF AN ALARM.

Denise and I sat facing each other, my passports and her fat manila folder on the table between us. Then Denise thought better of this configuration and shuffled her chair around so that we were positioned at a right angle to each other instead. Sitting very erect, she opened her folder and took out a small stack of paper that she tapped vertically into alignment. Then she explained that she was going to ask me a series of questions, my answers to which she would write down and give me the opportunity to review. If I were happy with what she had written, I would sign my name at the bottom of each page, indicating my approval. I could see no fairer alternative to this process, and yet as it was explained to me I began to have the sinking feeling you get when you agree to a game of Tic-Tac-Toe in which the other person gets to go first.

For the next twenty minutes, Denise and I repeated almost verbatim the same conversation we'd had nearly three hours earlier, when I'd first reached the end of the metal maze. This iteration took longer, of course, because Denise had to write everything down in her loopy, schoolgirlish handwriting, and then, whenever she reached the end of a sheet of paper, there was the time it took for her to swivel it toward me and wait while I read it over and signed my assent. Naturally, answering questions I'd already answered felt like a waste of time—but soon enough I regretted my impatience, because when we finally did move on it was into more sinister territory.

Have you ever been arrested?

No.

Is Amar Ala Jaafari the name you were given at birth?

Yes.

Have you ever used another name?

No.

Never?

Never.

You have never told a law enforcement officer that your name is anything other than Amar Ala Jaafari?

No.

Denise studied me intently for a moment before writing this last no down.

Can you tell me in more detail what you were doing here in 1998?

I'd just graduated from college and had a yearlong internship at the Toynbee Bioethics Council. I also volunteered at a hospital on weekends.

What was your address during your stay?

Thirty-Nine Tavistock Place. I don't remember the flat number.

And how was it that you came to live there?

It was my aunt's apartment.

Is it still?

No.

Why not?

She died.

I'm sorry. How?

Cancer.

The pen hovered.

Pancreatic, I said.

And now you're returning to London for the first time in ten years? To see some friends?

To meet up with Alastair Blunt, yes.

For only two days?

I looked at my watch. Yes.

I'm just thinking . . . It's a long way to come for only forty-eight hours. Not even forty-eight hours.

Well, like I said, I'm flying on to Istanbul on Sunday. It was the cheapest ticket I could find.

What is your relationship to Mr. Blunt?

We're friends.

Do you have a girlfriend? A partner?

No.

No partner?

Not at the moment, no.

And no job.

No.

Denise smiled at me sadly. Well, I guess it's not a good time to be looking, is it?

For a moment I thought she meant for a girlfriend. Oh, I said airily. Something will come along.

By the time she had run out of questions our combined hand-writing had filled nearly thirteen pages. All right, Denise said brightly, standing and tugging her trouser thighs back into place.

I'm just going to take you to our holding room while I make some general inquiries.

Then what?

Then I'll be discussing your case with the chief immigration officer on duty.

When?

I don't know.

I'm sorry, I said, I know you're just doing your job, but could you please give me a sense of what you're discussing? What the problem is?

There's no problem; we just need to check a few things. The background of your passports, that's all. As I've already explained to you. Just some general inquiries.

I looked at her.

Are you hungry?

No.

Do you need to use the toilet?

No. But I'm worried about my friend. I'm supposed to meet him in town in less than an hour.

We've explained things to Mr. Blunt. He knows you're here. He knows we're just making some general inquiries.

INITIALLY, I HAD MY eye on someone else. Then I went to see a performance of *Three Sisters* in which one of my roommates was playing Lieutenant Tuzenbach and Maddie was playing Olga, and now I can't even remember the other girl's name. Like many Ivy League student productions, this one had an overwrought quality that gave you the impression the twenty-year-old at the helm could now cross *direct a play* off his list of things to do before winning a Rhodes scholarship. The night I attended, the girl playing Anfisa had taken a morning-after pill at lunchtime and at the moment of her entrance at the top of Act 3 was in the bathroom retching into a toilet. Consequently, Maddie opened the act alone, accounting for both actresses' lines, the most crucial information being distilled into a riveting monologue premised upon (a) Anfisa having been too tired to complete the walk from town, where (b) a great fire was raging, traumatizing Olga such that she was hearing voices and talking to people who were not actually there. What if he is burnt! cried Maddie/Olga/Anfisa. What an idea . . . all undressed, too! [*Opening a closet and flinging clothes to the floor.*] We must take this gray dress, Anfisa . . . and this one . . . and this blouse, too . . . Oh, you're right, of course you're right, Nanny, you can't carry them all! . . . I'd better call Ferapont. By the time the imperious Natasha had come on, Maddie was huddled on a divan with a lace tablecloth over her head, trembling deliriously. Uh, Anfisa? Natasha ventured. What are you . . . ? Twisting under her hood, Maddie threw Natasha a meaningful look. Anfisa! said Natasha, when the penny dropped. Don't you dare to sit down in my presence! At which point Maddie stood, removed the improvised shawl from her head, and—playing Olga again—fixed her castmate with a withering stare. Excuse me, Natasha, but how rude you were to Nanny just now!

Well, I thought that was some of the best acting I'd ever seen. Were it not for the scandalized traditionalists whispering behind me, I would not have suspected anything amiss. That night, when Lieutenant Tuzenbach returned to our suite with a bit of pumpkin-colored makeup still collaring his neck, I learned that Maddalena Monti had had her pick of the semester's leading roles and was already hobnobbing with the seniors bound for graduate school in Los Angeles and New York. After that, like a word you come across for the first time and then it's everywhere, she began to appear in my path or periphery several times a week: reading in the dining hall, smoking a cigarette outside the language lab, legs outstretched in the library, roaring a silent yawn. I thought she was beautiful in the way some girls are beautiful despite having bypassed pretty entirely. It was a fickle beauty, undermined in an instant by her sardonic mouth, or by her eyebrows arching to angles of cartoon-ish depravity. A moment later, these same features that made her an electrifying Olga, or Sonya, or Lady Macbeth, would rearrange themselves into the radiant symmetry of a Yelena or Salomé. At first, I was wary of this inconsistency, which was reflected in her moods. I suspected it was deliberate, calculated to manipulate and seduce, and, worse, that Maddie possessed little awareness of the motives and consequences of her behavior. But in time I came to think that in fact Maddie more than anyone suffered her tenden-cies toward the mercurial, and moreover that this was probably the reason she was attracted to me: I was an antidote to what she liked least about herself. And contrary to the impression that she was not cognizant of her psyche's causes and effects, she was capable of startlingly articulate admissions of self-awareness. When we'd been having lunch together every Friday for a month, I asked her why she wasn't closer to her roommates. Oh, I'm not good with other women, Maddie replied simply. They make me feel inessential.

The night before Christmas break during our freshman year, she came to my room chewing on a thumb and consulted the calendar hanging on the back of my closet door. She was pregnant—by a graduate student in the Classics Department, though I never did learn his name nor how they'd wound up in bed—and someone at the campus health center had informed her that one must be at least five weeks along before a pregnancy may be terminated. December thirtieth, Maddie concluded, if she did not want to do it a day later than necessary. December thirtieth in 1994 fell on Isra and Mi'raj, by which time I was back at home in Bay Ridge, getting dressed to go to the mosque. Maddie called from her mother's house outside Albany and confessed that she had not been able to have it done after all. She was eager that I understand this was not owing to any late-breaking moral qualms. Undetected by her mother, she'd driven herself to the Planned Parenthood downtown, registered, paid for the procedure up front and in cash, changed into a paper gown, submitted the requisite blood and urine samples and lain down for a sonogram, then sat in a room with approximately half a dozen other women to wait. There had been a television on, and whatever they were watching was interrupted by a news report about what had just happened in Massachusetts. A man had taken a rifle to the Planned Parenthood in Brookline and shot and killed the receptionist there. Then he went up the street to a preterm clinic and shot and killed the receptionist there. Where's Brookline? the girl next to Maddie asked. Far away, Maddie had reassured her; there was no need to worry. But then the clinic's telephone began to ring and two policemen arrived to tell the women in the waiting room that they should all put their clothes back on and go home.

And now I don't know if I can go back.

Maddie, do you want a baby?

No.

Do you want to have a baby and give it up for adoption?

No.

I waited.

I know I need to do it, she said. I just don't want to go alone.

That night, I kneeled beside my father in the mosque and thought about what it would be like to accompany a girl I had not got pregnant to her abortion. There were children present, many more than usual, and as they listened with wide darting eyes to the story of Muhammad and Gabriel ascending into the heavens, I felt at once flattered and perverse. Afterward, in the parking lot, I was introduced by my parents to the daughter of some Lebanese friends, a pretty girl with long glossy hair and black eyeliner drawn expertly around each intelligent eye. She was home from Princeton, where she was a junior majoring in evolutionary biology, and I suggested that we meet for coffee one afternoon before we each went back to school. But I never did call her.

Maddie knocked on my door the following week wearing a skirt.

Was I supposed to dress up? I asked.

Oh, Maddie said quietly. No. I just thought it would make me feel better to look nice.

We did not say much after that. The cold felt so reproachful of our mission that when we came to a cheerful-looking coffee shop I suggested we stop in for some hot drinks. Maddie declined, on the basis that her stomach was supposed to be empty, so I went in to buy something for myself and we walked on. The clinic was not at all what I'd expected. Vaguely, I'd imagined something more, well, clinical, maybe a modern cinder-block affair, but instead Maddie was going to have her abortion in a three-story brick manor whose gabled roof, multiple chimneys, and lawn running the length of the block looked altogether more like a Victorian asylum. I was not allowed inside with my hot chocolate so to register she went in alone. Standing by the door I watched her walk to the receptionist's desk, where, with her hood up and her hands in her pockets, she looked like an Eskimo asking directions. Next to the receptionist's computer stood a miniature foil Christmas tree, strung with colored lights that blinked quickly, then slowly, then quadruple-time, like a disco strobe, then went dark for a long, suspenseful moment before the cycle started over again.

Why was I there? I was eighteen. I had had intercourse with only two girls, each of them once, both times with a condom employed so successfully that we might have been shooting a video for educational purposes. Maybe for this reason I felt faintly censorious of Maddie's condition—but then of course even the most conscientiously donned condom does not always stay on and/or intact. At any rate, this was not about me. You could draw a circle around me and my morals and another around Maddie and hers and the two needn't have overlapped. I had no share in this embryo. I had not asked her to do this. Later, Maddie would be in her room and I in mine, catching up on some reading over a Cup O'Noodle, having relinquished a few hours of my time but nothing more.

Anyway, would I mind so much if our circles overlapped?

All at once, my morals, whatever they were, felt too antiquated, too abstract. I threw the rest of my drink away and went inside to tell the receptionist that I was there with Maddalena Monti and how long did she think she would be? The receptionist said that it had been quiet and Maddie had not had long to wait but the anesthesiologist was running behind so it would probably be three hours at least. I sat down in the waiting room and picked up an old *New Yorker*. An unseen speaker softly played Ob-La-Di, Ob-La-Da. The only other person in the room was a woman knitting, of all things, a baby sweater. After watching her needles gently fencing for a while I flipped through the magazine until I became distracted by an ad offering Finest Ruby Red Grapefruit From Florida's Indian River! TREE-RIPENED—BRIMMING WITH JUICE—ORCHARD SWEET—NO SUGAR IS NEEDED—SATISFACTION GUARANTEED!

The receptionist's phone rang.

. . . No, not here. . . . No. . . . None of that matters here, honey. You can come here and it doesn't matter. . . . Between four and , seven, depending on how far along you are. . . . You do the exam and ultrasound here. . . . Do you live in the area? . . . Okay, talk to him, and why don't you guys call me together and we'll schedule an appointment for you to come in. . . . Everything is confidential here, hon. . . . No. . . . No. . . . Monday through Saturday. . . . Do you know his schedule enough to schedule an appointment now? . . . Okay. But just don't— . . . Just don't— . . . Uh-huh. You know what, don't . . . If I were you, hon, don't bring him in. Forget about that, and— . . . You don't have to call us back. Just come in before six thirty, okay? . . . My name is Michelle. . . . Okay? . . . Okay. . . . Okay . . . Bye.

Much later, when Maddie emerged, holding her coat, she looked smaller all over, though I couldn't imagine why she should have.

I'm starving, she said.

We bought doughnuts in the coffee shop on the way back to Silliman and when we got to my room Maddie asked if I had anything to drink. On the mantelpiece I found a bottle of Midori that belonged to my roommate who wasn't due to return until the following week. Maddie filled half a mug with the emerald syrup and drank, making a face. What's it supposed to taste like? she asked. I looked at the bottle. Melon, I said. Honeydew, I guess.

She took off her boots and lay down on my bed. I put a CD on and sat in a chair to flip through the spring course catalogue. The CD was Chet Baker, and the first three tracks were deeply mellow, depressing really, so I was about to get up and look for something else when we were saved by what I think is the only upbeat song on the album:

> *They all laughed at Christopher Columbus when he said the world was round.*
> *They all laughed when Edison recorded sound.*
> *They all laughed at Wilbur and his brother when they said that man could fly.*
> *They told Marconi, wireless was a phony; it's the same old cry!*

*They laughed at me, wanting you, said I was reaching for the
  moon.*
But oh, you came through; now they'll have to change their tune!
*They all said we never could be happy; they laughed at us, and
  how.*
But ho-ho-ho, who's got the last laugh now?

I thought Maddie was asleep, but when the trumpet interval
came around she spoke without opening her eyes.
Do you know who Bob Monkhouse is?
No. Who's Bob Monkhouse?
A British comedian my dad likes. Still alive, I think. And he tells
this joke that goes: When I was a kid, I told everyone I wanted to
be a comedian when I grew up, and they laughed. Well, they're not
laughing now.

Two years later, when Maddie told me that she too wanted to
become a doctor, I laughed. I laughed with the haughtiness of a
ballet mistress informing a dwarf that she will never be a prima
ballerina. But twenty-four hours later Maddie was sitting across
from her academic advisor discussing the logistics of changing
her major from theater studies to anthropology and applying to
postbaccalaureate conversion courses at many of the same medical schools to which I had applied. My reaction to this was febrile
indignation. And I suppose, I said, that next month you'll want to
be an astronaut. Or a Wimbledon champion. Or a clarinetist with
the New York Philharmonic. No, Maddie said quietly. I'll want
to be a doctor. I'll want to be a doctor because I've been reading
William Carlos Williams and I've decided his is an exemplary life.
Oh I see, I said contemptuously, even though I hadn't ever read
any William Carlos Williams. So you're going to become an over-
rated poet as well. And in the middle of a downpour Maddie left

my room and we did not speak for three days. What I decided
during this enforced period of reflection was that my girlfriend
would make a truly terrible doctor. I did not doubt her intelligence. Nor had I observed her to be unusually squeamish about
blood or pain. But her *being*! The clamorous, dizzying way she
inhabited the world—never on time, cardigan inside out, Amar
where are my glasses, my ID; has anyone seen my keys? On a good
day, the chaos was barely containable. But Maddie onstage was
something else. Acting organized her. It sorted her out. Like a
laned highway, it regulated her speeds and, for the most part, pre-
vented her emotions from colliding. She was good at acting, but
also, and this was the elegance of the fit, acting was good for her. It
made sense of her. It made sense of *us*. Maddie was the artist; I was
the empiricist. Together we had an impressive and mutually en-
riching range of humanity's disciplines covered. Or so I believed.
And so it seemed to me a perverse and even ungrateful surge of
whimsy that she should want to be something else, anything else,
but especially something so workaday, so unglamorous. A doctor!
Maddie! It seemed, if you will, not unlike a prima ballerina wanting to become a dwarf.

Undoubtedly, I felt this way in part because *I* did not want to
become a doctor. And maybe Maddie figured this out, and perhaps
even felt sorry for her poor boyfriend and his repressed condition,
because she tacitly forgave me my tantrum and went about reca-
librating her life's path with little regard for the cynical glances I
dealt her along the way. Meanwhile, of the eight medical schools
contemplating my candidacy, only one said yes. Curiously, it was
the one I most wanted to attend, yet after opening the deceptively
thin envelope I lay on my bed and stared at the ceiling for an hour
and a half. Then I walked to the Office of Career Services, feeling, I suppose, like a man slinking off to a strip club even as his
beautiful wife awaits him in lingerie at home. Most of the application deadlines in the binder labeled RESEARCH FELLOWSHIPS had

already passed. Of those that hadn't I narrowed the choice down to two: an assistant position in a cancer lab in Seattle and publications coordinator for a bioethics think tank in London. The latter was described as a nine-month post that came with free airfare and a stipend of one hundred pounds a week. I applied. Three weeks later, a man unforgettably named Colin Cabbagestalk phoned to say that if indeed I was still interested the position was mine. Something in his voice, hasty yet cagey, led me to think I had been selected from a candidate pool of one.

That summer, of 1998, I lived with Maddie in Morningside Heights. We subleased a studio on Broadway and spent eight weeks doing very little other than exactly what we wanted to do, which is to say a lot of drinking coffee, eating waffles, taking long walks around the reservoir or up and down Riverside Park and reading magazines cover to cover in the bath. Never have I felt so free, so unfettered by obligation. Also buoying our time together was something of the thrill of a clandestine affair, for Maddie had not told her parents about our living together and nor had I been altogether honest with mine. It seems foolish now, that we should have felt unable to tell them, and so went on acting like children even as we chafed at being treated as such. It is not implausible to think that my parents would have been relieved to learn I was in love with a lapsed Catholic bound for medical school in New York; a Muslim girl would have been preferable, of course, but at least with Maddie I was unlikely to join their only other child halfway around the world anytime soon. As for Maddie's mother, the presumed objection seemed to be less on religious grounds than simply a preference for someone with a whiter-sounding name. Still, we persisted with our ruse. When my parents came to visit, Maddie's things went into a closet. When her mother and stepfather took the train down from Loudonville, Maddie entertained them in the apartment of an old high school friend who lived over on York. We left our landlord's name on the mailbox, his voice on the answering machine, and steadfastly ignored the landline whenever it rang. It was not until Labor Day of that year that I bought my first cell phone, a Motorola the size of a shoe, and which had to be held out the window to get a signal, if there was a signal to be got at all.

We had dinner with the high school friend once. Maddie invited her over for pizza and wine and the conversation wound its way to a point where our guest felt comfortable asking whether I agreed religion stymies intellectual curiosity. On the contrary, I said. I consider seeking knowledge a religious obligation. After all, the first word received in the Quran is: Read! And the third line is: Read, because your Lord has taught you the pen; he taught mankind what mankind did not yet know. But religion, our guest insisted with impressive confidence, allows you to ask only so many questions before you get to: Just because. You have to have faith. Well, I said. Your problem with religion is virtually every faithless person's problem with religion: that it offers irreducible answers. But some questions in the end simply aren't empirically verifiable. Find me the empirical evidence as to whether you should derail the train and kill all three hundred passengers if it would mean saving the life of the one person tied to the tracks. Or: Is it true because I see it, or do I see it because it's true? The whole point of faith is that irreducible answers don't bother the faithful. The faithful take comfort and even pride in the knowledge that they have the strength to make the irreducible answers sincerely their own, as difficult as that is to do. Everyone—irreligious people included—relies on irreducible answers every day. All religion really does is to be honest about this, by giving the reliance a specific name: faith.

It was not a flawless speech, tipsy and improvising as I was, but still I was glad the subject had been broached, because it had seemed to me that a conversation along these lines had been looming on the horizon for me and Maddie for a while. Yet throughout dinner Maddie was unusually quiet, and the topic did not come up again the following day. Nor did it come up again at all before Maddie started her premed conversion classes and I flew abroad. All those walks. All those hours tangled up in bed. Sometimes I wonder whether we hide lovers from others because it makes it easier to hide ourselves from ourselves.

The bioethics council operated out of the basement of a Georgian town house in Bloomsbury's Bedford Square, a pretty oval garden popular at night with methadone addicts whose discarded syringes were a regular feature of my walk to work. My aunt's flat was a pleasant place, four well-kept rooms in a handsome prewar mansion block, but I did not spend much time there. Typically, I ran a bath (there was no showerhead), bought a coffee and pastry from the café at the end of the road, put in my eight hours at the bioethics council and then read in a pub or watched a film at the Renoir before calling Maddie from bed. On the weekends, I ran. Not in the parks, which with their manicured grass and mosaic flower beds were too unreal. You got nowhere running around Inner Circle. Instead, I dodged shoppers and strollers all the way down Southampton Row, onto Kingsway, a right onto Aldwych and over the Strand; then it was a race with the shadows of the double-deckers crossing Waterloo Bridge and a few bounces down the steps of Southbank to fall in with the ferries and barges, all of us purposefully gliding. I'd discovered in high school that I enjoyed running, not around a track but on my own in Shore Park, which in the early mornings afforded an ethereal view of lower Manhattan rising up like the Emerald City of Oz. I guess it would be more accurate to say I enjoyed running less than I enjoyed how running later made me feel. Still, there *were* immediate pleasures, namely the solitude, and the sense of myself as a person in motion, even if I wasn't sure in what direction that motion might be. Had someone told me that at twenty-two I'd be living in London, having secured myself a respectable internship *and* a spot in medical school *and* a serious girlfriend back in New York, it would have seemed to me a fabulous and enviable achievement. But Bloomsbury I found deeply gloomy. When I ran,

I would watch the indifferent pavement flowing under my feet and feel overwhelmed by the immense distance I'd put between myself and home. And although I liked the content of my work—I spent my weekdays editing newsletter articles on animal-to-human transplants, stem cell therapy, and genetically modified crops—the staff's median age was at least fifteen years older than I, and, after the onrush of college imperatives, this new learning curve felt too gentle, its revelations underwhelming and its pace grindingly slow. Rather than fabulous and enviable, then, I felt in London the way you do when you take one step too many at the bottom of a flight of stairs: brought up short by the unexpected plateau and its dull, unyielding thud.

The *Are you ready?* questionnaire that accompanied my application to volunteer at the local children's hospital threw into doubt a number of long-held presumptions:

> Are you emotionally mature and have the ability to deal with difficult situations and be sensitive?
>
> Are you a good listener?
>
> Are you reliable, trustworthy, motivated, receptive and flexible?
>
> Are you able to accept guidance and remain calm under pressure?
>
> Are you able to communicate well with patients, families and staff?

This sheet of paper was succeeded by something called an Equal Opportunities form, seeking confirmation of my gender, marital status, ethnicity, educational background, and disabilities, if any. It also presented me with a series of boxes to be checked depending on whether I considered myself Low Income, Homeless, Ex-Offender, Refugee/Asylum Seeker, Lone Parent, and/or Other. I could not help but think it would be easier to dispense opportunities equally if one did not know the answers to these questions. I answered them anyway, of course, hesitating only when it came to Low Income, which certainly described my stipend from the bioethics council, but which I somehow understood to mean something else.

For the interview, I got a haircut and bought a tie. A harried woman with a giraffe mural peering at me over her shoulder advised that the requisite police checks on my background could take up to eight weeks. In actuality, they took five, and my induction was scheduled for a Saturday that happened also to be Halloween. I call it an induction because that's what the harried woman said over the phone, but I'd hardly met her in the lobby and been shown to a playroom on the ground floor when she said that she had to attend to an emergency in the endocrinology ward and we did not see each other again for the rest of the day.

As I stood where she left me, charged with making myself useful as I saw fit, my first thought was that there was something sort of comical about having to pass five weeks of police checks in order to stand in a room full of children dressed as cats, clowns, princesses, bumblebees, ladybugs, pirates, superheroes, and, yes, policemen. My second thought was that I had never felt so out of place in my life. The lighting appeared inordinately bright. The din of the children laughing and shrieking and meowing seemed several decibels higher than what I was used to at the bioethics council, never mind my aunt's sepulchral flat. The other volunteers—we all wore sunflower-yellow T-shirts that read *Here to help* in blue across the back—sat on miniature chairs, their knees high like grasshoppers', or in that most uncomfortable position for non-yoga-practicing adults: cross-legged on the floor. Reluctantly, down I went, with pre-arthritic objections from my knees, and landed next to a Snow White absorbed in gluing glittered macaroni to a cardboard mask. What's that? I asked, in a voice higher and tighter than my own. A mask, the girl replied, without looking up. I watched her work for a while and then turned my attention to a tiny swashbuckler who, with his eye patch parked high on his forehead, was busy stacking blocks. To him I said nothing. These kids did not need me. *Here to help* might as well have been my own costume. In fact, as the afternoon wore on, I began to feel that *I* was the one being helped, and not least by this tireless demonstration of how very simple and egoless an existence can be: Put one block on top of another. Now another. Now another. Now knock 'em all down. Repeat.

I was not of use to no one that day. About an hour before the end of my shift, a woman wearing an abaya appeared in the doorway holding the hand of a little girl. This girl looked about seven or eight, and, other than being a little on the thin side, healthy as they come. Someone had drawn six whiskers on her face, but otherwise she did not have a costume—only a purple long-sleeved T-shirt and jeans that stopped a good inch above her frilly white socks. By this point I was leaning against a wall, my legs outstretched, while a couple of princesses (or ballerinas—one couldn't be sure) arranged and rearranged a Lilliputian gathering of stuffed animals around my ankles. The woman in the doorway stood watching for a long moment, then pointed in our direction and led the girl over. Hnana, she said, picking up a frog puppet. Here. The girl took the frog, inserted a hand inside it, and sank to the floor. She had a striking face, smooth and boyish, with long eyelashes and a sleek black bob tucked neatly behind her ears. The whiskers looked like an indignity she could have done without. She held the frog in her lap, belly-up, and at one point absentmindedly scratched her shoulder with its nose. Meanwhile, the princess-ballerinas continued setting up for some sort of stuffed-creatures convention. This involved lots of high-pitched ventriloquism and decidedly unballetic leaps over my legs and back again, the pink netting of their skirts rustling and jouncing with each unsteady jump. I thought maybe they hadn't noticed the new girl—until, unbidden, one of them picked up a rabbit, swiveled abruptly on her chubby pink legs, and held it out.

Want this?

The new girl shook her head.

This? The other princess held up an owl.

Again, the new girl shook her head. Then she removed her hand from the frog, pointed deep into the menagerie, and said a word so softly that none of us could hear.

Son, maybe. Or sun.

Hsan, I blurted. Horse.

The girl nodded, then turned to look at me with surprise. One of the other girls tossed her the horse. Discarding the frog, the new girl took up the horse and, blushing a little, began to comb its mane of yarn with her fingers. I reached behind her for the frog puppet and wriggled my own hand inside it. I wish I was a horse, I made the frog say, in Arabic. The girl smiled.

When the costumes came off, you saw the iniquity of illness more clearly. You saw its symptoms, or rather the invisibility thereof, and you could not resist trying to predict the poor child's chances. An arm or a leg in a cast was not so bad. Often just a playground casualty that in eight weeks would have already faded into family lore. A port-wine stain covering half a face seemed much more unfair— although, with time and lasers, it too could be persuaded to fade. Harder to behold were the more structural disfigurements, like Microtia, Latin for little ear, or Ollier disease, a hyperproliferation of cartilage that could turn a hand as knobby and twisted as ginger root. I read about these and all manner of other disorders in the basement of the bioethics council, where a bookshelf jammed with medical dictionaries became my most reliable lunchtime companion. It wasn't always easy to arrive at a diagnosis. The doctors at the hospital did not readily share their conclusions and, being a mere playtime volunteer, I generally did not feel in a position to ask. So I went on what I could see: Bulging joints. Buckling legs. Full-body tremors. What you could see could be apprehended. Leukemia, on the other hand, or a brain tumor, even one as big as a tangerine: their stealth was terrifying. It is not a logical theory. It is not even a theory. How can it be a theory when there are such blatant exceptions? Indisputably, there is no correlation between the visibility and severity of diseases, and yet the invisible ones have a special power. Maybe because they seem dishonest. Disingenuous. A birthmark may be unfortunate, but at least it doesn't sneak up on you. So whenever I saw a new child coming through the lobby I could not help but search hopefully for a sign: of something tolerable, maybe even curable, like a sole that with a squirt of glue can be reattached to a shoe. Please, just don't let it be attacking her from the inside out. Please don't let her have one of the invisible things.

Practically speaking, I was doing this for professional reasons, to get a feel for the hospital setting and to work on my bedside manner, but in truth I found it so emotionally draining that all I seemed to be working on was my desire for a beer. One Saturday, toward the end of my shift, a fellow volunteer called Lachlan suggested that I join him and some friends for a pint in a pub around the corner. Alastair was there, along with two or three others eager to explain to me the true significance of New Labour, the inanity of Cool Britannia, and the flatulence-inducing qualities of Young's Bitter. We also, that night or another night, talked about Afghanistan, or rather Clinton's missile strikes of a few months before, which in the table's majority opinion were an all-too-convenient distraction from his so-called domestic problems. I doubted that—after all, Clinton had not ordered the embassy attacks in Dar es Salaam and Nairobi as well—and I kept one eye on Alastair as I said this, for I'd already understood that he was a shrewd and independent thinker and I was anxious not to preclude myself from aligning with his opinion. But Alastair did not contribute much to this sort of talk. He sat in the corner, under a shelf of board games that cast a shadow over half his face, blearily surveying the far side of the room like someone involuntarily consigned to a long wait. Lit from above, the other half of him looked sallow and haggard beyond its years, and had I not known him—had I been there on my own, observing him from a distance as he swallowed pint after pint—I would have taken him for a has-been, or a never-been; in any case, for a derelict alcoholic. To be fair, Alastair probably spent the first several of our

evenings together taking me for a tedious newcomer. But of course
I *was* the tedious newcomer, and while Alastair may have been an
alcoholic, he was not derelict. Not yet.

One night, I asked him where he was from.

Bournemouth, he replied, and then got up to go to the bathroom.

Another night, the girl wiping our table asked me where I was
from.

Brooklyn.

But his parents grew up in Baghdad, Lachlan said.

Alastair leaned over the table to look at me with fresh interest.
Where in Baghdad?

Karrada.

When did they leave?

Seventy-six.

Muslim?

I nodded.

Sunni or Shiite?

Caught in the volley, Lachlan got up to give me his seat, but it
wasn't long after I'd slid over that it became apparent Alastair knew
quite a bit more about contemporary Iraq than I did. I hadn't been
in ten years and couldn't remember the name of the Shiite tribe
my family belonged to; moreover, when I admitted I'd never tasted
sheep's-head soup he gave me a look of such incredulity you'd think
I was a man from Parma claiming never to have tasted ham. Still, a
certain spirit of fellowship had been established, and soon while the
others carried on about cricket or the barmaids' backsides Alastair
was telling me about his various stints not only in Baghdad but in
El Salvador, Rwanda, Bosnia, and Beirut—where, while I'd been
a teenager in Bay Ridge, alphabetizing my baseball cards and taking the PSATs, he'd been dodging Hezbollah and smoking hash-
ish in the old Commodore Hotel. Stories such as these rendered
me spellbound and even a little envious. I did not desire my own
run-in with paramilitary extremists, of course, but I wouldn't have
minded being able to say I'd dodged them.

When I'd taken up drinking with the locals on Saturday nights, my Sunday runs gave way to entire days of Radio 4 and the quicksands of rumination in bed. It wasn't so much that I was hungover— although I did drink too much, and, one morning, having awoken to the surreal cadences of the Shipping Forecast, thought for a moment I'd done irreversible damage to my brain. It was more that my new Saturday nights, quintessentially British and brimming with camaraderie, felt like whatever I'd been running to, which no longer needed to be found. The first *Desert Island Discs* castaway I ever heard was Joseph Rotblat, the Nobel Peace Prize laureate who'd helped to invent the atomic bomb and then spent much of the rest of his life trying to undo the consequences. In his nineties now, he spoke urgently, with a Polish accent and the ragged rasp of age, and he described for the interviewer how, after Hiroshima, he'd vowed to change his life in two major ways. One was to redirect his research from nuclear reactions to medical operations. The other was to raise awareness of the potential dangers of science and make its practitioners more responsible for their work. His musical selections—the eight records he'd take with him if banished to a desert island— strayed little from these ideals: Kol Nidrei, Last Night I Had the Strangest Dream, Where Have All the Flowers Gone?, A Rill Will Be A Stream, A Stream Will Be A Flood, performed by the Swedish Physicians in Concert for the Prevention of Nuclear War . . .

Your ambition, said Sue Lawley, when the Swedish Physicians had faded out, goes beyond a nuclear-weapons-free world. You want to see a world free of war. Do you believe that it will happen, or do you simply dream that it might?

It *must* happen. I've got two objectives in my life, what's still left of it. The short-term objective and a long-term objective. The short-term objective is the elimination of nuclear weapons, and the long-term objective is the elimination of war. And the reason why I felt that one is important is because even if we eliminate nuclear weapons, we cannot disinvent them. Should there be a serious conflict in the future between great powers, they could be reintroduced.

Moreover, and this comes back to the responsibility of scientists: certain other fields of science, particularly genetic engineering, could result in the development of another weapon of mass destruction, maybe more readily available than nuclear weapons. And therefore the only way is to prevent war. So there would be no need at all. Any type of war. We have got to remove war as a recognized social institution. We have got to learn to sort out disputes without military confrontation.

And do you believe there is a real chance of that happening?

I believe we are already moving towards it! In my lifetime, I have seen the changes that have occurred in society. I've lived through two world wars. In both of these wars, France and Germany, for example, were mortal enemies. They killed each other off. Now, the idea of war between these two countries is quite inconceivable. And this applies to other nations in the European Union. This is an enormous revolution. People don't realize how big a change has occurred. We have to educate ourselves to the culture of peace, rather than the culture of violence in which we live now. . . . In the words of Friedrich von Schiller: Alle Menschen werden Brüder. All men will be brothers. This, I hope, will be achieved.

Before the interview concluded and the theme music with squawking seagulls resumed, Rotblat also recounted how, in 1939, having accepted an invitation to study physics in Liverpool, he'd left his wife alone in Poland because his stipend was not sufficient to support them both. The following summer, after receiving a small raise, he returned to Warsaw to collect her, but Tola had come down with appendicitis and was unable to travel. So Rotblat went back to England alone, expecting her to follow as soon as she was well, but two days after he arrived in England Germany invaded Poland, and all means of contact between him and his wife were suspended. Only after several months did he manage to reach her with the assistance of the Red Cross and make plans to get her out through a friend in Denmark. Then Germany invaded Denmark. Now he tried through some friends in Belgium, and Belgium was invaded. Then he tried Italy, where one of his professors knew a willing convoy in Milan, but the day Tola set off to meet the liaison there Mussolini declared war on Britain and she was turned back at the Italian border. This was the last Rotblat heard of her.

That evening, when I relayed this story to Maddie, she sounded distant and unmoved. When I pressed her, she remained silent for a moment and then cleared her throat and said something about how, once we know the end of an unfortunate story, it's tempting to ask why its protagonist did not do better to swerve his fate.

Or do you think it's all up to God? she asked a moment later, in a voice that did not invite the affirmative. God's decision? God's will?

And if I did?

That I didn't see the end of me and Maddie coming seems impossible to me now. But at the time I had this notion that even though my own feelings for my girlfriend had begun to cool not long after the spectacular prize of her was attained, to part ways on this basis would be as much an act of infidelity toward myself. It unsettled me that the Amar of a year ago could be so inconsistent with the Amar of today, and I suppose that in my determination to pretend, at least, that nothing had changed—that I was not so fickle and vain as to want a woman only until she had been won—I did not sufficiently entertain the possibility that Maddie herself was capable of changing, too. Then, on the last Sunday before Christmas, Sue Lawley announced her castaway that week to be the English comedian Bob Monkhouse. Amazed, I picked up the phone and dialed the many digits that were Maddie, but there was no answer.

Stormy Weather started up, and I tried her again. Vaughn Monroe, Racing With the Moon. Ravel. Barber's Adagio for Strings. During You Have Cast Your Shadow on the Sea, performed by Monkhouse and Cast, I tried her a fourth time, my hangover compounded now by my bilious anxiety over why my girlfriend of three and a half years was not answering her cell phone at six forty-five Eastern Standard Time on a Sunday morning.

What about your book? Sue Lawley asked.

That would be the complete works of Lewis Carroll.

What if you could only have—

One?

—one bit of Lewis Carroll?

Well, *Hunting of the Snark*, I suppose, is my favorite piece of work by Lewis Carroll. But then again, I couldn't do without the characters in *Wonderland* and *Through the Looking Glass*. Now would it be . . . Can I please have the *Complete Adventures of Alice*?

I could see why she thought me hypocritical. On the face of it, it's paradoxical to be so cautious in life, so orderly and fastidious, while also claiming to place one's faith in the ultimate agency of God. Why give up cigarettes if He has already written you off in a bus accident next week? But theological predestination and free will are not necessarily incompatible. If God has a definite power over the whole of existence, one can imagine this power extending to His ability, whenever He wills, to replace any given destiny with another destiny. In other words, destiny is not definite but indefinite, mutable by the deliberate actions of man himself; Allah will not change the condition of a people until they change what is in themselves. God has not predetermined the course of human history but rather is aware of all its possible courses and may alter the one we're on in accordance with our will and the bounds of His universe. Or, as I'd put it to Maddie the week before: Think of a bumper cars rink. Seated in a bumper car, you're free to steer yourself in any direction you like, while at the same time your vehicle is connected by a pole to a ceiling that supplies energy to the car and ultimately limits its movements to those predetermined by a grid. Similarly, with his enormous bumper cars rink, God creates and presides over the possibility of human action, which humans then take it upon themselves to carry out. And in so doing—turning left or right, advancing or reversing, slamming into your neighbors or respectfully veering clear of them—we decide what we shall become and assume responsibility for these choices that define us.

I could tell from the softening silence on the line that Maddie was not immediately opposed to what I was saying. But I could also tell, by the length of said silence, that diverging views on the scope of God's will were not really our problem. Our problem was a forty-nine-year-old medical professor named Geoffrey Stubblebine. But never mind. We all disappear down the rabbit hole now and again. Sometimes it can seem the only way to escape the boredom or exigencies of your prior existence—the only way to press reset on the mess you've made of all that free will. Sometimes you just want someone else to take over for a while, to rein in freedom that has become a little too free. Too lonely, too lacking in structure, too exhaustingly autonomous. Sometimes we jump into the hole, sometimes we allow ourselves to be pulled in, and sometimes, not entirely inadvertently, we trip.

I'm not talking about coercion. Being pushed is another matter.

IN THE LITTLE ANTECHAMBER to the holding room, a large man wearing a fluorescent yellow vest tagged my luggage and swung it like a bag of feathers onto a shelf. A second man, less burly but only just, relieved me of my backpack and frisked me through my clothes. I was allowed to keep what cash I had in my pockets—$11.36, in stale American tender—but not my phone, because it had a camera. While we waited for Denise to fill out a new flurry of paperwork, the man whose hands I could still feel warmly pawing my groin gestured amiably toward a vending machine.

Cuppa tea?

No thanks.

Banana? Cheese-and-pickle sandwich? Crisps?

These were arranged lemonade-stand-style on the table between us.

I shook my head. I'm fine.

Denise handed me a new slip of paper. In you go then. Be quick as I can.

The holding room was a large space, low-ceilinged and windowless—except for the window through which the guards watched us, and we watched the guards—with seating enough for seventy or eighty people. En route, I'd imagined I might be reunited there with the young Chinese woman who'd flown halfway around the world at the questionable behest of Professor Ken, but in this moment the only other person in residence was a tall black man pacing agitatedly against the far wall. He was wearing a red knit cap and a long cream dashiki and as he moved back and forth between the convex mirror-cameras suspended high in each corner his cherry-topped reflection in them grew and shrank, grew and shrank. I sat down several seats away. A television bolted to the ceiling was tuned quietly to some sort of talk show. One woman was showing another woman how to make a Greek New Year's cake. This included an elaborate tutorial on where to hide the good-luck coin, followed by how one should cut the cake so as to avoid what was referred to as a serious confrontation over coin ownership. After watching this dully for a while I got up to read the notices taped to the walls.

Pillows and blankets as well as fire evacuation procedures were offered in eleven languages. Next to a pay phone were numbers for Refugee and Migrant Justice, as well as the Immigration Advisory Service, in English only. Also beside the phone were numbers for the Airport Chaplaincy and community ministers on call: The Reverend Jeremy Benfield. The Reverend Gerald T. Pritchard. Friar Okpalaonwuka Chinelo, Rabbi Schmuley Vogel, Sonesh Prakash Singh. Automatically, my eyes scanned for an Arabic name. Mohammad Usman. Imam Mohammed Usman. Heathrow Community Muslim Centre, 654 Bath Road, Cranford, Middlesex, TW5 9TN.

A few feet away, on another folding table with a fake wooden grain, someone had arranged, giving equal prominence to each: a Hebrew Bible, a King James Bible, a Spanish Reina-Valera, and two Qurans (English and Arabic). Affixed to the table beside the Qurans was a qibla arrow, showing Mecca to be in roughly the same direction as the Female toilet. Underneath the table, three prayer mats stood loosely rolled up in a basket like jumbo baguettes, while a respectful yet implicit distance away someone had taped up another sign, this one also in English only: SLEEPING ON THE FLOOR IS NOT ALLOWED.

The black man sat down and began rubbing his eyes with the heels of his hands. On his feet were dusty penny loafers, but no socks, and the skin around his ankles had turned the color of ash. The forecast for London that weekend had been for temperatures barely above freezing, and for a fantastic moment I imagined this was why he had been detained: for lack of suitable footwear. After all, the NHS cannot be in the business of hospitalizing every under-dressed guest for hypothermia or gangrene. No socks in December, sir? Very well then. Take a seat. Just some general inquiries. Be quick as I can.

On the other side of the room stood a second table, this one more carelessly strewn with secular material: newspapers in English, Spanish, French, and Chinese; a dog-eared copy of Japanese *Vogue*; two French installments of *Twilight*; a Spanish romance novel; and a German edition of *Eat, Pray, Love*. I resigned myself to my earlier position in front of the television. The black man had gone back to his pacing. He was also making noises now: short, intermittent, involuntary-sounding grunts and moans that reminded me of a pianist my brother likes, an eccentric who makes similar sounds when he plays, as though with the effort or ecstasy of his art. The book I'd held on to lay unopened in my lap. The hour of my re-union with Alastair at The Lamb came and went. The Greek New Year's cake was cut.

GROZNY WAS THE WORST. Twenty-five thousand civilians killed in eight weeks. Dark winter days dodging shellholes and tripping over bodies tagged with martyr ribbons in Minutka Square. Some of the Chechens not already killed by the bombs were captured by Russian conscripts and herded into cellars while in the streets their mothers wept and pleaded for their release. At night, Alastair and the other journalists slept fifty miles away, in an appropriated kindergarten in Khasavyurt, on tiny cots pushed together to make beds that were still too small. They held handkerchiefs to their noses against the stink of unwashed bodies in a room that remained decorated with children's drawings and watercolors: bunnies and wizards, butterflies and unicorns, stick-figure families holding hands under a rainbow pouring into a pot of gold. Green grass on the bottom. The sky a firm stripe of blue along the top. You didn't dream, or remember dreaming; trying to run under the plodding weight of a flak jacket all day was dream enough. Whereas the Chechens: the Chechen fighters seemed only too glad to die. And why shouldn't they be? A willingness to die is a powerful thing. Especially when leveraged against those who would really rather not die. Starve me, humiliate me, raze my cities and take away my hope, and what do you expect? That I shouldn't be reduced to fighting you with my life? That I shouldn't want to be a martyr, the only distinction left me? You, weak man, sucker for Russian mothers and rainbows: go home to your English New Year, to your party crackers and prix fixe with complimentary coupe. We do not need your acknowledgment. We do not need you to 'bear witness.' Your 'empathy'

lacks imagination. Even the Russians are better than you; even the
Russians are not too good to drink their Champagne out of dented
mess cups, blowing on their fingers and stomping their feet in the
piss-riddled snow. For you, this is a novelty. For us, it is a cage.
And then the world asks why. Why are they killing each other?
Why can't they sort it out? Why do so many people have to die?
But maybe a better question is: Why do so many people not want
to live?

Some Saturdays, when the sun was shining, a few of us volunteers would take a couple of the sick children out to play in one
of the public garden squares nearby. My usual companion on such
outings was Lachlan, a man of comfortable silences and exceptional trivia. One afternoon we were sitting in Bloomsbury Square,
keeping half an eye on our charges, when Lachlan pointed toward
the iron railings on the far side of the park and said that the original ones had been dismantled and melted down for ammunition
during the Second World War. These new ones were shorter, and
unlocked all day; square's been open to the public ever since. I could
not pass Bloomsbury Square after that without wondering where
the old iron had wound up. On which fronts. In whose bodies. It
was around this time that the avowal to do away with Saddam's
weapons of mass destruction was accelerating toward its first anti-
climax. Blair had declared it time to repay America for its help sixty
years earlier and pledged Britain's commitment to sniffing out all
remaining stockpiles of genocidal intent. Forty-eight hours later,
Clinton announced that Iraq intended to cooperate; a month after
that, UNSCOM reported that in fact Iraq was *not* cooperating, and
lo, the British-American bombing began. I watched the Desert Fox
air strikes with Alastair, sitting in our usual spot in The Lamb,
whose ceiling had been strung with Christmas bunting and the bar
transformed into a lukewarm buffet of mince pies and a faux caul-
dron of brandy-spiked mulled wine. Throughout its broadcast of
the blitz—a final frenzy before the allies would respectfully adjourn
in honor of Ramadan—the BBC toggled between footage in two

contrasting but equally mesmerizing palettes: one dim and grainy, with palm trees silhouetted against sepia plumes and orange flares, the other awash in the Midori-green of night vision. An explosion over the Tigris abruptly illuminated the water with the innocent quality of daylight. Leave me alone, the river seemed to say, under the fleeting white glare. I've done nothing to you. Leave me in peace.

Also on the television that night was an item about how the House of Representatives had voted to impeach Clinton on two counts. This time, when the sniggering about his foreign policy calendar started up, I said nothing.

Beside me, Alastair too said little, and drank with a darker determination than usual. By then I'd begun to wonder whether, at some point in the previous decade—in Rwanda, maybe, or Grozny, or perhaps so gradually that you could not pin it on any one abomination—the man had, as they say, lost his mind. He did not still seem to be without it; it was as if it had been taken away from him temporarily, for safekeeping, and then returned some time later with a stern warning to use it for only innocuous thoughts. This, I imagined, was why he was there, watching things unfold from a pub in Bloomsbury rather than from the roof of some Baghdad hotel. I asked him why night vision was green.

Phosphor, Alastair replied. They use green because the human eye can differentiate between more shades of green than any other color.

You could write a book, I said, a long moment later.

Alastair inhaled and watched the foamy residue of his lager slide slowly down the inside of his glass. When an answer came to him, he looked relieved. It was not a real answer, but it would do.

There's an old saying, he said, about how the foreign journalist who travels to the Middle East and stays a week goes home to write a book in which he presents a pat solution to all of its problems. If he stays a month, he writes a magazine or a newspaper article filled with 'ifs,' 'buts,' and 'on the other hands.' If he stays a year, he writes nothing at all.

Well, I said, you wouldn't necessarily have to solve anything.

No, said Alastair, picking up his glass. And neither do you.

That no live chemical, biological, radiological or nuclear arsenals were found that winter seemed only to fan the Manichean panic. Against this backdrop, melting park railings down into cannonballs and rifleshot seemed quaint to the point of inducing nostalgia. Certainly, as I sat in sunny Bloomsbury Square, listening to the song thrushes tweeting overhead, it did not seem likely that the spires surrounding us now would ever be drafted into combat. Then again, had someone suggested that steering commercial airplanes into enemy skyscrapers might be an effective means of modern warfare, I suppose I would not have thought that very likely either.

One day a little boy with a bandage taped to one ear came over to ask if we had anything to eat. I gave him a HobNob.

Raining crumbs from his mouth, the boy announced: I'm eating a biscuit.

So you are, said Lachlan.

I love you, said the boy.

I love you too, said Lachlan.

The boy watched the pigeons pecking the ground for a moment before turning to me.

I'm eating a biscuit, he said.

I see that, I replied.

I love you.

I nodded. I love you too.

Three or four times these lines were repeated to us—*I love you* and *I'm eating a biscuit*—until, having finished the HobNob, and perhaps having finished loving us as well, the boy ran back to the pigeons, who scattered lamely.

Presently, my little Arabic-speaking friend came over, eyeing me slyly. I offered her a HobNob, which she declined.

Turning to Lachlan she said carefully, in English:

My daddy wants me to be a boy.

. . . Say again?

Baba says I'm a boy!

Then, abruptly, she turned on a heel and darted away.

Blimey, said Lachlan. What was that?

I've no idea. Do you know what's wrong with her?

Lachlan shook his head. Only that she's younger than she looks.

Sometime later, we would learn that the little girl had a rare form of something called congenital adrenal hyperplasia. Normally, a stimulant called adrenocorticotropic hormone, or ACTH, is produced by the pituitary gland and carried by blood down to the adrenal glands, which sit atop the kidneys. There, ACTH announces the need for cortisol, a steroidal hormone having many essential everyday functions. But cortisol doesn't come spontaneously into existence; it derives from precursors that enzymes convert into cortisol. In a body affected by CAH, the key enzyme is missing, causing the assembly line to break down just before cortisol is made. The result is a buildup of precursors—but never enough cortisol. And since it's the presence of cortisol that suppresses the dispatching of more ACTH, the pituitary gland sends out more and more ACTH, stimulating the adrenal glands such that they swell to an abnormal size.

Cortisol is required for normal endocrine activity, regulating growth, metabolism, tissue function, sleep patterns, and mood. Untreated, a cortisol deficiency can be fatal, causing hypoglycemia, dehydration, weight loss, dizziness, low blood pressure, even cardiovascular collapse. Also problematic are the symptoms arising from the thwarted cortisol precursors, which include an excess of androgens, otherwise known as the male sex hormones. As a result, a three-year-old boy affected by CAH could develop hair under his arms and acne as bad as his babysitter's. Likewise, a little girl with it could also exhibit masculine features from an early age: body hair, a growth spurt, even a preference for trucks and tractors over teacups and dolls. When she reaches the normal age of puberty, her voice might deepen, her chest might remain flat, and she might menstruate very lightly, if at all. In theory, few cases should reach this stage

of virilization, because earlier signs would have prompted a trip to
the doctor, who in turn would have prescribed synthetic steroids to
lower the androgen levels in the system.

Sometimes, the problem is even apparent at birth. Instead of
having a normal-sized clitoris, a baby having two X chromosomes
might be born with an enlarged clitoris that looks like a tiny penis.
Her urethra and vagina might have merged toward a single opening and the labia may have fused entirely, resembling a scrotum.
Yet an ultrasound will reveal that, inside, she has a perfectly normal uterus, fallopian tubes, ovaries, and a cervix. In fact, were she
to have external reconstructive surgery, she would have everything
she needs (save someone else's sperm, of course) in order one day
to conceive. My little Arab friend had been born with ambiguous
genitalia, but not so ambiguous that her parents, nor an obstetri-
cian back in Syria, had seen fit at the time to call her anything but
a girl. More recently, however, certain other signs, including the
increasingly phallic anomaly between her legs, had raised eyebrows
at home and she was brought in. Indisputably, her cortisol levels
needed to be regulated. But there remained the question of what
to do about her gender. Her doctors were of the opinion that she
should be given hormone-replacement therapy and perhaps also
a genitoplasty and carry on as a girl. Her mother was inclined to
agree. But her father had a different perspective. Where he was
from, a boy is superior. A boy is prestige. A boy brings you pride.
Where he was from, one might even say: Better an infertile man
than a fertile woman. In fact, said the father, I always thought she
was a boy. It was a mistake from the beginning. She looks like a boy.
She acts like a boy. Her life would be so much easier if she were a
boy. He's a boy.

There's no cure for CAH. It's a genetic condition whereby the
double helix inherits two copies of a faulty gene, one copy from
each parent. Usually, the gene is recessive to a dominant counter-
part. But if both parents are carriers, there's a 25 percent chance
their child will inherit both faulty genes and express the condition.

This leaves a 50 percent chance the child will inherit only one faulty gene (and become another carrier), and a 25 percent chance the child will inherit only normal genes, and be unaffected. Owing to the probability that two partners will have inherited the same mutant gene from a common ancestor, autosomal recessive disorders are especially common among the offspring of consanguineous couples. The closer the relationship, the greater the proportion of shared genes. The greater the proportion of shared genes, the greater the risk their offspring will be homozygous for the shared gene. In other words, autosomal recessive disorders are especially common in certain cultures in which, for enduring tribal reasons—to strengthen family ties, maintain a woman's status within the hierarchy, facilitate the finding of suitable partners, and preserve a family's traditions, values, property, and wealth—it is not only acceptable but standard and even encouraged to marry your first cousin.

IN DECEMBER OF 2003, approximately seven months after Bush declared his mission accomplished and the UN lifted a majority of its sanctions against Iraq, I saw my brother again for the first time in thirteen years. I was living in West Hollywood, three semesters into my economics PhD, and I had flown from LAX to Paris to Amman, at which point a driver was supposed to pick me up at the airport and take me to the hotel where my parents, who had traveled from Bay Ridge, were waiting for me to meet them. From Amman we would be driven across the desert to Baghdad, a journey that takes some ten hours. Before sanctions, and then the invasion, one could fly from Amman to Baghdad in less than one hour, such that reaching Amman meant you were almost there. Now, it meant you were only about halfway there.

When I got to the airport, there was no driver. Or rather, there were plenty of drivers, all of them keen for my custom, but none holding a sign bearing my name. At some point I realized that the address of the hotel in which my parents were staying was written in a notebook I'd left in the facing seat back of my flight to Charles de Gaulle. After about an hour, I gave up trying to find our arranged liaison and, via a series of leery interviews, identified a man willing to take me to up to five different hotels for a flat fare of 250,000 dinars, or about eighty dollars.

In the car, when this man heard that I was ultimately destined for Baghdad, he became delirious with ambition. I take you! I take you right now! Be there by morning!

Quite possibly, this was an offer made with the intention of selling me to kidnappers in the desert. I thanked the man and explained politely that I wanted to rest a little at my hotel before continuing my journey. At this the driver looked not only undaunted but delighted. Yes! Perfect. You rest, and I'll come back later and take you in the morning. He might as well have said: Even better. I'll just make some arrangements to sell you in the desert and then we'll be ready to go.

My parents were at the third hotel. When I approached the front desk, the receptionist was on the phone. After a moment he placed the receiver on his shoulder and I asked if a Mr. Ala Jaafari and his wife were among his guests. And you are? Their son. The receptionist's eyebrows went up. He pointed at the receiver on his shoulder. This is your driver. He wants to know where you are. Where is *he*? I asked. At the airport, said the receptionist. No, I said. I've just come from the airport, and I swear it to you: he wasn't there. The receptionist nodded, inspecting me kindly, then returned the receiver to his ear and communicated my message into the phone. A muffled string of invective ensued, making both of us wince. Then the receptionist gave me another long look, as if he were listening to someone describe me—as one describes a wallet or a watch that has been lost—and, as the voice on the other end continued to chew him out, he hung up.

You know what? said the receptionist, shaking his head. I know this guy. He wasn't there.

When my mother opened the door she was wearing a head scarf. Typically she did not wear one in Bay Ridge and for the first time I thought the hard black oval around her face gave unflattering emphasis to her jowls. She had also, owing to her age, taken to walking at a slight forward angle, as if leaning in the right direction might preserve or even generate momentum. Lately, when I called home and spoke to my father, he would answer questions as to how he and my mother were doing with a report on how well or badly my mother had slept the night before. It was like a poltergeist, her insomnia and its effects, and my father warned me of its presence the way he used to warn me approximately once a month that Fatima is not herself today. Now, in Amman, even as she beamed maternally on my arrival, I could tell that my mother needed sleep, and I hoped she'd be able to get some rest in the car. I hoped *I'd* be able to get some rest in the car. But shortly after we'd embraced my father took me to one side and said that while it was all right for my mother to sleep one of us would have to remain awake at all times. We were leaving in the middle of the night, in order to reach Iraq around dawn; moreover, night or day most of the journey would be monotonous—mile after mile of scrubland and dunes—so it was equally important that we be on alert that our driver should not nod off, or, in my father's words, pull something funny.

This was the same driver who'd been supposed to meet me at the airport, and who greeted me now with an air of superior and charitably suppressed exasperation. His armored Chevy Suburban, with its tinted windows and long boxy rear, looked like a hearse. I could not have slept if I'd tried. Every uptake in speed made me start. Every pair of headlights advancing toward us seemed to push through the dark with an ominous stealth. Our driver gripped his steering wheel tightly, with both hands, bouncing his unoccupied knee and chewing his lip. He was a smoker, obviously; the car stank of it, and every spare compartment had been stuffed with cigarettes—dozens of Marlboro boxes marked CHINA DUTY FREE wedged over the visors and into the pockets behind the seats—but before we'd set off my father had asked if he wouldn't mind abstaining. Much of the first hour of our ride I spent silently debating the pros and cons of this request. If our escort needed nicotine to deliver us safely into Baghdad, let him have it. We would not die of secondhand smoke in ten hours. On the other hand, my father, who had only recently given up tobacco himself, had paid dearly for this service: three and a half thousand dollars. Why shouldn't he have his way?

We arrived at the border a little before four. Slowing, our driver opened the glove compartment and removed a billfold of American twenties, which, after powering down his window, he began peeling off and passing out to the border patrol officers as though they were the standard toll. Any foreigners? one of the officers asked, in Arabic.

Our driver shook his head. All Iraqis.

Now he was handing out Marlboros: two packets per officer. Then he powered the window back up and it seemed we would be waved through until one of the officers standing in the road turned around and held up a hand.

The window went back down and two more packets of cigarettes were offered through and pocketed unceremoniously. Then the officer said something about Baghdad. Our driver nodded. The officer walked away.

Sitting in one of the SUV's middle seats, I turned around to face my father inquiringly. My mother, with her dark eyes and snug headwear, looked like an owl.

What's happening?

They want us to take someone to Baghdad.

An officer?

Our driver nodded.

An Iraqi intelligence officer?

Jiggling his leg, our driver ducked to peer under the rearview mirror and didn't answer.

What should we do? asked my father.

Please, said the driver. Pretend to sleep. Do not speak.

I have to go to the bathroom, my mother said quietly.

I am sorry, our driver said urgently, turning around to face us now. We cannot stop unless he says to stop. You must be quiet. Your accent will discover you. I will try to take you quickly, quickly as possible, but please: do not speak.

By now a large man with a beard and gray army fatigues was approaching. Our driver unlocked the SUV and the officer opened the passenger-side door and sat down in front of me, causing the vehicle to cant. Sabah al-khair, said the officer. Sabah al-noor, our driver replied. Good morning. We Jaafaris said nothing. Our driver relocked the Suburban, put it into gear, and resumed driving, waved off by the officers in the road. Our new passenger adjusted and readjusted his seat, reducing my own legroom by half. Then he reached up above the visor, removed a pack of Marlboros, peeled the cellophane away, drew out a cigarette, and did not stop smoking for the next six hours.

My grandmother's house was smaller than I'd remembered it, whereas my brother was larger. Not fatter. Not softer and wider, as some of us become when we age, but bigger all over, in a solid and proportionate sort of way, as though to save space my mind had shrunk him down by 20 percent.

He was also handsomer than I'd remembered: ruddier in the cheeks and readier with a smile, sprouting long lines around his eyes. When at last my parents and I entered our grandmother's living room, Sami stood, put his hands on his hips, and grinned at me for a long moment, as if he knew my preconceptions were in the process of being dashed. And what had my preconceptions been? That he would be both more and less the Sami I'd remembered. More boyish. Less boyish. Going a little gray behind the ears. He *was* going a little gray behind the ears, but this was less uncanny than the ways in which he seemed almost exactly the same. The squareness of his hairline. The singular shadows around his mouth. They unnerved me, these animated relics, but in an oddly pleasant sort of way—as it can be oddly pleasant to pass a stranger on the street and catch a whiff of your high school chemistry teacher's shampoo for the first time in twelve years. We think we have evolved, we think the dross of consciousness is shed, and then all it takes to splice in a frame from 1992 is a noseful of Prell.

One afternoon we sat out in the garden and while Sami smoked a cigarette he plucked an orange off the grass and tossed it to me for peeling. He'd graduated from medical school a few years earlier and was now a junior doctor at al-Wasati, the hospital for corrective surgery. Prior to the war, the majority of his cases had been nose jobs, breast jobs, liposuction, and hip replacements; now he spent his days staunching rocket wounds, tweezing shrapnel, and swaddling burns. There'd been talk of the Health Ministry funding ear replacements for the men who'd had one or both of their own cut off for deserting Saddam's army in the nineties, and my brother seemed to look forward to this. After all, he said, if he were reconstructing ears instead of staunching rocket wounds, it would mean the fighting had died down a little. Wouldn't it?

We were quiet for a while, and then I mentioned the little boy I'd known at the children's hospital in London, born with what looked like a butter bean for an ear. Putting his cigarette out in the grass, my brother responded wryly: I wish we had only nature's mistakes to fix.

And yet he seemed mostly serene. Not with the situation, of course, but with his choices in life. Certainly no one could accuse him of doing a job that did not matter. After the invasion, and despite the presence of overwhelmed American troops patrolling the city, al-Wasati had been the only public hospital in Baghdad not plundered to the point of incapacitation. Nine months later, it was still undersupplied and understaffed, as an increasing number of doctors refused to make the commute into town or had fled the country altogether. The day my father and I went to see my brother at work, a drive that in peacetime would have taken twenty-five minutes took us an hour and a half. Somewhere, a tanker had exploded, bottlenecking traffic and burdening the hospital with a fresh influx of casualties. Outside the entrance, a man sobbed as the body of another was loaded onto a gurney. The sobbing man covered his face with his hands. Then he lifted his arms to the sky and cried, Why? Why? Why are they doing this? What do they want? Is it money? Why? Just inside the entrance, another gurney contained a child of about ten, his legs wrapped in blood-soaked gauze and his eyes blinking with an otherworldly sort of resignation. No one appeared to be with him, and as my father and

I waited to one side, looking for Sami, a doctor came over to us and pointed at the boy.

Who is dealing with him?

We don't know, my father replied.

The doctor turned to the rest of the lobby and shouted into the rabble of people milling, weeping, praying:

Who is dealing with him?!

Waleed! someone shouted back.

While the doctor continued frowning at the child in a way that suggested only minimal satisfaction, a nurse led us off to the staff mess, where an Arabic soap opera was playing on a television in the corner and my brother presently appeared wearing scrubs. A young man who'd been hit by shrapnel the evening before was waiting for him in the operating theater. My father asked if we could watch.

This happened yesterday? Sami asked the man on the operating table.

The man nodded. At sundown. I was just going out for some bread.

Sami gouged two holes in the man's torso, just under his arms, to drain the blood from his lungs. The man screamed. He'd been given a small dose of anesthesia, but because anesthesia was one of the things the hospital had too little of, no one gave him more.

Allahu Akbar! cried the man.

Give me more light, said Sami.

An assistant changed the angle of the lamp over the man's body while two more men, one on either side of him, held him down. My brother fed tubes into the holes under his arms and then adjusted their position so that the man's skin was drawn away from his rib cage this way and that, like Silly Putty.

No Muslim would do this to another Muslim! cried the man. My son, he is two, his face was blown off! Why are they doing this? Why?

Sami sunk a syringe into the man's abdomen. When he began digging around in the intubated holes again, I closed my eyes and

turned to leave. About half an hour later, when I looked back
into the operating theater, it was empty. In the doctors' mess, the
television had been turned off and two men waiting for a kettle
to boil were arguing over whether Saddam's capture of four days
earlier was real or a lie propagated by the Americans for publicity.
I found my father and brother back in the lobby, standing over the
boy with the bloody legs, my father with his arms folded as if he
were cold and my brother smoking. Another doctor stood beside
Sami, also smoking. Waleed, I guessed. On the other side of the
gurney stood three more men, two in dishdashas and the third in
a red-and-white keffiyeh knotted under a thick black beard. We
found him on Wathiq, one of the men was saying. Says he lives in
Zayouna. Says his name is Mustafa. Says he hasn't seen his parents
since last week. It wasn't until that point that I looked more closely
at the men standing over the boy—who even as he was being discussed continued his preternatural blinking at the wall—and saw
that the one with the very black beard and the red-and-white scarf
tied around his neck was Alastair.

PLEASE NOTES read a sign taped to the front door of the Al-Hamra.
GUNS MUST BE LEFT AT SECURITY DESK. THANS FOR YOUR COOP-
ERATION.

   Inside, a man wearing a camel-colored turtleneck sat at the hotel's reception desk doing a crossword in Arabic. On his desk were
a pocket watch, a security wand, and a Kalashnikov, the barrel of
which lay aimed at my groin as Sami and I lifted our arms to be
frisked.

   Through a pair of heavy wooden doors, the journalists' Christmas party was already under way. The restaurant's red walls, red
tablecloths, and dimly glowing wall sconces all suggested a supper
club in purgatory. In one corner, two waiters in bow ties stood quietly at attention, the fabric of their shirts so thin you could plainly

see the outline of their tank tops underneath. In another corner, a third Iraqi sat playing big band standards on a piano. The instrument was a blond old upright that faced into the room, its crisscrossed innards partly veiled by a floral-print curtain that matched those on the windows. Although: it was dark outside, and the hotel's windowpanes had been reinforced with dense argyle iron grids; there might as well have been no windows at all.

In the center of the room a crowd of correspondents, cameramen, photographers, and contractors mingled festively, pouring drinks and cutting cigars. Most of them were men, although there were also a few women present, including one in tight white jeans being cornered by a man who, in a French accent, was explaining how the situation was not unlike Vietnam. You try to crush the resistance and in so doing you inflame the neutral population. We found Alastair out by the pool, sitting at a candlelit table cluttered with bottles and ashtrays and talking to a young American man whose hat identified him as with the United Nations High Commissioner for Refugees. Each man was working his way through a cigar, the American rather less adroitly, and because Alastair was no longer wearing his keffiyeh I saw now that while his beard was real, the black was not.

Anyone who was paying attention in the nineties, he was saying—anyone who learned anything from Yugoslavia, Bosnia, and Somalia—would have anticipated this. If you disband the military, if you fire everyone who ever worked for the government, if you take away people's jobs, their income and their pride, what do you expect? That they're going to sit around playing Parcheesi until you show up at their door and hand them a ballot? And if they know where the old munitions are hidden, and you aren't guarding those either—is it really a surprise when they turn them against you?

In the pool, a series of fluorescent deck lamps reflected like a row of shimmering moons. A chin-ups bar had been installed on the far side of the water, where, as we talked, an impressively muscled silhouette strode over, sprang up, and began vigorously pistoning himself into the air. The UNHCR man, who had a Southern accent and continuously shifted his cigar from one hand to the other as though even its unlit end were unbearably hot, said:

Well, what choice did we have?

For that matter, said one of the other Americans, why wasn't anything done sooner? Like when Saddam was murdering Kurds and Shiites for staging a rebellion at our own not-so-subtle suggestion? Leading to thousands of them being killed right under our noses, because our troops were under inexplicable orders not to intervene? Even though they were *there*. Even though the attack arguably breached Schwarzkopf's cease-fire treaty. Why didn't we do anything then?

You sound like an exceptionalist, said Alastair.

So? said the American. Exceptionalism is only a problem when it's used to justify bad policies. Ignorance is a problem. Complacency is a problem. But to aspire to exceptional behavior—exceptionally generous, judicious, humane behavior—as anyone lucky enough to have been born in an exceptionally rich, exceptionally educated, exceptionally democratic country should do . . .

The man in the UNHCR cap nodded sagely and blew smoke rings that stretched oblong before dissolving into the collective haze above the pool. Less than two years later, the same pool would have the body parts of suicide bombers floating in it, but on this night, an Iraqi Christmas of relative calm, Saddam had been captured and it was impossible not to hope that the arc of the moral universe was not, after all, so very long and unyielding. I watched my brother light a cigarette without taking his eyes off the man on the pull-ups bar and thought maybe he wasn't listening to the conversation, or listening but dismissing it as unworthy of his own participation. But then, still with his eyes on the exercising silhouette, Sami exhaled and said:

Isn't it possible that what the West really wants is simply not to be inconvenienced by the Middle East? Not to be terrorized, not to

be charged too much for its gas, not to be threatened with chemical
or nuclear weapons? And otherwise you couldn't really care less?

No, said the man with the UNHCR. I believe the average American is sincere when he says he wants Iraq to become a peaceful and
democratic nation. A free and secular nation. Though we understand this may not be possible for some time.

But you wouldn't want us to become richer than you. More powerful than you. To have greater international clout and the same
seemingly boundless potential.

The man in the UNHCR cap looked nonplussed.

Well, Alastair put in quietly, it's hard to imagine. But it would
make for an interesting development, geopolitically speaking, yes.

Inside, the journalists, cameramen, and contractors were sitting
around one long table now, carving up a Honey Baked Ham someone's mother had FedExed from Maine. I sat down with Alastair at
one end of the table, where two plates of meat were passed down to
us and Alastair ate them both. While he did, I noted that he seemed
more alive than when I'd last seen him, which had been in London
five years earlier; his body now appeared more charged and alert—
as though, casualties aside, he really rather preferred life in a war
zone. I asked whether it didn't occasionally feel hypocritical to be
censorious of a war while at the same time drawn to its energies. Still
chewing, Alastair nodded and said, Yes, it's true, there's something
thrilling, addictive even, about the idea you're living every moment
only half a step ahead of death. But if it weren't for those willing to
do it, those willing to risk their lives to witness and record what's
happening, how would the rest of us know what our governments
are doing in our names? I pointed out that the very proliferation
of pseudo journalism these days, the cacophony of conjecture and
partisan agendas and sensationalism that seem orchestrated above
all to provoke and entertain, tended to leave me feeling as though
I know less than ever what my government is doing in my name.
Drinking, Alastair shrugged and nodded as if to concede: Yes, well,
there's always the moronic inferno.

It was also on this night that Alastair told me about how, eight years earlier, in Kabul, he and his crew had been packing up after a segment when an Afghan boy darted over and snatched his cameraman's bag. A few minutes later a policeman happened by and Alastair stopped him to describe the boy: five foot seven maybe, fourteen or fifteen, wearing a light-blue shirt and a dark-green shemagh. Went thataway. A few minutes later the policeman returned with the boy and handed Alastair the bag. Alastair thanked him, and the policeman told the boy to apologize, which the boy did. Then the policeman drew his pistol from his holster and shot the boy in the head. You can imagine, said Alastair, the number of times I've replayed that scene in my mind and regretted my unwitting participation. And if it's violence driving up your employer's advertising revenue and you're the one reporting the violence it's hard to see how in that respect, too, you aren't one of the ones perpetuating the violence. So, no, I don't always sleep soundly at night. But if I quit, which I considered very seriously after that day, I think I'd go mad from the alternative. When I'm working, when I'm high on adrenaline, I'm not exactly in what you would call a contemplative state. But when I go home, when I go out to dinner or sit on the Tube or push my trolley around Waitrose with all the other punters and their meticulous lists, I start to spin out. You observe what people do with their freedom—what they don't do—and it's impossible not to judge them for it. You come to see a mostly peaceful and democratic society as being in a state of incredibly delicate suspension, suspension that requires equilibrium down to the smallest molecule, such that even the tiniest jolt, just one person neglecting its fragility with her complacency or self-absorption, could cause the whole fucking thing to collapse. You think about how we all belong to this species capable of such horrifying evil, and you wonder what your responsibility to humanity is while you're here, and what sort of game God is playing with us—not to mention what it means that generally you'd prefer to be back in Baghdad than at home in Angel with your wife and son reading *If You Give a Mouse*

a Cookie. If I am unnerved by peace and contemplation, if something biochemical in me craves the stimulus of violent spectacle and
proximity to conflict, where am *I* on the spectrum? What am I capable of, under another set of circumstances? How different am I,
really, from 'them'?

I didn't know you believe in God.

I don't. Or rather, I'm agnostic. A foxhole agnostic. There's a
Mandelstam poem that goes: '*Your form, agonizing and fleeting / I
couldn't make it out in the haze /—God!—I said by mistake / Without
having thought to speak.*' That about sums it up. You?

Yeah.

As in Allah?

I nodded.

Alastair lowered his beer.

What?

Nothing. I just . . . You're an economist. A scientist. I didn't
know.

Beside us, four men in flak jackets sat down with a deck of cards.
It was one of those military-issue packs, with ranks comprising the
fifty-two most-wanted Ba'athists and Revolutionary Commanders;
the game was Texas Hold'em and Chemical Ali led the flop. Designed and distributed to familiarize American soldiers with the
names and faces of those they've been charged with capturing or
killing in a raid, the concept is a descendant of one also employed
in the Second World War, when air force pilots played gin rummy
with cards sporting the silhouettes of German and Japanese fighter
aircraft. It's a curious tactic, this teaching of whom we should target
and exterminate through a medium traditionally associated with
playtime entertainment; one wonders whether the instructional
advantage isn't undermined by the incendiary implication that, to
the Americans, war is akin to a game. In the one under way beside me, Saddam was the ace of spades, his sons Qusay and Uday
that of clubs and hearts, respectively, and the only woman—the
American-educated Huda Salih Mahdi Ammash, aka Chemical

Sally—the five of hearts. Thirteen of the cards, including all four deuces, had in lieu of a photo only a generic black oval that resembled the outline of a head wearing a hood like the grim reaper's. And yet it was these cards, I thought, as the man nearest me laid down a flush—the cards without faces—that had the most humanizing effect. Maybe because their featurelessness more readily suggested that you, too, could have been born Adil Abdallah Mahdi (deuce of diamonds) or Ugla Abid Saqr al-Kubaysi (deuce of clubs) or Ghazi Hammud al-Ubaydi (deuce of hearts) or Rashid Taan Kazim (deuce of spades). If only your great-grandfather had met a different woman. If only your parents had taken a later flight. If only your soul had sparked into being on a different continent, a different hemisphere, a different day.

Meanwhile, the din of laughing and clinking and drunken caroling had begun to compete now with a slow but steady crescendo emanating from the piano in the corner. I looked up to see my brother there, sharing the instrument's bench with its hired player, each man looking after his own half of the keyboard while also carrying on a conversation that made their cigarettes bounce between their lips. The music was no longer Cole Porter and Irving Berlin but instead a sort of jazz fever that had no beginning, middle, or end—just a cycle of surges, looping swells and contractions, long frenetic improvisations that managed to sound both triumphant and apocalyptic at once. It reminded me, in places, of the sort of music that accompanies a silent-movie brawl, or a Charlie Chaplin chase, or the headlines of history being peeled away one by one. And it went on late into the night—long after the ham had been finished and most of the journalists and contractors and cameramen had gone up to bed, long after the waiters had cleared the soiled tablecloths away and the camouflage-backed cards had gone back into their box, long after the cerulean pool had settled into a state like glass and the tiny column of ash on my brother's cigarette had grown long enough to bow downward and drop off.

I PUT DOWN JAPANESE *Vogue* and went over to the observation window, through which I could see the guards trying to coax a bottle of juice out of the vending machine from where it had become trapped, midfall. When I tapped on the glass, the two men straightened up simultaneously and the one nearer me lunged for the door.

Come to think of it, I said, I *could* use something to drink.

While they fetched me some water, a new officer, a man I hadn't seen previously, passed wordlessly through the antechamber into the holding room, where he approached the black man and sat down. As the officer spoke, the black man stared intently at the floor, rubbing his eyes and blinking reasonably. Something about Lagos. Arik Air. No record of a Miss Odilichi in Croydon. Holding my water, I sat down again a few yards away and resumed my analphabetic perusal of *Vogue*. It was time for Asr, or past it—there was no telling in that room lit exclusively by fluorescence—but under the circumstances I decided it best to remain where I was, inconspicuously upright, innocuously absorbed in my Coco Rocha and chiffon.

When the officer had left, several uneventful minutes passed. Then the black man got up, went into the Male toilet, and began to moan.

A moment later the moaning became a thumping that grew louder and faster.

I got up and went back to the observation window. Having liberated their juice, the guards were now sitting with their feet up on the table, chatting and passing a bag of potato chips between them.

When they'd taken note of my presence and opened up again I said I thought the man in the toilet might be hurting himself.

The guards hurried past me and wrestled the man out by his arms. Then they dragged him to a seat, forced him down, and perched on either side of his body in an attempt to subdue its fitful writhing. Every now and again the black man would endeavor to wrench free of them with a violent sideways jerk; then he would collapse, head back and palms facing the ceiling, and in this position looked something like a martyr awaiting the stigmata.

The guards seemed uncertain what to do next. One and then the other glanced in my direction, as if to gauge whether I might be sufficiently trustworthy to fetch a fifth party. Meanwhile, the muted television scrolled a headline about an apartment that had exploded in Yevpatoria. A state of emergency had been declared in the Marshall Islands and Suzuki was considering production cuts amidst the financial crisis. Funny, I thought, how when you've been involuntarily subtracted from the world its problems begin to seem less the random luck of a mostly innocent people and more the consequences of their own had-it-coming stupidity. And so we remained: me sipping my Evian by the door, the guards holding fast to their unpredictable Nigerian. Until Denise, for whom I'd begun to feel an almost filial affection, returned at ten past five with a cold curried-chicken sandwich and a redhead named Duncan who was going to take over my case because Denise's own shift was up.

AT FIRST, SULAYMANIYAH DID not seem to me all that different from Baghdad. The nearest usable airport was a fourteen-hour drive and at least one international border crossing away. Slightly older than middle-aged men waddled around with their heads down and their hands clasped behind their backs, prayer beads dangling from three fingers. Most of the electrical power was being produced by backyard or rooftop generators. There was running water for only half the day, so as soon as it came on people started filling the gigantic drums they'd placed on their roofs just for that purpose. Practically everyone smoked. Actually, that might be the entire list of similarities.

Among the differences was language, for one. Our first morning there, walking in search of a money changer, my father and I got as far as a block before I noted how eerie it was that we could read all of the signs well enough to make out the letters and their pronunciation, but neither of us had a clue as to their significance. Both Kurdish and Arabic are spelled phonetically, and the alphabets are basically identical—although Kurdish, like Persian, has a handful more letters. So we were looking for a bank, or a money changer, and hoping that the words in Kurdish for bank or money changer were cognates with the Arabic, but we didn't find one until Sami's Kurdish driver came and took us to one. The word for bank is the same, but the word for money changer is not, and while I have never learned the etymology behind this minor asymmetry I can imagine it represents centuries of cultural and ideological dissidence.

Another difference: security. There's a fork in the road not far from Dohuk. Bear right and before long you're on the outskirts of Mosul. Bear left and you remain well inside Kurdistan. Waving an American passport around would have yielded very different results, depending on which way we went. We went left. This was not without cost: the drive to Sulaymaniyah from Zakho, on the Iraqi-Turkish border, took about nine hours that way. If we'd cut the corner and gone down to Mosul and then across to Kirkuk, it would've taken about five. That's if we would have arrived at all. My grandmother and cousin came up via Kirkuk and it was of considerable concern whether Hussein would be able to carry both his American and Iraqi passports without the wrong one being glimpsed on the wrong side of the Kurdish border.

A year after my last visit to Iraq, we were in Kurdistan for my brother's engagement to Zahra, a recent University of Baghdad graduate who'd grown up in Sulaymaniyah and persuaded Sami to take a job at the teaching hospital there so that they might start a family in the relatively peaceful north. Short of returning to Bay Ridge and establishing his own practice over the Irish ophthalmologist's on Fourth, my brother could not have made my parents much happier with this news, and I too felt a certain precipitous relief. Eleven months earlier, a double suicide attack at the offices of Kurdistan's two main political parties had killed more than a hundred people and wounded at least as many more, but even this contributed to an incidence of violence less frequent, less pervasive, and less indiscriminate than what had been mounting in Baghdad. And, in Sulaymaniyah, things worked. Not by Western standards, of course, but compared to the rest of the country it was encouraging to see how functional Kurdistan was. Elections for the new National Assembly were less than a month away and the Kurds really seemed to believe that they were part of something momentous. The Kurdish Democratic Party dominated in the two states east, and the Patriotic Union of Kurdistan dominated in Sulaymaniyah itself, but the Kurdish flag—the Italian tricolore rotated ninety degrees, with a golden burst of sun at its center—flew everywhere.

On the rare occasions when I saw the Iraqi flag flying, it was the old one, the pre-Saddam one, the one that doesn't have God is great written on it. Of course we believe God is great, Sami's Kurdish driver told me; we just don't think Saddam should have written it on the flag so that he could pretend to be a champion of the faith.

On the day of the engagement, Zahra's father Hassan and I went out for a walk. The weather left a bit to be desired: rain every morning, clouds all day, exceedingly early sunsets because we were in a deep valley. But the landscape was stunning—mountains in every direction, and covered with a shrubby vegetation similar to that one sees on the mountains of Santa Monica. In fact it was striking how much Iraq reminded me of Southern California; if the area around Baghdad is like the deserts east of Los Angeles, then Sulaymaniyah would be up around Santa Clarita, where the mountains just start to get big enough to collect snow at the top.

For a man in his sixties, Hassan was an impressive walker. He was also a schoolteacher by trade, and, as far as I could tell, perfectly suited to it. Whenever I asked him a question, even something innocuous like, Is it always cloudy in the winter up here?, he would smile delightedly and say, Aaaahhh, yes, now that is an excellent question, and there is an amazing story behind the answer. Following which you could expect a forty-five-minute disquisition that would begin directly related to your query but then spiral outward to include anecdotes and observations regarding many other intriguing if not entirely innocuous matters as well. Thus in our three hours switchbacking up Goizha we discussed Aristotle, Lamarck, Debussy, Zoroastrianism, Abu Ghraib, Hannah Arendt, and the as-yet-unknown contingencies of de-Ba'athification, Hassan managing even with respect to the more sobering of these topics to display a certain philosophical resilience. At one point I said I'd heard there was a new hotel going up in town, and that this seemed to me a positive sign, and Hassan halted to announce that even if they built a *hundred* new hotels there still wouldn't be sufficient accommodation because the number of tourists coming to Kurdistan was going to overwhelm. No no, he said, when I looked at him askance. Don't think about the present. Think about the future. I wish you were staying with us longer. I'd show you some of the wonderful places we have, in the mountains and the valleys. You'll see. They'll come from everywhere.

Think about the future. And yet: if I were to articulate the prevailing impression of the seven cumulative weeks I spent in Iraq between December 2003 and January 2005, it would be to venture that the future meant something very different there from what it means in, say, America. In Iraq—even in the comparatively auspicious north—the future has long been viewed as a much more nebulous eventuality, if indeed one expects to be around for its eventuality at all. Over dinner on the night of his engagement, my brother was trying to explain to his soon-to-be in-laws about New Year's resolutions. In America, he said, it's traditional for people to promise themselves they'll change aspects of their behavior in the coming year. Zahra's family thought that was crazy. Who are you, they asked, to think you can control your behavior in the future? Well, you know, my brother replied, some things you can control. You can decide you're going to eat more vegetables. Or that you're going to exercise more. Or that you're going to read a little each night before you fall asleep. To which Zahra's mother, an X-ray technician at the teaching hospital, replied: But how do you know you're going to be able to afford vegetables next month? Or who says there won't be a curfew tomorrow, preventing you from going to the gym or running in the park after work? Or who says your generator won't give out and then you'll have to read with a flashlight until the batteries die and then with a candle until that burns down, and then you won't be able to read in bed at all—you'll just have to sleep, if you can?

By contrast: the following day, having driven across town to check out a used Yamaha my brother had seen advertised online, he and I found ourselves eating breakfast in a café next to three journalists, two American and one Scottish, who were telling their driver the plan. First we want to go here. Then at eleven we'll leave there for here, and then at one thirty we'll go here. The driver listened with brow-furrowing bemusement. It got better. Oh! said one of the Americans. And on the fifteenth, there's this meeting that I want to go to in Arbil. Now the driver looked as though he'd been asked to drive to Shanghai and back by Tuesday. Arbil was a ways from here. The fifteenth was a ways from now. In Iraq, when so remote a prospect is raised, a common response is: Well, look . . . God is generous. Meaning: Well, okay, fine. Let's talk about it when it's relevant. But if this journalist isn't in Arbil in two weeks' time, it's going to come as a surprise to her. In the interim, she's going to plan her life as though she's going to be in Arbil on the fifteenth. If she learns of another meeting somewhere else on that day, she'll probably say, Oh, I can't go to that; I'm going to be in Arbil. Arbil is two weeks from now, and 125 miles from here, but meanwhile our resolute American is already then and there in her mind. Well, let us see. God is generous.

The Yamaha was a glossy black baby grand that had belonged to a British woman who'd lived in Sulaymaniyah for thirty years until her husband had died and she'd returned to Shepherd's Bush. In addition, she'd also evidently left behind this disaffected-looking young man whose biceps implied less interest in the piano he was trying to sell us than in the weightlifting equipment densely arrayed on the Persian rug underneath it. When Sami asked if he might lift the Yamaha's lid and play a little something to get a sense of its sound, the man gave us a disinterested wave and went back to frying garlic in his kitchen. Unsurprisingly, the piano was out of tune, but instead of discouraging my brother its dissonance appeared to intrigue him like a benign and fascinating medical mystery to be solved: after a brief flurry of warped Mozart he pressed and held down one long note after another, then another, and another, presumably to confirm that each on its own had the purity and resonance of a respectable instrument; only in combination did they jar and jam. Meanwhile, I toured the little room with my hands in my

pockets, still thinking about Arbil. I was determined not to con-
template the future or even the past but only what was happening
to me *right now*—which unfortunately can be a little like trying to
fall asleep and failing to do so because you cannot stop thinking
about how you are trying to fall asleep. A poster of Che Guevara
rendered in calligraphic Arabic reminded me that I hadn't yet re-
scheduled a meeting with my Argentinian dissertation advisor. A
stack of *Hawlati*s on a ring-stained coffee table conjured the ardent
recycler I'd broken up with two months before. Also on this table
were an open can of Wild Tiger and a porcelain ashtray made to
look like a crumpled Camels pack, completing a sort of Kurdish
bachelor-pad tableau that inevitably led to comparisons with my
own hermitic home life. But for a few moments there, distracted by
the ashtray's uncanny verisimilitude, I did succeed in not thinking
about my singleness, nor about my dissertation, nor about when I
was going to learn the results of my latest grant application and not
about the long drive to Baghdad my parents and I were intending
to make the following day—I was not even thinking about the drift
and worthiness of my thinking—and I suppose another way of saying all this is I was happy.

While Sami counted out a stack of American hundreds, I
stepped over a barbell to approach the piano as if for a better look.
Behind it hung a large, gilt-framed mirror that did not, when I
caught my reflection in it, fail to disappoint, in that like all mirrors
it gave back startlingly little a sense of the worlds within worlds
a single consciousness comprises, too dull and static a human surface to convey the incessant kaleidoscope within. Invigorated by my
new surroundings, my brisk mountain walks and the spirit of possibility that accompanies the advent of a year, I'd been feeling in Sulaymaniyah more attuned to life and richer in potential than I'd felt
in a long time—maybe not even since that first summer after college, with Maddie. In Sulaymaniyah, unburdened by routine and
inspired by my brother's apparent tranquility and contentment, I
envisioned myself approaching a kind of bifurcation, a meaningful

deviation that would steer my life closer to his and our Iraqi ancestry than ever before. *Here* was the future; here was where one of the most important revolutions of my earthly tenure was taking place, and emboldened by the extra passport in my pocket I wanted to witness it and play a part in its fruition.

This is how I *felt*. But in the mirror on the other side of Sami's new piano I didn't *look* like a man teeming with so much potential. On the contrary, in my eleven-year-old jeans, a week's worth of stubble, and a fraying windbreaker from the Gap, I looked rather more like the embodiment of a line I would later read—something about the metaphysical claustrophobia and bleak fate of being always one person. A problem, I suppose, that it is entirely up to our imaginations to solve. But then even someone who imagines for a living is forever bound by the ultimate constraint: she can hold her mirror up to whatever subject she chooses, at whatever angle she likes—she can even hold it such that she herself remains outside its frame, the better to de-narcissize the view—but there's no getting around the fact that she's always the one holding the mirror. And just because you can't see yourself in a reflection doesn't mean no one can.

Having agreed on terms of delivery, my brother and the taciturn Kurd were now emptying the piano's bench of its contents. I watched as out came a stack of old sheet music, some composition paper with a smattering of handwritten notes that ended after only a few bars, and a book of poems by Muhamad Salih Dilan. There was also an antique postcard of the Royal Opera House that my brother lodged admiringly into the bottom left-hand corner of the mirror's frame, and a 1977 copy of *The Portable Stephen Crane*. This last item was entrusted to me for the inventory's duration, and, after a bit of idle leafing through An Experiment in Misery, An Experiment in Luxury, and An Episode of War, I landed on this: It perhaps might be said—if anyone dared—that the most worthless literature of the world has been that which has been written by the men of one nation concerning the men of another. The context was an essay written about Mexico in 1895, but under the circumstances, the grievance felt personal and prescient, and in the car on the way back to my brother's I said it reminded me of something Alastair had once said, about how the more time a foreign journalist spends in the Middle East the more difficult it becomes for him to write about it. I said that when I'd first heard this it had sounded like an excuse, an alibi for failing to do the hard work of writing well, but that the more time I'd spent with Alastair—and for that matter in the Middle East—the more sympathetic to it I'd become. After all, humility and silence are surely preferable to ignorance and imperiousness. And maybe East and West really are eternally irreconcilable—like a curve and its asymptote, geometrically fated never to intersect. My brother looked unimpressed. I see what you're saying, he said, as we slowed for a group of teenagers exiting a fast-food restaurant called MaDonal. But wasn't it also Crane who said that an artist is nothing but a powerful memory that can move itself at will through certain experiences sideways?

My parents and I arrived in Baghdad the same day its governor Ali al-Haidari and six of his bodyguards were assassinated, sinking my optimism and adding to my growing list of differences between north and south that the latter was much more politicized. Though this made sense: Baghdad was the capital, the situation up north was much more stable, and as far as the Kurds were concerned the election results were a foregone conclusion. Of course, aside from my brother and his driver and Zahra and her relatives, I knew no one in Sulaymaniyah, whereas in Baghdad my parents and I were surrounded by my large extended family, who have always been a pretty political bunch: of my eight aunts and uncles still living in the city, two worked in the Green Zone and three, including Zaid, were running for office. But it was also what one saw in the streets, like the billboard at the end of my grandmother's road that read: So that we might leave a better country for our children. This appeared over a picture of a ballot box and the date on which everyone should vote, making it somewhat difficult not to interpret the caption to mean: Yes, for our generation it's probably a lost cause, a hopeless and terrifying mess, but maybe if we vote first our children will still inherit a better country. God is generous.

Indeed, everyone I observed in Baghdad was afraid, much more than the year before. They were afraid of being robbed, shot, stabbed, taken hostage or blown apart by an explosion. They weren't going out at night. They were changing their paths to work each day. One afternoon Zaid's driver noticed that a car, the same car, had been in our sight nonstop the whole way from Hayy al-Jihad to al-Jadriya. Sometimes it was ahead of us, sometimes behind, sometimes a lane or two over, but always in our vicinity. Zaid's driver insisted this was probably a fluke, but all the same he turned off the main road and we drove around al-Bayaa for a while before getting back on track. It worked. Or rather, it turned out we needn't have worried, or that our casers gave up, or had concluded their reconnoitering for the day. The point is that these things were always on Baghda- dis' minds, much more than the year before. The year before—in late 2003 and early 2004—people had been perplexed. Wary. Con- versations had revolved around questions such as: Who are these people and why are they suddenly so interested in bringing us free- dom? What do they really want? How long will they stay? By Jan- uary of 2005, however, the questions at the heart of such discussions had become: Why are they such bastards? Were they planning for things to go like this all along? Or is it really possible they are this incompetent? And: Are they going to let us run our own country even if they don't like the constitution?

You went to the *moon*, one of my uncles' friends reminded me, when he learned I was American. We *know* you could fix this if you really wanted to.

But I did want to. Didn't I? Or did I only want it to be done? A week earlier—inspired, paradoxically, by the conversation I'd had with my brother about the seeming futility of just this—I'd renewed my efforts to keep a journal. (A New Year's resolution, it's true.) But whenever I sat down with it the following week in Baghdad I was reminded of the moment in *The Red and the Black* when the narrator announces that in lieu of a political conversation the author had wished to put in a page full of dots. This is because politics in imaginative work is like a shot in the middle of a concert. The noise is deafening but it imparts no energy. It doesn't harmonize with the sound of any other instrument. (That would show very little grace, warns the author's editor, and if so frivolous a piece of writing lacks grace it is fatal. If your characters don't talk politics, this is no longer France in 1830, and your book is not the mirror you pretend it to be. . . .) Well, I too would have liked to substitute every political conversation I had in Baghdad in January of 2005 with a page of dots. But if I had, all I would have had at the end of it was a Moleskine full of dots. And in any case my family and their friends and I weren't characters in an imaginative work; we were real people weathering real lives, in which politics aren't merely *like* a gunshot in the middle of a music concert; sometimes they actually *are* a gunshot in the middle of a music concert, making the urgency one feels in talking about them all the more urgent. Imploringly, as though I had my own line to the Situation Room and the exclusive wherewithal to plead their case, my relatives would describe to me what Baghdad used to look like. They told me that as recently as the seventies it looked like Istanbul does now: bustling with tourists and businesspeople, a thriving cosmopolitan capital in an ascendant Middle East. Before Iran, before Saddam, before sanctions and Operation Iraqi Freedom and now this, theirs too had been a country of culture, of education and commerce and beauty, and people came from all over to see it and be a part of it. And now? Do you see, Amar, this chaos outside our doors, this madness? In the evenings, mindful of the inadequacy of dots, I pored over the books and photographs and letters that my grandfather had saved from his government days, and these too described a Baghdad vividly at odds with what I saw when I dared to step outside—which was a place in which you could not forget about politics for one minute, never mind the time it takes to eat a meal or read a poem or make love. Very little worked. Very little was beautiful. The order and security that undergirded even my unhappiest moments back home seemed here the wondrous luxuries of another world. Baghdad, to borrow four words from *If This Is a Man*, was the negation of beauty.

Around midmorning on our last full day in Iraq, my father and uncle and I returned from visiting Zaid's grandchildren to find we had a visitor. My grandmother made some coffee and the six of us, including my mother and Zaid, sat around in the front garden and talked. Like most conversations, this one had its lulls, and each time there was a lull our visitor would attempt to dispel it by saying: This will pass eventually. It was like a nervous tic, repeated maybe half a dozen times in our presence: This will pass eventually. This will pass eventually. At one point after saying it the man looked up and caught the doubtful expression on my face.

I mean, he said, it's not as though things can continue like this forever, right?

Under the circumstances, this is what passed for optimism in liberated Baghdad: the vaguely morbid notion that things couldn't possibly go on so very awfully indefinitely. In truth, I found it difficult to endure, and even more so when the pervasive dejection was joined by a creeping guilt: the guilt of an inveterately forward-thinking American counting down the days before he and his parents would be boarding their flights home. But not everyone is fatalist, Zaid tried to reassure me. The political activists are smarter and more sophisticated than they were last year. And last year they were smarter and more sophisticated than they'd been the year before. They see opportunities they've been waiting for for decades and they're moving hard and fast to exploit them. They're thinking ahead while also being mindful of past mistakes. Their political opponents have chosen violence over competition, which means that if people do make it to the polls, they'll win, and they'll write the constitution, and then the game will be theirs to lose unless it's stolen from them. A nontrivial condition. If the elections really are free and fair, Americans are not going to like the outcome. But assuming it doesn't get stolen things will only get harder after the constitution is writ.

I must have looked convinced, or at least open to persuasion, because when my mother and father and I had loaded our bags into the car and were coming back up my grandmother's driveway to say goodbye, Zaid pulled me aside and asked whether I might be willing to consider a job in the Green Zone. A friend of his had been named the government's liaison to the UN regarding a fledgling economic project and the liaison wanted someone he could trust to keep up with the technical aspects of the initiative and advise over the course of its negotiations with the various parties involved. Not dishonestly, I told my uncle that I was flattered, and that naturally it would be an honor to help, but also that I couldn't be sure of when I'd be able to make it back to Iraq, as it was becoming of critical importance to my psychological welfare that I prioritize finishing my PhD. But yes, I added quickly, when I saw the disappointment in his eyes. I'll think about it. Think about it very carefully, said Zaid, and let us know your decision as soon as you are able. You are in a unique position to help us help our country, Amar. You understand as well as anyone that we will not be remade in Amrika's image, but nor should Amrika want us to be. So, come back to us. Come back to us soon. This last line he repeated while also giving my shoulder a gentle shake, as if to wake me from a dream.

By the summer of 2007 I had finished my coursework and teaching requirements and had only to conquer my dissertation, which had been growing at the dilatory rate of one paragraph per day. I decided that Los Angeles was the problem, or rather that my Los Angeles-born addiction to Internet browsing was the problem, so I subleased my apartment in West Hollywood and moved for the summer out to a cabin on Big Bear Lake, one hundred miles east, in the San Bernardino Forest. There I had a woodstove, mountain views, and an Ansel Adams print on the wall where you'd expect a flat-screen to be. The first thing I did after arriving and flushing a spider down the toilet was to move the kitchen table into the living room, where I envisioned myself surrounded by textbooks and datasets, working easily and ingeniously into the night. The second thing I did was to get back into the car and go in search of an Internet café. I had only just turned out of the driveway when my cell phone beeped and it was my father calling to tell me that Zaid had been kidnapped.

It had happened right in front of his house. His driver had come to pick him up for work and was opening the rear passenger door when another car pulled into the driveway and two men got out and pointed Kalashnikovs at Zaid's head. Tafadhal, ammu, one of the men said, opening the front door to their car. Be our guest, uncle.

The following morning my aunt Alia received a phone call requesting fifty thousand dollars.

But Kareem's offered them half, said my father.

Who's Kareem? I asked.

Our broker.

Ten days later, anti-Shiite factions bombed al-Askari for the second time in sixteen months. Curfews were imposed in Samarra and Baghdad while in retaliation Shiites set fire to Sunni mosques—and Zaid remained missing. On being hired, Kareem had asked my uncle's driver where the kidnappers had put him. In the front seat, said the driver. Good, Kareem said. The front seat is good. If you put your hostage in the trunk, you're probably going to kill him, for political reasons, whereas if you give him the front seat you don't care if he's Sunni or Shiite; you're just in it for the ransom and you're looking after your hostage in order to get paid. So, let's negotiate. But as time passed with only curt and sporadic communication from the kidnappers, followed by even terser and more infrequent instructions from someone who identified himself as Big Yazid and complained he'd bought Zaid from his original captors at too high a price, the more difficult it became to believe Kareem's theory was sound. Meanwhile, holed up in my Californian idyll, checking and rechecking my phone and listening to the lake water lap placidly at the dock, I was not getting much work done. In the afternoons, I went for long bike rides or loitered in the Internet café, where I met a girl named Farrah who lived over in Fawnskin and with whom I went to bed a couple of times before she invited me to a cookout on the Fourth of July. It turned out to be a small party, less raucously collegiate than I'd expected, and while we were waiting for the sun to go down and the fireworks over the lake to begin someone suggested a game of Pictionary. I was on Farrah's team, along with two other women whose sundresses, when they leaned over the table, gaped to reveal the lace trim on their pastel-colored bras, and shortly after I'd removed the cap on my first bottle of beer in six years someone drew an All Play. The timer was upended and everyone leaned in, shouting guesses that became predictably louder and more urgent as the sand trickled down: Person. People. People holding hands. People dancing. Angry person. Mean person. Mean person holding a letter. Parking ticket. Manifesto. *Mein Kampf.* Karl Marx. Bag. Sack. Money. Robber. Bank robber. Heist. Bandits. Butch Cassidy. *Bonnie and Clyde. Dog Day Afternoon.* Heist. Somebody already said that. No grunting! Sounds like . . . Eyelashes. Hair. Beautiful. Handsome. Sounds like handsome! Bandsome, candsome, dandsome, fandsome, gandsome . . .

At one point, Farrah looked up and gave me a meaningfully exasperated look. Then she drew a car.

Then she drew two stick figures holding hands next to the car.

Then she drew an arrow between one of the figures and the front seat of the car. Then she x-ed out the trunk.

Oh, I said. Kidnap.

Widening her eyes, Farrah nodded, and stabbed her pencil at what looked like a scrunched-up paper bag with a dollar sign on it. She was a pretty good drawer.

Ransom! shrieked the girl on my other side.

Ransom note! someone else shouted, on the other side of the table. He wasn't on our team. Anyway, the sand in the little imitation hourglass had already run down. And when the drawings were passed around for inspection more than one noble stickler for rules pointed out that symbols, including dollar signs, aren't allowed. I don't remember who won. It tends to be the regrettable things, the details that in retrospect seem to reflect your own pettiness and a certain incurable myopia, that you remember most clearly of the prelude to a shock. The next day my father called to tell me that even though Alia had wired the forty thousand dollars agreed for her husband's release Zaid's body had been left in a plastic bag under the porch, a bullet in his head.

MR. JAAFARI? WOULD YOU come here, please?

Slowly, I backed away from Imam Usman's contact details and went to meet Duncan by the door.

I'm afraid it's not good news, he said, carrot-colored eyebrows straining empathetically. You *are* going to be refused entry to the UK today.

I waited.

I'm sorry. I'm afraid my chief is not satisfied that you are not here for reasons you have not disclosed to us.

I'm here on a layover to Istanbul!

And we have no reason to disbelieve that claim. I'm sorry. I did try to find a loophole for you. I did. But unfortunately the burden of proof is on the passenger to convince us he's not going to take advantage of the system—

Why would I—

—or pose a threat.

I closed my mouth.

I'm sorry, he repeated. You just don't qualify *today*. If you can satisfy another clearance officer in future that you qualify for entry on another day, then your case will be viewed on its merits. This does not automatically exclude you from coming back to the UK in future.

What about tomorrow?

What about tomorrow?

Is there a chance I'll qualify tomorrow?

No.

So what happens now?

Well, we've spoken with BA, and they have a flight going back to Los Angeles that leaves in one hour, which is a bit tight, but if we can get you and your luggage screened and checked in right away we might be able to get you on that.

Why can't I just stay here?

Duncan smirked.

I'm serious, I said. If I'm trying to get to Iraq and I'm booked on a flight to Istanbul that leaves here on Sunday morning, is there any reason I can't just stay here, in your detention room, until then? Why would I want to go all the way back to Los Angeles?

. . . I'd have to ask.

I wish you would.

You might have to sleep in here.

That's fine.

He was gone another hour. Another hour of not knowing. Another 1/24th of a rotation. Another sixty minutes of trying not to think about what I might be doing and what I should have done before. Four years earlier, when we were hiking up Goizha on the afternoon of his daughter and my brother's engagement, Hassan had told me that during the good old days male Ba'ath party members secretly identified themselves with mustaches that were slightly shorter on one side than the other, like the hands of a clock. Specifically, the left side would be shorter than the right, like a timepiece at 8:20, and as the one on the wall opposite me now crept steadily through the same configuration my heart began to race and my fingers to go blue with cold. Where was my brother now? Was he comfortable? Was he warm? Did he have food and water and light, enough to see a clock? Eight twenty-five. Eight thirty. On the muted television, *EastEnders* gave way to *It's a Wonderful Life*. El dunya maqluba—America on Christmas indeed. There is yet another use for El dunya maqluba, by the way, and that is to express disapproval, or incredulity, typically with respect to the perceived lunacy of some modern development. Have you heard

there's going to be a black man in the White House? El dunya maqluba! The world is upside down! In this spirit, the phrase has an
English cousin, The World Turned Upside Down, which is the title
of at least two songs with anarchist origins as well as that of a book
by the Marxist historian Christopher Hill, writing about radicalism
during the English Revolution. The first song is said to have surfaced as a ballad published in a British newspaper in 1643, written
in protest against Parliament's declaration that Christmas ought to
be a strictly solemn occasion and therefore all happy traditions associated with the holiday abolished. *The Angels did good tidings bring,
the Sheepheards did rejoyce and sing. / . . . Why should we from good
Laws be bound? / Yet let's be content, and the times lament, you see the
world turn'd upside down.* Of course, to the English protestors who
wanted to keep their Christmas celebrations, it was Parliament
turning the world on its head. To my beautiful cousin Rania, it was
the celebrations themselves.

Nine ten. Nine fifteen. Nine twenty-five. A thousand miles
eastwise, 66,666 to orbit the sun, 420,000 around our galactic center
and 2,237,000 across the universe. Cumulatively, we are traveling
through space at 2,724,666 miles per hour—and all of us in near
sync, like a flock of starlings swirling patterns through the sky. An-
chored, more or less, to the same astronomical nonpareil, whose car-
dinal directions are only a recent invention, specifically by humans
who happened to call the northern continents home. The mile and
the hour, too, were each invented north of the equator—the former by Roman invaders who, marching through Europe, planted
a stick in the ground after every mille passuum, or thousand paces,
the latter by the Ancient Egyptians when they divided into twelve
segments the sunlit part of the day. Whereas Islam's day begins at
sundown. A mile in Imperial Russia was 24,500 feet. Australians
measure liquid volume by the amount of water in their most pop-
ulous city's harbor. It's nothing new, disunity. Disparity. Termino-
logical conflict. There have always been dissenters, always those for
whom the world is due a revolution and spilling a little blood is

the only way. The problem with the idea that history repeats itself is that when it isn't making us wiser it's making us complacent. We should have learned something from Yugoslavia, Bosnia, and Somalia, yes. On the other hand: humans kill. They take what isn't theirs and they defend what is, however little that may be. They use violence when words don't work, but sometimes the reason words don't work is because the ones holding all the cards don't appear to be listening. Whose fault is it, then, when a good man, a man who works hard and lives in accordance with generous and peaceable principles, can't leave his house in Sulaymaniyah at five o'clock in the afternoon to walk a child home from a piano lesson without being kidnapped at gunpoint by men who can conceive of no better way to make a hundred thousand dollars in American bills?

And even more than your brother, Alastair had warned me the night before, in an email I'd read standing in line to board my flight—as he would be warning me now, in The Lamb, had his exemplary Border Force seen fit to let me through—someone like you would be the richest prize these people could ever hope to run across. A Shiite from a political family affiliated with two of the political parties they hate, *and* who's got connections in the Green Zone, *and* is an American citizen with family in the US and savings in dollars? Can you imagine? 'So many birds! One stone!'

All right then, Mr. Jaafari. You can stay. But if you're going to be our responsibility for the next thirty-four hours, we're going to have to get you checked out by a doctor.

America is America again, I said to myself the night Obama was elected. I said it not by mistake, but certainly without thinking—without, as Mandelstam wrote of God, having thought to speak. A little more than one month earlier, Eid had fallen on the second of October, the same evening Joe Biden braved Sarah Palin in the vice-presidential debate—the night Palin quoted Ronald Reagan as having said that freedom is always just one generation away from extinction. We don't pass it to our children in the bloodstream. We have to fight for it and protect it, and then hand it to them, so that they shall do the same, or we're gonna find ourselves spending our sunset years telling our children, and our children's children, about a time in America, back in the day, when men and women were free. But Reagan hadn't been talking about national security. He'd been speaking, in 1961, on behalf of the Women's Auxiliary of the American Medical Association, about the perils of socialized medicine—specifically, Medicare.

I was alone on Eid, in my apartment in West Hollywood, breaking the fast with some klaicha my mother had sent me, and as my dissertation was due to my advisor the following morning I was struggling to install a new ink cartridge with which to finish printing its forty-three pages of tables and notes. Meanwhile, listening to Governor Palin fire off her arsenal of errata, I began to wonder whether I hadn't left it too late to go into politics after all. If you don't like the way things are, change them. No use sitting around rolling your eyes. All that is necessary for the triumph of evil is that good men do nothing, etc. But then Obama won and suddenly I did like the way things were, or were going to be, provided the damage done by his predecessors didn't prove too tenacious or even irreparable. The political depression I'd suffered for nigh on eight years had lifted, and I even dared to imagine that the apparently superior qualities of our president-elect would ingratiate us anew beyond our shores. Or: Do those who hate us even care whom we vote into office? Or does our having elected someone who would seem to be intelligent and well-spoken, charming and prudent, farsighted and diplomatic—an altogether enviable leader—only make them hate us more?

The socialized medic examining me now was a pleasant man— gentle, efficient, and studiously indifferent to my crimes, whatever they were—but it was nonetheless a peculiar experience, this undergoing a checkup when I didn't need one, when I hadn't the mildest complaint other than the agony of my helplessness, when the physical well-being I wanted most to have confirmed was not my own but that of my now twice vanished brother. Dr. Lalwani had a strong Indian accent but otherwise flawless English and no fewer than four university certificates displayed on his wall, prompting me to wonder what level of success a British doctor must achieve in order to avoid working the Boxing Day night shift in the windowless innards of Terminal Five. Height: Five nine. Weight: Sixty-seven kilos—about ten and a half stone. Is that normal for you? Yes? Good. Now say Ahhhhhh. Now touch your tongue to the roof of your mouth. Now raise your arms. Now make two fists. Now push them against me. Good. Good. Touch your finger to your nose? Touch my finger? Now alternate as fast as you can. Bladder problems? Trouble ejaculating? Good. Now bend over. Now stand up, vertebra by vertebra. Now walk over there. Now come back to me. Good.

I'm just going to take some blood. Do you want to know if you test positive for HIV?

Well, I said, it's extremely unlikely. But yes, I guess I would like to know.

He picked up a metal file and held it between us like a tiny orchestral baton. Now I want you to close your eyes, and each time you feel me touching this to one of your cheeks say *now*.

. . . Now.

Now.

Now.

Now.

Now.

Now.

Now.

Now.

Good. Now, still keeping your eyes closed, tell me: Does this feel sharp or dull?

Sharp.

Dull.

Sharp.

Dull.

Sharp.

Sharp.

Dull.

Dull.

Sharp.

Dull.

Good. Now, still keeping your eyes closed, tell me what each of these objects is, that I place in your hand.

A paper clip.

A key.

A pencil.

A dime.

He laughed. It was a five-pence piece. Trick question.

I watched him ride his swivel chair across the room to collect an ophthalmoscope from a mirrored tray before wheeling back and bringing his face so close to mine we could have kissed. His skin had a clean, rubbery smell. As I listened to the breath whistling in his nostrils my pupils flooded with white.

I can see the veins pulsing behind your eyes.

Oh?

Yes. We like that.

The last item on his list was a complete abdominal X-ray— something about checking for any foreign objects, which I under-stood to mean balloons of heroin hiding in my bowels—and while I got dressed he asked:

So, what do you do?

I'm an economist.

Oh? What kind?

Well, I replied, zipping up my fly, my dissertation was on risk aversion. And now I'm looking for a job.

Lalwani nodded kindly.

And then, I suppose because I sensed in him a tolerant man, an

intelligent and liberal-minded ally whom in any case I would probably never see again, I added:

I'm also thinking of running for public office.

For a moment, Lalwani's face froze in a kind of cautious delight—
as if I'd just mentioned an acquaintance we had in common, but
our respective opinions of said acquaintance weren't yet clear. To be
fair, I'd surprised even myself with this announcement—yet I was
serious, as serious as my detention was looking to be long, and when
it became apparent Lalwani clapped his hands together and fairly
shouted: Marvelous! Where?

In California, I replied. Thirtieth congressional district, I think.

Lalwani nodded with something like impressed deference now,
and when I'd tied my sneakers and straightened up again his eyes
had assumed the squinty, professorial gaze of distant recall. 'I have
not the art of divination,' he said a touch theatrically. 'In the course
of four or five hundred years, who can say how it will work. But
this is most certain: Papists may occupy the position, and even
Mahometans may take it. I see nothing against it.' Then, looking
pleased with himself, he removed the rubber glove from one hand
and extended it. Well, Dr. Jaafari. I think it's a fine idea. Congress-
man Jaafari. *President* Jaafari. Good luck to you. Maybe, one way or
another, when you're done visiting your brother you'll be able to get
us out of this mess.

Walking back to the holding room, I felt unburdened somehow,
lighter and even a little effervescent—as though, in the very process
of having its robustness confirmed, I'd shed my body and left it on
the floor of the examination room behind me. Are the veins behind
Sami's eyes still pulsing? Are they still behind his eyes? Three sum-
mers ago, shortly after my mother was diagnosed with Alzheimer's,
my father had sent me an email containing a link to a story in *The
Seattle Times* about a two-year-old named Muhammed who'd been
shot in the face on the road between Baghdad and Baqubah. He
and some family members had been driving home from visiting
a relative when militants stopped their SUV and turned AK-47s

on four of the five unarmed people inside. Muhammed's uncle was killed, and his mother badly wounded; only his four-year-old sister had not been harmed. The bullet fired at Muhammed destroyed his right eye and grazed his left, such that after months of hospitalization in Iraq and then Iran he'd been flown by a humanitarian organization to a medical center in Seattle so that his vision might be saved by a cornea transplant there. I'm sorry to be conveying depressing stories, my father had written, as though all our correspondence over the previous month had not been depressing. But I thought you should know that the uncle who died was the same man who came to see us at your grandmother's last January, the one who sat in the garden saying repeatedly: This will pass eventually.

I suppose he was right.

It was nearly midnight now, but overhead the holding room's fluorescent lights persisted with their colorless buzzing like some sickly polar sun. And it was so cold, surprisingly cold for a room with no windows; I'd been given a thin blanket sticky with static and a miniature pillow encased in disposable gauze, neither of which did much to replicate the warmth or comfort of a bed. Meanwhile, I was no longer alone. A limping woman swept the floor along with my feet while a blonde who looked to be in her late twenties sat on the other side of the room, crying quietly. She was sitting in what many hours earlier had been the black man's seat, a pillow and blanket like my own left neatly on the chair beside her, her legs crossed and her coat folded over on itself in her lap, the black fur on its hood riffling a little whenever she exhaled or blew her nose. My own coat was in my suitcase, rolled up between a pair of hiking boots and a toy abacus. All I had on me now was the light parka in which I'd departed Los Angeles twenty-three hours earlier, anticipating a tomorrow very different from today. In West Hollywood, it had been fifty-six degrees—not exactly springlike but still mild enough that on my way home from a farewell meeting with my dissertation advisor I'd decided to sit down outside the café at the end of my road and order a plate of eggs. I'd had a book with

me, the same book on post-Keynesian price theory I'm not reading
now, and after ordering my brunch and checking in for my flight
I'd opened it up and read with a highly tenuous concentration until
my five dollars of freshly squeezed sanguinello arrived and I drank
it down all at once. The juice was pulpy and sweet and the words on
the page looked denser and farther away after that. High in the sky
an afternoon moon threw back the light of the sun. Then my phone
beeped, the screen flashing PARENTS; then it beeped again, and this
time Maddie left me a message saying Merry Christmas, inshallah;
then it beeped a third time, just as a basket of bread and jam was
set down by my elbow, and as I listened to my father tell me what
Zahra had told him only half an hour before I laid down my knife
and watched the traffic on Beverly Boulevard fleeting west. It was
SUVs, mostly, SUVs plus the odd old hatchback or sedan; there was
also a white stretch limo, a van painted to look like a shark, and a
gleaming red fire truck leisurely trailing an American flag. They've
asked for a hundred thousand, my father told me, through tears.
Hassan's offered seventy-five. Approaching their own reflections in
the open window opposite my chair the vehicles appeared to drive
into themselves, to glide eastward and westward at once—their
hoods and wheels and windshields to disappear into antimatter, the
flag to devour itself.

III

EZRA BLAZER'S DESERT ISLAND DISCS

[recorded at BBC Broadcasting House in London on February 14, 2011]

INTERVIEWER: My castaway this week is a writer. A clever boy originally from the Squirrel Hill neighborhood of East Pittsburgh, Pennsylvania, he graduated from Allegheny College swiftly into the pages of *Playboy*, *The New Yorker*, and *The Paris Review*, where his short stories about postwar working-class Americans earned him a reputation as a fiercely candid and unconventional talent. By the time he was twenty-nine, he had published his first novel, *Nine Mile Run*, which won him the first of three National Book Awards; since then he's published twenty more books, and received dozens more awards, including the Pen/Faulkner Award, a Gold Medal in Fiction from the American Academy of Arts and Letters, two Pulitzer Prizes, the National Medal of Arts, and, just this past December—"for his exuberant ingenuity and exquisite powers of ventriloquism, which with irony and compassion evince the extraordinary heterogeneity of modern American life"—literature's most coveted honor: the Nobel Prize. Widely admired in the States as well as here in the UK and abroad, he's been translated into more than thirty languages—and yet, off the page, he remains a recluse, preferring the sanctity of his longtime residence on the eastern end of Long Island to what he calls the "fatal froth and frenzy" of Manhattan literary life. "Be audacious in your writing," he says, "and conservative in your days." He is Ezra Blazer.

Are we to take it from that, Ezra Blazer, that the decidedly unconventional protagonists in your novels are entirely the products of a wild imagination?

EZRA BLAZER: [*Laughs.*] If only my imagination were so wild. No. Certainly not. And yet it would be equally wrong to call them autobiographical, or to become caught up in that inane exercise of trying to separate "truth" from "fiction," as if those boxes weren't kicked aside by the novelist for good reason to begin with.

INTERVIEWER: And what reason is that?

EZRA BLAZER: Our memories are no more reliable than our imaginations, after all. But I'm the first to admit it can be irresistible, contemplating what's "real" versus "imagined" in a novel. Checking for seams, trying to figure out how it's been done. It's as old as time, this practice of dishing out advice you don't always follow yourself. "Be audacious in your hieroglyphs, conservative in your hunting and gathering."

INTERVIEWER: Critics have not always been kind to you. Do you mind?

EZRA BLAZER: I try as best I can not to have any contact with what's written about my work. I don't find it does me any good and if it's laudatory or negative I have to conclude it's all the same thing. I know my work better than anybody. I know my shortcomings. I know what I can't do. By this point I certainly know what I can do. In the beginning, of course, I read every word I could find about myself. But what did I get from that? Sure, there are intelligent people who have written about my writing, but I'd rather read these intelligent people on writers other than myself. Maybe praise does something for your confidence, but your confidence has to be able to exist without it. The review of your last book doesn't help you eighteen months into the new book that's driving you crazy. Book reviews are for readers, not writers.

INTERVIEWER: Tell me about your childhood.

EZRA BLAZER: I think everyone's heard enough about my childhood.

INTERVIEWER: You were the youngest of three children—

EZRA BLAZER: Really, I'd rather talk about how music came into my life. I never heard classical music growing up. In fact I had a kind of ignorant boy's disdain for it. I thought it was all phony, and especially opera. But my father liked to listen to opera, strangely, although he wasn't educated—

INTERVIEWER: He was a steelworker.

EZRA BLAZER: He was an accountant for Edgewater Steel. But on weekends he'd listen to opera, on the radio, I think it was on Saturday afternoons, and . . . Milton Cross, that was the name of the announcer. He had a deep, mellifluous voice, and the opera was broadcast from the Metropolitan Opera House, and there'd be my father, on the sofa, with his dog-eared copy of *The Story of a Hundred Operas*, listening to *La Traviata* or *Der Rosenkavalier* on the radio. And, well, I found it all a little strange. We had no phonograph, and no books, so the center of our entertainment was the radio, and on Saturday afternoons my father monopolized it for hours.

INTERVIEWER: Was he himself a musical man?

EZRA BLAZER: Sometimes he would sing in the shower, arias, little passages of the arias, and my mother would come out of the kitchen with a dreamy smile on her face and say, "Your father has a beautiful voice." Unlike my protagonists I'm from a happy family.

INTERVIEWER: *Did* he have a beautiful voice?

EZRA BLAZER: He didn't have a bad voice. But I was in the thrall of the popular music. I was eight when the war began, in 1941, so I heard all the songs from the war years, and then when I got to be an adolescent it was all that romantic stuff—

INTERVIEWER: For example?

EZRA BLAZER: [*Pauses, then sings:*] "*A small café, Mam'selle. A rendezvous, Mam'selle. La-da-da-da-da-da-da—*" Or: "*How are things in Glocca M-o-o-o-r-r-r-a-a-a-a?*" And *that* song I remember because it was popular just before my older brother went into the army. At dinnertime we were always listening to the

radio and whenever "How Are Things in Glocca Morra?" came
on, my brother would sing along in a not-bad Irish accent that
just thrilled me. And then he left for the service and whenever
that song was played my mother cried. She'd start to cry and I'd
stand up from the table and say, Come on, Ma, let's dance.

INTERVIEWER: How old were you?

EZRA BLAZER: In 1947? Thirteen, fourteen. So that's my first record. "How Are Things in Glocca Morra?," sung by Ella Logan,
the Irish Ethel Merman.

INTERVIEWER: She's Scottish, actually.

EZRA BLAZER: Really? Does everyone know that?

INTERVIEWER: I think so.

EZRA BLAZER: Ella Logan is Scottish?

INTERVIEWER: She is.

*   *   *   *   *

*   *   *   *

*   *   *   *

INTERVIEWER: That was "How Are Things in Glocca Morra?,"
from the musical *Finian's Rainbow*, performed by Ella Logan.
But tell me, Ezra Blazer, surely you didn't dance only with your
mother. What were the origins of your romantic life?

EZRA BLAZER: Well, as you imply, I soon began dancing with
girls. At the prom. At parties. One of my friends had a *finished
basement*, for parties. The rest of us didn't have much money
and lived in flats, but his parents had a one-family house and a
finished basement and we had our parties there. And the singer
who drove us wild at those parties was Billy Eckstine. He had a
rich baritone voice, and his blackness, which enchanted us. He
wasn't a jazz singer, though he did sing some jazz songs. [*Sings:*]
"*I left my HAT in HAI-ti! In some forgot—*" But no. That's not
the one I want. The ones we loved most were the ones we could
dance to, very slowly, with the girls, holding them as close to us

as we could, because that was the only thing approaching sex that we had, there on the basement dance floor. The girls were virgins and they would remain virginal right through college. But on the dance floor you could press your groin against your girlfriend and if she loved you she would press back, and if she was suspicious of you she would dance with her ass backing away.

INTERVIEWER: This is a family program.

EZRA BLAZER: I beg your pardon. With her tuchis backing away.

INTERVIEWER: And Eckstine?

EZRA BLAZER: Eckstine used to wear suits called the "one-button roll": the lapels were long and narrow and held together below the waist with a single button. He wore his tie in a wide Windsor knot and there was a big rolled collar on his shirt—a "Billy Eckstine collar." Wednesday nights and Saturdays I worked in the Monogramming Shop at Kaufmann's and what with my employee discount I saved enough money to buy a pearl-gray, one-button-roll suit. My first suit. And when Billy Eckstine came back to Pittsburgh to sing in the Crawford Grill my friend and I sneaked in wearing our suits, and, oh, bliss was it to be alive, but to be young was very heaven!

INTERVIEWER: Second record?

EZRA BLAZER: "Somehow."

*   *   *   *   *
    *   *   *   *
*   *   *   *   *

INTERVIEWER: Billy Eckstine singing "Somehow." After graduating from Allegheny College, Ezra Blazer, you too went into the service. What was that like?

EZRA BLAZER: I was in the army for two years. I was drafted, in the Korean War draft, and luckily I wasn't sent to Korea but to Germany, along with something like a quarter million other Americans bracing themselves for World War III. And I was an MP. A military policeman. At Lee Barracks, in Mainz. Before age and illness laid waste to my frame and reduced my proportions to what you see now, I was six feet two and two hundred pounds. A big muscular MP with a pistol and a billy club. And my specialty as an MP was directing traffic. We didn't have World War III, but we did have traffic. I was taught in MP school that the key to directing traffic is to let the traffic flow through your hips. Would you like to see?

INTERVIEWER: It sounds like dancing.

EZRA BLAZER: It sounds like dancing, yes! Do you know that joke?

INTERVIEWER: I don't think I do.

EZRA BLAZER: A young rabbi-in-training is about to get married and so he goes to the wise old rabbi with a beard down to the ground, and he says, "Rabbi, I'd like to know what's permissible and what isn't. I don't want to do what's forbidden. Is it all right," he asks the old rabbi, "if we get into bed together, and I get on top of her, and we have intercourse like that?" "Fine!" says the rabbi. "Absolutely fine." "And is it all right if she rolls over on her stomach and we have intercourse that way? With me on top like that?" "Fine!" says the rabbi. "Absolutely fine. Poifect." "And if we sit on the edge of the bed, and she sits on top of me, facing me, and we do it like that?" "Fine! Absolutely fine." "And what if we do it facing each other standing up?" "No!" cries the rabbi. "Absolutely NOT! That's like *dancing*!"

INTERVIEWER: Next record.

EZRA BLAZER: Well, it often happens to young fellows in the army that you meet someone who becomes your teacher, someone who knows worlds unknown to you. In Germany, I was stationed with a guy who'd gone to Yale, and at night—he had a phonograph with him, in the barracks—he'd play Dvořák. Dvořák! I didn't know how to pronounce it, never mind spell it. I was ignorant of classical music. Ignorant of it and hostile to it, in a coarse kid's way. Well, one night I heard him playing something that stunned me. It was the cello concerto, of course. I think it was Casals. Later on, I'd hear Jacqueline du Pré play it, marvelously of course, but it was Casals's that I heard first, so let's play him. What I liked was the electricity of it, the drama that was like voltage entering your veins . . .

   *   *   *   *   *
    *   *   *   *
   *   *   *   *   *

INTERVIEWER: That was Pablo Casals playing Dvořák's Cello Concerto in B Minor, with the Czech Philharmonic Orchestra conducted by George Szell. And how was it, Ezra Blazer, being a soldier in Germany?

EZRA BLAZER: Well, it was not entirely pleasant for me. I liked directing traffic. I liked wearing a uniform, and being a tough-guy MP. But this was 1954. The war had ended only nine years earlier. And it was only in the years after the war that the total destruction of European Jewry by the Nazis had been revealed in all its horror. So I had no love for Germans. I couldn't stand them, couldn't bear to hear them speaking in German. That language! And then, alas, what should happen but that I met a girl. A pretty, blond, blue-eyed, strong-jawed, one-hundred-percent Aryan German girl. She was a student at the university, and I saw her in town carrying some books and I asked her what she was reading. She was lovely, and she knew a little English—not a lot, but the way she spoke it I found charming. Her father had been in the war, and this to me was not so charming. I was ashamed to imagine what my family would think of my falling in love with a Nazi's daughter. So it was a very fraught affair, and I tried to make it the subject of my first book. I couldn't do it, of course. But yes, the first book I wanted to write was about this love affair with a German girl when I was a soldier, and the war having ended only nine years earlier. I couldn't even bring myself to go to her house to pick her up because I didn't want to meet her family, and this was crushing for her. We never fought, but she cried. And I cried. We were young and we were in love and we cried. Life's first big blow. Katja was her name. I don't know what became of her, where she is now. I wonder if somewhere in Germany she reads my books in German.

INTERVIEWER: And your efforts on this first book? Where are they? In a drawer somewhere?

EZRA BLAZER: Gone. Long gone. I wrote fifty terrible pages full of rage. I was twenty-one. She was nineteen. Lovely girl. That's the story.

INTERVIEWER: Record number four.

EZRA BLAZER: Well, I wanted to see more of Europe after my service, so I took my discharge there, and I stayed. I had a big duffel bag, my army duffel, and my army overcoat, and my separation pay, which amounted to about three hundred bucks, and I took a train to Paris and moved into a shabby little hotel in the Sixth. One of those hotels where you get up to use the bathroom in the middle of the night and go out to the hallway and you can't find the light, or if you do blindly find the switch you turn it on and go six steps and the light goes off again. And if you ever do find the bathroom, you're in worse trouble, because the toilet paper in those postwar years—May I speak about toilet paper on a family program?

INTERVIEWER: You may.

EZRA BLAZER: The toilet paper was like emery board. Not sandpaper: emery board.

INTERVIEWER: So you lived in Paris for a year—

EZRA BLAZER: A year and a half.

INTERVIEWER:—after your service in the army.

EZRA BLAZER: Yes. I lived near the Odéon Métro station and I used to go to the Café Odéon and of course I met a girl. Geneviève. And Geneviève had a sputtering little black motorbike—they were all over Paris then—and she would roll up to the Odéon at night and meet me there, and somehow, this girl, who was not . . . Well, she was pretty, certainly, but she was kind of a street girl, and yet she too had musical taste, like my army pal, and it was she who introduced me to the chamber music of Fauré. And that's also when I learned about the beauty of the cello, which of course I have Marina Makovsky play in *The Running Gag*. For months that was the only instrument I wanted to hear. The sound of it thrilled me. There are beautiful piano passages in Fauré, but it's the cello, that wonderful [*growls like a cello*]—Those sounds whose depths only the cello can reach. That got me. It has this lilt, this freshness, just gorgeous. I'd never heard music like it before—a long way from "Mam'selle," you see, though we're in the right city. It's crazy how everything comes at you. Everything is an accident. Life is one big accident. I didn't love this girl the way I loved the German girl, by the way. Maybe because there wasn't so much *sturm und drang*.

*   *   *   *   *
  *   *   *   *
*   *   *   *   *

INTERVIEWER: That was Gabriel Fauré's Cello Sonata no. 1 in D minor, performed by Thomas Igloi with Clifford Benson on the piano. Now remind me, Ezra Blazer, wasn't it around this time *The Paris Review* started up?

EZRA BLAZER: Oh, yes. I think those fellows got there in fifty-three, fifty-four. So this was just a year or two later. And sure, I knew everybody. George, Peter, Tom. Blair. Bill. Doc.

Wonderful guys. Charming, adventurous, serious about literature, and, blessedly, wholly unacademic. Paris then still had that
aura of the American expatriate adventure: Fitzgerald, Hemingway, Malcolm Cowley, *Transition*, Shakespeare & Company,
Sylvia Beach, Joyce. And the *Paris Review* crew, they were romantic about what they were doing. You know that E. E. Cummings poem? *"let's start a magazine / to hell with literature . . .
something fearlessly obscene . . ."* They were romantic but they
were hard-nosed, too, and they were doing something brand-
new. Though in the end, like me, they were in Paris because it
was fun. And plenty of fun there was.

INTERVIEWER: Were you writing by this time?

EZRA BLAZER: Trying to. I wrote some delightfully poetic little
short stories, very sensitive short stories, about . . . Oh, I don't
know. World peace. Pink sunlight on the Seine. That was one
problem: the rampant sentimentality of youth. Another was that
I was constantly trying to shoehorn characters into each other's
lives, planting them on street corners or in cafés together so that
they could *talk*. So that they could *explain* things to each other,
from across the great human divide. But it was all so contrived.
Contrived and meddlesome, really, because sometimes you just
have to let your characters get on with it, which is to say coexist.
If their paths cross and they can teach each other something, fine.
If they don't, well, that's interesting, too. Or, if it isn't interesting,
then maybe you need to back up and start again. But at least
you haven't betrayed the reality of things. In my twenties, I was
always fighting this, always trying to force meaningful conver-
gence with my ravishing prose. And the result was these airless
little short stories that could not be faulted on the sentence level
but that had no resonance, no reason for being, no spontaneity.
Nothing *happened*. I showed one to George once and he sent me
a note that began, "You plainly have gifts, dear Ez, but you need
a subject. This is like *Babar* written by E. M. Forster."

INTERVIEWER: Next record.

EZRA BLAZER: Well, at one of the clubs we used to go to we heard Chet Baker play, with Bobby Jaspar, I think, and Maurice Vander, a wonderful pianist, he was around a lot, too. I remember one night listening to them play "How About You?" and feeling just overcome by where I was and what I still had in front of me. All of it! When you're young you can't wait for the main event to begin. I couldn't wait for anything back then. No *thinking*, just *charging*—always charging ahead! Do you remember that feeling?

*   *   *   *   *

  *   *   *   *

*   *   *   *   *

INTERVIEWER: That was "How About You?," performed by Chet Baker, Bobby Jaspar, Maurice Vander, Benoit Quersin, and Jean-Louis Viale. And can you tell us, Ezra Blazer, why did you leave Paris?

EZRA BLAZER: Why did I leave. A part of me has always wondered. A part of me—the audacious part—has always said to the sensible part: Why didn't you just stay? If only for the women. Because the erotic life in Paris had nothing to do with what I'd known as a boy at Allegheny. But then, after about a year and a half of it, I really had to come home. My writing, if you can call it that—Well, I didn't know what I was doing. As I said, it was all this lyrical sentimental crap about nothing. So I came home. To Pittsburgh. My parents were there, and my sister was there, married with children now, and certainly after Paris that wasn't for me. I've always loved Pittsburgh, especially when it looked its worst. I've written about that, of course: Pittsburgh before they cleaned it up. Now it's this immaculate city, all finance and technology, but back then you could die just from taking a breath on the street. The air was black and steaming with smog—"hell with the lid off," they used to say—and there was the clanging of trains, and the great mills, a very dramatic place, and maybe had I stayed and got lucky I might have been the Balzac of Pittsburgh. But I had to escape my family. I had to go to New York.

INTERVIEWER: Where you discovered ballet.

EZRA BLAZER: Ballet and *ballerinas*. These were Balanchine's great days, after all. Spectacular stuff. All new. I discovered Stravinsky, I discovered Bartók, Shostakovich. That changed everything.

INTERVIEWER: Your first wife was a dancer.

EZRA BLAZER: My first *two* wives were dancers. Who didn't like each other, as you can imagine. But that was another education. I married Erika—

INTERVIEWER: Erika Seidl.

EZRA BLAZER: Yes, Erika Seidl. Later she became famous, but when we married she was still a girl in the corps and I was enchanted. Everything was new. Everything! It just burst upon me. And the newness, the thrill of discovery, became embodied for me in this exquisitely beautiful young woman. Born in Vienna. Trained in the Vienna State Opera Ballet School and her family lived there until she was fourteen and then her parents divorced and her mother, who was American, took her to New York, and she just disappeared into Balanchine. It was about a year after we married that she soloed in *The Seven Deadly Sins* and that was it, I never saw her again. It was like being married to a boxer. She was always in training. When I went backstage to see her after a performance she stank like a boxer. All of the girls stank; it was like Stillman's Gym on Eighth Avenue. She had this little monkey face—not onstage; onstage it was a great skull, all eyes and ears, but backstage she looked like she'd gone fifteen rounds with Muhammad Ali. Anyway, I never saw her. I'd found what few men found in that era,

which was a woman wholly occupied by what she did, and
wedded to it. So we parted. And I drifted to another dancer.
Not smart. Dana.

INTERVIEWER: Dana Pollock.

EZRA BLAZER: Dana was never the dancer Erika was, but she
was something. I don't know why I did it again. I did the same
thing again, and the same thing happened. So next I married a
bartender. But she was out nights, too.

INTERVIEWER: You never had children?

EZRA BLAZER: After the fact, I consider my girlfriends my children.

INTERVIEWER: Do you regret never having children?

EZRA BLAZER: No. I love my friends' children. I think about
them and I call them and attend their birthday parties, but I
had other fish to fry. And monogamy, insofar as it's conducive
to good parenting . . . Well, I've never been inordinately fond
of monogamy. But ballet, and ballet music, that was the next
education. And then came everything else. Mozart, Bach, Beethoven, Schubert, the Schubert piano pieces I love, the Beethoven quartets, the great Bach sonatas, the partitas, the Goldberg
variations, Casals playing those growling cello pieces. Everyone
loves those; by now they're a little like "Mam'selle."

INTERVIEWER: Let's hear about your sixth record then.

EZRA BLAZER: A friend recently gave me a copy of Nijinsky's
diary, the first edition, which was put together by his widow, Ro-
mola, who I'm told suppressed what she didn't like. Having to
do with Diaghilev, I suppose. Because she was jealous of Diaghilev and his power over Nijinsky and she blamed Diaghilev for
Nijinsky's illness. Anyway, there's a new edition out now, where
the edited-out parts have been restored, but it's the widow's I
read, and whatever may have been done to it it's still marvelous.
All of this sent me back to "Afternoon of a Faun," another first
love. [*Laughs.*] But now I can hear the rebellion in it—the per-
versity, the enslavement to imagined forces. Alas, we don't have

any footage of Nijinsky dancing the Faun, so we have to make do with what we do have, which is Debussy.

*   *   *   *   *

*   *   *   *

*   *   *   *   *

INTERVIEWER: That was Debussy's "Prélude à l'après-midi d'un faune," performed by Emmanuel Pahud and the Berlin Philharmonic, conducted by Claudio Abbado. Ezra Blazer, you've written that depression is "the inevitable crash after an untenable happiness." How often has that been true for you?

EZRA BLAZER: Well, it's true whenever depression hits, which fortunately for me has been only two or three times. Once when I was left by a woman I hugely loved. Twice when I was left by a woman I hugely loved. A third time when my brother died, and I was the only Blazer left. All right, maybe four times. But anyway, it's true of any sort of depression—emotional, economic: it occurs only after you've been riding too high. We ride too high on deceptive notions of power and security and control and then when it all comes crashing down on us the low is made deeper by the high. By its precipitousness, but also by the humiliation you feel for having failed to see the plummet coming. As I said: sometimes it's personal, sometimes it's economic, sometimes even a kind of political depression sets in. Lulled by years of relative peace and prosperity we settle into micromanaging our lives with our fancy technologies and custom interest rates and eleven different kinds of milk, and this leads to a certain inwardness, an unchecked narrowing of perspective, the vague expectation that even if we don't earn them and nurture them the truly essential amenities will endure forever as they are. We trust that someone else is looking after the civil liberties shop, so we don't have to. Our military might is unmatched and in any case the madness is at least an ocean away. And then all of a sudden we look up from ordering paper towels online to find ourselves delivered right into the madness. And we wonder: How did this happen? What was *I* doing when this was in the works? Is it too late to think about it now? Anyway, what good will it do, the willful and belated broadening of my imagination? A young friend of mine has written a rather surprising little novel about this, in its way. About the extent to which we're able to penetrate the looking-glass and imagine a life, indeed a consciousness, that goes some way to reduce the blind spots in our own. It's a novel that on the surface would seem to have nothing to do with its author, but in fact is a kind of veiled portrait of someone determined to transcend her provenance, her privilege, her naiveté. [*Laughs softly.*] Incidentally, this friend, she was one of the—Well, no. I won't say that. I won't say her name. Never mind. There it is. What's the line? War is God's way of teaching Americans geography.

INTERVIEWER: You don't believe that.

EZRA BLAZER: I think an impressive number of us cannot read-ily point to Mosul on a map. But I also think God is too busy arranging David Ortiz's home runs to be much concerned with teaching us geography.

INTERVIEWER: More music.

EZRA BLAZER: How many do I have left?

INTERVIEWER: Two.

EZRA BLAZER: Two. And we've only gotten up to my thirties. We'll be here forever. My next record is from Strauss's *Four Last Songs*. I didn't listen to them in Germany. I couldn't listen to Wagner, either. Only later did I come to my senses. I love the *Four Last Songs*, with Kiri Te Kanawa singing. Who doesn't?

*   *   *   *   *   *

*   *   *   *   *

*   *   *   *   *

INTERVIEWER: That was Dame Kiri Te Kanawa singing "Im Abendrot," with the London Symphony Orchestra, conducted

by Andrew Davis. Ezra Blazer, you said earlier that you have
no regrets about not having had children, but there have been
rumors that you *did* in fact father a child, in Europe. Is there any
truth to those rumors?

EZRA BLAZER: I fathered two children.

INTERVIEWER: You did?

EZRA BLAZER: Twins. Since you asked. Impertinently, I must say.
I told you about my friend? With the little black motorbike, who
introduced me to Fauré? Well, she became pregnant, just as I
was about to leave Paris, and I didn't know it at the time, and I
came back to America. I had to. I had nothing left to live on.

INTERVIEWER: You didn't keep in touch?

EZRA BLAZER: We corresponded for a while, but then she disappeared. That was 1956. In 1977 I happened to be spending a week in
Paris, promoting the French publication of one of my books. I was
staying at the Montalembert, near my publishing house, and I was in
the bar, talking to my editor, when a young woman came up to me,
very pretty, and said, in French: Excuse me, sir, but I believe you're
my father. I thought, Fine, if that's the way she wants to play it. So
I said, Sit down, mademoiselle. And she told me her name, and of
course the last name I recognized. My French lover, Geneviève, had
been the same age as this girl when I knew her. So I said, Are you the
daughter of Geneviève so-and-so? And she said, *Oui. Je suis la fille de
Geneviève et je suis* votre *fille.* And I said, Can that be? How old are
you? And she told me. And I said, But how can you be sure I'm your
father? And she said, My mother told me. I said, Were you waiting
for me here? *Oui.* You knew I was in Paris? *Oui.* Then she said: My
brother's on his way. Oh? said I. How old is he? The same age. That's
right, you have a daughter *and* a son. And at this point my editor
stood up and said, "We can discuss the translation another time."

INTERVIEWER: You tell this story so calmly, but it must have
been a shock.

EZRA BLAZER: A colossal shock and a colossal delight. I hadn't
had to raise them, you see. I met them as adults, and the next

night we had supper with their mother, and we had a wonderful
time. And now they have children, my grandchildren, and I'm
besotted by them. I like my children, but I'm besotted by my
little French grandchildren.

INTERVIEWER: Do you see this secret family?

EZRA BLAZER: I go to Paris once a year. I see them in France,
but rarely in America, to keep the gossip at bay. Maybe now I'll
see them in America. I help them out financially. I love them. I
didn't know there were rumors. How did you hear? How did
you know?

INTERVIEWER: A little bird told me.

EZRA BLAZER: A little boid told you. That's delicious, you know,
in an English accent.

INTERVIEWER: A Scottish accent.

EZRA BLAZER: You're Scottish. Everyone's Scottish. You'll be telling me next Obama is Scottish.

INTERVIEWER: Anyway, Ezra Blazer, I thought you might appreciate an opportunity to set the record straight. In your own
voice.

EZRA BLAZER: Well, it's certainly been a more significant Q & A
on the radio than I was expecting. I've been outed as a father.
There it is. It's a wonderful thing, what happened to me. A mi-
raculous thing. As I told you earlier, life is all accidents. Even
what doesn't appear to be an accident is an accident. Beginning
with conception, of course. That sets the tone.

INTERVIEWER: Has this particular accident affected your work?

EZRA BLAZER: It would have, if I'd had to raise them. But I
didn't. And no, I've never written about them, not obviously.
I'm amazed even to find myself talking about them now. I don't
know why I didn't lie to you. You took me by surprise. And
you're just such a charming young woman yourself. And I'm a
decrepit old man. It doesn't matter any longer what biographical
facts get added to or subtracted from my life.

INTERVIEWER: You're not decrepit.

EZRA BLAZER: I am the soul of decrepitude.

INTERVIEWER: Last record. What are we going to hear?

EZRA BLAZER: Something from Albéniz's *Iberia*, which he wrote in the last years of his life—he died in his late forties, of kidney disease, I think—and bear this in mind, while you're listening to it: that it sprang from a mind, a sensibility, that so soon afterward would be snuffed out, leaving behind this magnificent burst, this smoking flare . . . If I were in charge, we'd sit here and listen to the whole hour and a half of it, because each of the pieces builds on the last, they're discrete and yet all the richer for being heard together, and you just ache with the mounting intensity of it. The vibrancy. The innocence. The concentration. I like Barenboim's version, partly because of his association with Edward Said, who of course before *he* died wrote an essay on late style—the notion that an awareness of one's life and therefore one's artistic contribution coming to an end affects the artist's style, whether by imbuing it with a sense of resolution and serenity or with intransigence, difficulty, contradiction. But can you call it a "late style" if the artist died at only forty-eight years old? How did he compose such a marvelous, buoyant, triumphant masterpiece while contending with the excruciating pain of kidney stones? As I said, I'd like to listen to the whole thing with you, but as you're motioning for me to wind this up, let's go with the second track, which is called "El Puerto." The technical term, I understand, is *zapateado*, which I suspect is Mexican for tap music.

          *   *   *   *   *

             *   *   *   *

       *   *   *   *

INTERVIEWER: "El Puerto," from Isaac Albéniz's *Iberia*, performed on the piano by Daniel Barenboim. Now tell me, Ezra Blazer. Why *not* monogamy?

EZRA BLAZER: Why not monogamy. That's good. Because monogamy is against nature.

INTERVIEWER: So is writing novels.

EZRA BLAZER: Agreed.

INTERVIEWER: But certainly you've experienced benefits, pleasures, from monogamy.

EZRA BLAZER: When I've been monogamous, yes. But now I'm celibate, and have been, for some years. And to my astonishment celibacy is the greatest pleasure. Wasn't it Socrates, or one of his ilk, who said that the celibacy of old age is like finally being unstrapped from the back of a wild horse?

INTERVIEWER: Surely celibacy is against nature.

EZRA BLAZER: Not in the old. Nature loves celibacy in the old. Anyway, I contributed my twins to the longevity of the species. They've contributed their children. I did my job.

INTERVIEWER: Unwittingly.

EZRA BLAZER: Which is perhaps the best way. I've enjoyed being a tool of evolution. Usually it's when you're young, young and charging, that Evolution says, "I want YOU."

INTERVIEWER: Like Uncle Sam.

EZRA BLAZER: Yes, like Uncle Sam. Not bad for a Scot. Evolution dons his top hat and tugs on his goatee and he points at you and he says, I. WANT. YOU. It is in the unwitting service of evolution that people are crazed by sex.

INTERVIEWER: Which I suppose makes you a highly decorated soldier.

EZRA BLAZER: I saw some action. I have a Purple Heart. I hit the beaches. Long before the sexual revolution began in the sixties I was one of the generation who hit the beaches in the fifties and struggled under fire up the shore. We valiantly fought our way up the beaches against heavy opposition and then the flower children traipsed right over our bloody corpses having their multiple orgasms along the way. But you asked about decrepitude. What it's like to be so old. The short answer is that you go about your business reminding yourself to look at everything as though you're looking at it for the last time. Probably you are.

INTERVIEWER: Do you worry about the end?

EZRA BLAZER: I am cognizant of the end. Maybe I have three, five, seven years, at most nine or ten years. After that, you're beyond decrepit. [*Laughs.*] Unless you're Casals. Casals, who also played the piano, by the way, once told a reporter when he was in his nineties that he had played the same Bach piano piece every day for the past eighty-five years. When the reporter asked whether this didn't get boring, Casals said, No, on the contrary, each playing was a new experience, a new act of discovery. So maybe Casals never became decrepit. Maybe he took his last breath playing a bourrée. But I'm not Casals. I didn't draw the Mediterranean-diet straw. What do I think about the end? I don't think about the end. I think about the totality, my whole life.

INTERVIEWER: And are you happy with what you've accomplished over your whole life?

EZRA BLAZER: I'm satisfied that I couldn't have done any better. I never shirked my duty to my work. I worked hard. I did the best I could. I never let anything out into the world that I didn't think I had taken as far as I could. Do I regret the publication of certain lesser books? Not really. You only get to book three by writing books one and two. You're not writing one long book; that's too poetic a way of looking at it. But it's a single career. And each piece is, after the fact, necessary to going on.

INTERVIEWER: Are you working on something now?

EZRA BLAZER: I've just begun a massive trilogy. In fact I wrote the first page earlier today.

INTERVIEWER: Oh?

EZRA BLAZER: Yep. Each volume is going to be 352 pages. The significance of the number I needn't go into. And I'm writing the end first, so it'll be end, beginning, middle. The first two books will be middle, beginning, end. The last will be only beginnings. And this is a scheme that I think will prove to the world that I don't know what I'm doing, and never have.

INTERVIEWER: How long do you think it will take you?

EZRA BLAZER: Oh, a month or two.

INTERVIEWER: And tell me, Ezra Blazer, if the waves were to crash upon the shore, threatening to wash all of the discs off your desert island, which one would you run to save?

EZRA BLAZER: Oh my. Only one? Where is this island?

INTERVIEWER: Very far away.

EZRA BLAZER: Very far away. Is there nobody else around?

INTERVIEWER: No.

EZRA BLAZER: Just me on a desert island.

INTERVIEWER: That's right.

EZRA BLAZER: What else can I take?

INTERVIEWER: The Bible. Or the Torah, if you prefer. Or the Koran.

EZRA BLAZER: Those are the last books I would take. If I never see those books again I'll be quite happy.

INTERVIEWER: *The Complete Works of Shakespeare.*

EZRA BLAZER: Very good.

INTERVIEWER: And one more book of your choosing.

EZRA BLAZER: I'll come back to that. What else?

INTERVIEWER: A luxury.

EZRA BLAZER: Food.

INTERVIEWER: We'll take care of food. Don't worry about food.

EZRA BLAZER: Then I'll take a woman.

INTERVIEWER: I'm sorry, I should have said. You can't take another person.

EZRA BLAZER: Not even you?

INTERVIEWER: No.

EZRA BLAZER: Then I'll take a doll. A blow-up doll. Of my own choosing. In whatever color I want.

INTERVIEWER: We'll give you that. And your record?

EZRA BLAZER: Well, I've chosen only ones I truly love, so it's hard to say what I would like to hear over and over. Some days you're in a *Finian's Rainbow* frame of mind and other days the mood is Debussy. But I think it would have to be one of the great classical pieces, and that I could always appreciate the soaring—that's S-O-A-R-I-N-G—in Strauss's *Four Last Songs*. May I take all four of them with me?

INTERVIEWER: I'm sorry . . .

EZRA BLAZER: You drive a hard bargain.

INTERVIEWER: I didn't make the rules.

EZRA BLAZER: Who did?

INTERVIEWER: Roy Plomley.

EZRA BLAZER: Is he Scottish?

INTERVIEWER: I'm afraid we're running out of time.

EZRA BLAZER: Fine. "Im Abendrot." And with that I think I would have the spirit to get through my island days, me and my blow-up woman. We might even have a nice life together. Very quiet.

INTERVIEWER: And your book?

EZRA BLAZER: Well, certainly not any of my books. I suppose I'd take *Ulysses*. Which I've read twice in my life. So far. It's endlessly rich and endlessly baffling. However many times you've read it, you confront new enigmas. But it yields its pleasures up to steady concentration. And I would have plenty of time, of course, so, yes, Joyce's *Ulysses*, with the notes. And I'll tell you why you need the notes. His genius, his comic genius, keeps you splendidly entertained, the erudition is exciting, and then this city of Dublin, which is the landscape of the book, it *is* the book, is not my city. I wish I could have done as he did with Pittsburgh. But I could only have done this if I'd stayed in Pittsburgh with my sister and my mother and my father and my aunts and my uncles and my nephews and my nieces. Not that Joyce did that, mind you; as soon as he could get out of Dublin he fled, to Trieste, to Zurich, and then eventually to Paris. I don't think he ever went back to Dublin, but he was obsessed with the city and its billion particulars all his life. Obsessed with capturing it in a way utterly new in fiction. The erudition, the wit, the richness, the great novelty of it all . . . My God, it's magnificent! But without the notes I'd be lost. The Homeric analogue doesn't interest me too much, by the way. In fact, it doesn't interest me at all. But I suppose on a desert island it would start to, because what else would? You can only spend so much time with your blow-up woman, perfect though she may be. So yes, I'll go out with Joyce.

INTERVIEWER: Thank you, Ezra Blazer, for letting us hear your—

EZRA BLAZER: The thing I like best about a blow-up woman, though, is that—and I don't mean this in the physical sense, I mean it in the emotional sense—there's no friction. Much as I loved my darling dancers, there was friction constantly. Because they belonged to Mr. Balanchine, not me.

INTERVIEWER: . . . Do you always use the language of possession when talking about love?

EZRA BLAZER: It's impossible not to! Love is volatile. Recalcitrant. Irrepressible. We do our best to tame it, to name it and plan for it and maybe even to contain it between the hours of six and twelve, or if you're Parisian five and seven, but like much of what is adorable and irresistible in this world it eventually tears free of you and, yes, sometimes you get scratched up in the process. It's human nature to try to impose order and form on even the most defiantly chaotic and amorphous stuff of life. Some of us do it by drafting laws, or by painting lines on the road, or by damming rivers or isolating isotopes or building a better bra. Some of us wage wars. Others write books. The most delusional ones write books. We have very little choice other than to spend our waking hours trying to sort out and make sense of the perennial pandemonium. To forge patterns and proportions where they don't actually exist. And it is this same urge, this mania to tame and possess—this necessary folly—that sparks and sustains love.

INTERVIEWER: But don't you think it's important to cultivate freedom in love? Freedom and trust? Appreciation without expectation?

EZRA BLAZER: Next record.

INTERVIEWER: Now that we know you *do* have children, Ezra Blazer . . . Any regrets?

EZRA BLAZER: That I didn't meet you sooner. Is this what you do for a living?

INTERVIEWER: Yes.

EZRA BLAZER: Do you enjoy it?

INTERVIEWER: Of course.

EZRA BLAZER: Of course. You know, I know a poet, who lives in Spain, a wonderful Spanish poet who's in her sixties now, but when she was in her thirties, late twenties or early thirties, she was extremely adventurous, and she went around to all the bars in Madrid, trying to find the oldest man there, so that she could take him home with her. That was her mission: to sleep with the oldest man in Madrid. Have you ever done something like that?

INTERVIEWER: No.

EZRA BLAZER: Would you like to begin now?

INTERVIEWER: . . . That would be with you?

EZRA BLAZER: That would be with me. Are you married?

INTERVIEWER: Yes.

EZRA BLAZER: Married. Well. That didn't stand in Anna Karenina's way.

INTERVIEWER: No.

EZRA BLAZER: It didn't stand in Emma Bovary's way.

INTERVIEWER: No.

EZRA BLAZER: Should it stand in your way?

INTERVIEWER: Anna and Emma came to no good end.

EZRA BLAZER: Children?

INTERVIEWER: Two.

EZRA BLAZER: Two children and a husband.

INTERVIEWER: Correct.

EZRA BLAZER: Well [*laughs*], let's forget about him. I find you a very attractive woman and I've enjoyed this enormously. I'm going to a concert tomorrow night and I have two tickets. A friend of mine was going to go with me but I'm sure he'll be content to go another time. Pollini is here, the wonderful Maurizio Pollini is here, and he's playing Beethoven's last three piano sonatas. So, my final question for you? On *Desert Island Discs*? Tomorrow night, Maurizio Pollini, at Royal Festival Hall, and I can bring only one woman, and I would like that woman to be you. So. What do you say, miss? Are you game?

ACKNOWLEDGMENTS

The two passages read by Alice on pages 19 and 20 are from *Adventures of Huckleberry Finn* by Mark Twain, specifically the Modern Library paperback edition published in 2001.

The passage on pages 20 and 21 is from *The Thief's Journal* by Jean Genet, specifically the Grove Press edition reissued in 1994.

The second passage on page 21 is from *The First Man* by Albert Camus, specifically the First Vintage International edition published in 1996.

The third and fourth passages on page 21 are from *Tropic of Cancer* by Henry Miller, specifically the Grove Press edition reissued in 1994.

The passage on pages 22 and 23 is adapted from the text of an information pamphlet provided by Parkmed Physicians of New York.

The passage read aloud by Ezra on page 37 is from a letter written by James Joyce to his wife, Nora, on December 8, 1909. It is quoted from *Selected Letters of James Joyce*, originally published by Faber and Faber Limited in 1975 and reprinted in 1992.

As Alice says, the lyrics Ezra sings on page 39 are from "My Heart Stood Still" and "September Song." "September Song" is from the musical *Knickerbocker Holiday*, with lyrics by Maxwell Anderson and music by Kurt Weill. Copyright © 1938 (renewed)

Chappell & Co., Inc. and Tro-Hampshire House Publishing Corp. All rights reserved. Used by permission of Alfred Publishing, LLC. The lyrics to "My Heart Stood Still" are by Lorenz Hart, with music by Richard Rodgers. Copyright © 1927 (renewed) WB Music Corp. and Williamson Music Co. All rights reserved. Used by permission of Alfred Publishing, LLC. Copyright © 1927 Harms, Inc. Copyright renewed. Copyright assigned to Williamson Music and WB Music Corp. for the extended renewal period of copyright in the USA. International copyright secured. All rights reserved.

The passage underlined by Alice on page 47 is also from *The First Man* by Albert Camus, specifically the First Vintage International edition published in 1996.

As Ezra notes, the "bargeman" passage he reads aloud on page 48 is from *The Personal History of David Copperfield* by Charles Dickens, specifically the Bradbury & Evans edition published in 1850.

The lyrics on page 55 are from the song "Beyond the Blue Horizon." Ezra sings along to the Lou Christie version. "Beyond the Blue Horizon" is from the Paramount Picture *Monte Carlo*. Words by Leo Robin. Music by Richard A. Whiting and W. Franke Harling. Copyright © 1930 Sony/ATV Music Publishing LLC. Copyright renewed. All rights administered by Sony/ATV Music Publishing LLC, 424 Church Street, Suite 1200, Nashville, TN, 37219. International copyright secured. All rights reserved. Reprinted by permission of Hal Leonard LLC.

The passage read by Alice on pages 58 and 59 is from *Into that Darkness: An Examination of Conscience* by Gitta Sereny, specifically the First Vintage Books edition published in 1983.

The first passage on page 60 is from *Eichmann in Jerusalem: A Report on the Banality of Evil* by Hannah Arendt, specifically the Penguin Classics edition published in 1994.

The second passage on pages 60 and 61 is also from *Into that Darkness: An Examination of Conscience* by Gitta Sereny, specifically the First Vintage Books edition published in 1983.

The passage on pages 63 and 64 is from *Survival in Auschwitz: The Nazi Assault on Humanity* by Primo Levi, specifically the Collier Books/Macmillan Company edition published in 1993.

The lyrics sung by Alice on page 66 are from the "Nonsense Song" performed by Charlie Chaplin in *Modern Times*, with music composed by Leo Daniderff and lyrics by Charles Chaplin.

The passage about Jordy the Tailor on page 74 is from an issue of *Lickety Split* published in 1978.

The voiceover quoted on page 107 is from the jury duty orientation film entitled *Your Turn*, written and produced by Ted Steeg.

As Amar notes, the lyrics quoted on pages 174 and 175 are from the song "They All Laughed," performed by Chet Baker with minor modifications. Music and Lyrics by George Gershwin and Ira Gershwin. © 1936 (Renewed) NOKAWI MUSIC, FRANKIE G. SONGS, IRA GERSHWIN MUSIC. © 1936 (Renewed) IRA GERSHWIN MUSIC and GEORGE GERSHWIN MUSIC. All rights for NOKAWI MUSIC administered by IMAGEM SOUNDS. All rights for FRANKIE G. SONGS administered by SONGS MUSIC PUBLISHING. All rights on behalf of IRA GERSHWIN MUSIC administered by WB MUSIC CORP. All Rights Reserved. Used by permission of ALFRED PUBLISHING, LLC. Reprinted by permission of Hal Leonard LLC.

The *Desert Island Discs* episode summarized and quoted from on pages 186 through 189 is Sue Lawley's interview with Joseph Rotblat, broadcast on BBC Radio 4 on November 8, 1998.

The poem referred to by Alastair on page 215 is an untitled one by Osip Mandelstam. The English is Alastair's paraphrasing of a translation from the original Russian by Leeore Schnairsohn.

As Ezra recalls, the poem he paraphrases on page 256 is by E. E. Cummings: #24 in the book *No Thanks*, originally published by Cummings himself in 1935.